The Price of Silence

Ulla Håkanson

Till Christina,
Tack för vänskap & stöd!

XO
Ulla

First published in 2013

This edition published 2013

Copyright © Ulla Håkanson 2013

The right of Ulla Håkanson to be identified as the author of this work has been asserted in accordance with the Copyright, Designs and Patents Act 1988.

All rights reserved. No part of this publication may be reproduced, stored in a retrieval system, or transmitted in any form or by any means, without the written permission of the author or publisher.

ISBN 978-1481063210

Design and layout by Artsgraphique.com
Photo of author by Shayd Johnson

Published by BroadPen Books, St Albans, Hertfordshire, UK

For Ingrid and Ulf

Thrills and romance, caught between a beautiful landscape and an ugly underworld

Possessed of a bright, entrepreneurial spirit, Amy and her fiancé Tyler looked forward to a promising future. But Tyler finds greater allure in seductive white powder than in the arms of his fiancé and Amy soon discovers just how destructive his drug habit and ensuing business deals could be.

The Price of Silence is a powerful portrayal of the seedy life of illicit drug involvement and the misery of those who fall victim to addiction. Tyler's need plunges him and Amy into the depraved underworld of the drug trade. Gang involvement, Tyler's complicity in murder, kidnapping, and physical brutality bring Amy's life crashing around her until she is rescued by Ben, a policeman and new love in her life.

Often genuinely chilling, *The Price of Silence* is set in the stark beauty of central British Columbia. This story intimately captures the lives of those characters caught in the wake of drug addiction, but despite its dramatic ending, it offers hope that the human spirit can overcome even seemingly insurmountable obstacles.

Dan Lundine, author of *Signpost – A Prairie Town*

Chapter 1

A rust-riddled Dodge crept into a lonely gas station. With headlights off, its dark shape blended with the night. The driver stopped by the phone booth, cut the motor and scanned the area. He slipped from the car, then entered the booth. The light flicked on above his unkempt hair, highlighting his blood-covered face as he reached up to smash the bulb with the butt of his pistol. His haunted eyes probed the darkness. No traffic on the road, no movement, no sign of life.

He spat blood on the floor and picked up the receiver. Squinting at the numbers in the weak light from the station, he dialled his ex-fiancée's number. "Hi there, this is Amy … I'm unable to answer …" He cursed, slamming the phone down. It was past ten; she should be home by now.

He waited, peering into the night to see if anyone might be creeping up on him. After a moment, he dialled again. No answer. He soon fell into a routine: call, hang up, wait, scan the roadside, repeat – one foot tapping a nervous rhythm on the floor.

* * *

Amy Robinson waved to her last customer of the day and locked the door to Tresses, her Vancouver beauty salon. She flipped the sign in the window to 'Closed', watching her customer jaywalk through the stop-and-go rush-hour traffic on Fourth Avenue, coat over head to shield her new 'do' from the rain.

She swept the floor, made a few notes in the ledger, collected towels and smocks and put them in the washing machine. Her feet were tired. It had been a long day, busier than usual. She sank down in a chair, kicked her shoes off and stretched out her long slender legs with a sigh of relief. Standing all day was more tiring than a couple of hours' workout at the gym and sparring with her trainer. She pulled the elastic out of her thick auburn hair and shook it loose with her fingers. She was proud of her business. It had grown swiftly over the past two years. It wouldn't be long until she'd be able to pay off the loan from her father. Then Tresses would be all hers.

Her co-worker Meg was singing along with Abba on the radio, cleaning combs and brushes over a sink. Meg, with her short blonde hair curling around her ears and wide smile, had walked in one day looking for a job. She'd explained that her last job at a Unisex salon in the small town of Castlegar, watching AC flights, made her yearn for Vancouver action. So when George, her boss, started to become too friendly, she opted for a change. She'd been with Amy for five months now. Great with hair, good with people, easy to work with.

"So you're all set for the next week?" Amy asked.

"Yes, I am." Meg put the brushes and combs on a rack and wiped her hands. "I rescheduled three customers. The rest I can handle."

"I was just thinking how lucky I am to have you here."

"Thanks," Meg smiled. "I like it here."

"I'm glad." Amy pushed her feet back in her shoes, then went to the kitchenette and picked up chicken sandwiches and drinks she'd bought at Tim Hortons next-door. "Let's eat and do the inventory, then call it a night."

They finished inventory at ten and left through the backdoor. "Have a great time, Amy," Meg said. "Don't worry about Tresses. Everything will be fine."

"I'm sure it will. You've the number to the lodge, in case you want to reach me?"

Meg patted her shoulder bag, "Right here." She gave Amy a quick hug, waved and walked off toward the parking lot.

Amy enjoyed the twenty minute brisk walk to her apartment. The rain had stopped and a few stars were visible in the night sky. It looked like a promising start for her mini-vacation.

Weeks earlier, Amy's cousin Willa had asked her to come along with her and six of her friends on a kayaking trip in Bowron Lake Provincial Park, about 800 kilometers northeast of Vancouver. "We'll be moving across several interconnecting lakes and rivers. They go in a circuit inside the park," she said. "I hear the scenery is stunning, and we'll see plenty of wildlife."

"Thanks Willa, but I don't think so," Amy had said. "I've enough drama in my life. Being around rapids, bears and cougars doesn't sound like my idea of getting away from it all."

But Willa wouldn't take no for an answer. She trotted out scenic pictures and glowing articles. Finally, Amy had agreed.

A similar tug-of-war went on regarding a tip-and-recovery course. "What's the point?" Amy asked. "Sea kayaks don't capsize."

Willa kept insisting. Eventually, Amy relented. The course took place in a sheltered bay. They'd tipped their kayak and learned how to turn it upright again with the help of paddles and floats.

That course hooked Amy on kayaking. Now her waterproof dry bags were packed and she couldn't wait to go.

Back in her apartment, Amy pushed the blinking message button on the phone. She heard someone say, "Fuck," but nothing more. The rest of the messages were blank. She watered her plants, poured juice in a glass and looked around for her cigarettes. The phone rang.

"Ya."

"Hi, it's Tyler."

No, not again. Amy's heart sped up. "What do you want?"

"I want my desk."

"Like I told you before, your desk is in the garage. If you don't pick it up soon, the super's going to give it away."

"I need your help."

"Sorry." Amy paced the floor.

"Listen, Amy. I'm in trouble. I have to come up with a few thousand dollars."

"Not my problem."

"Dammit, Amy, you have to help me."

"You're out of your mind. We're finished, Tyler. Stop calling me." Amy hung up and dropped the phone on the sofa. *Get away from me.* She clutched her T-shirt with damp hands, trying to calm down. She found her cigarettes, picked up the juice and moved onto the balcony.

She smoked, looking out over English Bay where cargo ships from different parts of the world had anchored for the night. *Damn you, Tyler.* It drove her crazy that he kept calling after all this time.

She thought back to the time they met, four months after she opened her salon business. It was early January. Heavy, wet snow had fallen since noon, reducing the four-lane street to one lane in each direction. Traffic was inching its way, cars gassing, braking, sliding.

She'd been about to close up for the day when a well-dressed, good-looking man entered, asking if he could have a haircut without an appointment. He'd made her heart skip with his charm, his baritone voice and light friendly smile.

Seven months later, they got engaged. Amy blushed at the thought of their dinner out that warm night in July. They'd picked a table on the patio at a small Italian restaurant with checkered red-and-white tablecloths and dripping candles. They shared a bottle of red wine, but she couldn't remember what they ate, only that they couldn't stop smiling, looking into each other's eyes, touching, reaching over the small table, whispering loving things. They'd noticed other guests' amused looks, but didn't care. They were happy.

Three months later, they rented a small apartment on Pine Street in Vancouver and moved in together. All Tyler brought from his old place was his personal effects, his desk and chair that he placed in the small den to use as his office. He told Amy she could do whatever she wanted with the rest of the place. He'd share the cost with her.

Amy gave her used furniture to SOS, except for the TV, then went to Ikea in Richmond, a city adjacent to the southern part of Vancouver. She bought a white area rug, a shark-grey sofa, two red armchairs, a glass coffee table and dining set, two end tables, two lamps, a TV stand, a bookcase for her collection of suspense novels, a large ficus plant and a palm tree. In another store, she found a set of three big Art Deco posters of women with extreme hairdos, had them framed and hung them in a row on a wall.

Tyler made good money in his investment business, and Amy's

salon business kept her busy. But she longed for a baby, longed to have a close family. She knew Tyler wanted children, too, but when she brought it up with him, he thought it was too early. "I'm not ready to get married yet," he said.

The pill had never agreed with Amy, so they always used condoms. Three-and-a-half months later, she found out she was pregnant. Even though it was an accident, she'd never been happier.

Six weeks into her pregnancy, things started to go wrong. Tyler lost money on a land deal. "I'm off to Winnipeg to meet with the investor," he said. "We'll straighten it out."

Two days later he came back, restless and edgy. Amy tried to comfort him, but he pulled away, asking if she could lend him some money to tide him over for a month.

"What happened?"

"Someone's trying to pull out of a deal. Money is coming, but it'll be a few weeks."

Amy wanted to suggest he ask his parents for a loan, but realized that wouldn't happen. His upper-middle-class parents had cut Tyler off, and he refused to talk about it.

"But honey, after paying my share for groceries and rent, I don't have any extra cash," she explained. "You know whatever I've left goes to paying off the loan from my father."

"Yeah, but you've money in your business account, don't you?"

"Yes, because I have running costs for my business. For inventory, taxes, heat, water, rent, phone, unexpected expenses."

"This is an unexpected expense."

"Unexpected business expenses."

"Can't your father wait with the payments for a few months? Give us a break?"

"He might. But you'll have to ask him."

"Fine."

The next evening, Tyler had stormed back into the apartment, his face a dark mask. "Your precious father is playing games with me," he said, crashing down on the sofa beside her.

"What are you talking about?"

"I asked him for a loan. A small one. I even promised not to ask again." Tyler let his head flop back and stared at the ceiling. "He told me he'd think about it after taking a look at my business plan. Bloody insulting. I bet he was enjoying himself."

"Why do you say that?"

"His tone suggested I grovel."

"That's just my controlling father tugging the leash. He won't lend me a dime until I explain every detail about what I'm going to do with it. Why should it be any different with you?"

Tyler sat up and sneered. "You're taking his side against me now?"

Amy frowned at his sudden hostility. "No, I'm not, but under the circumstances, I don't think he's being unreasonable. So what did you say to him?"

"Nothing. I took off."

"That's really going to help."

"The two of you are just alike. Tight with your damn money."

"How can you say that? I've paid half of our bills ever since we moved in together. Even though you earn twice as much as I do."

"Business can be unpredictable sometimes."

"What business are we talking about? All I know is that you're investing in land with someone. You keep me in the dark. Why? I'd like to know how things are going, too. See some progress."

"There's been a delay … you know how some people take their

time. No big deal. I just need a little help to carry me over."

"Then *tell* my father. Except you've got to be more specific."

The sound of a distant ship's siren snapped Amy back to the present. A large cruise ship crossed the bay, lit up like a giant birthday cake. She felt lonely. Tyler's friends had disappeared after the break-up. She didn't miss them. But she'd neglected her own friends during that time, which had created some distance.

She shivered. The wind had turned cold. Muffled voices seeped through open windows. Footsteps echoed on the pavement below.

I've got to quit these things. She pushed the cigarette butt into a sand-filled can on the floor. Tired of thinking, she called it a day.

Chapter 2

"Fuck!" Tyler groped for another coin after Amy hung up on him and dialled her number again. No answer. Deciding to confront her instead, he got back in the car and drove south through the night.

Blood still oozed from the deep cut along his jaw. The pain played games with his vision. It took all of his concentration just to stay on the road. After his third near crash, he pulled onto the shoulder and stretched out on the seat.

Still in shock, he wondered why he hadn't seen it coming. Months earlier, he'd screwed up on a shady land deal and needed cash. A couple of his new buddies put him in contact with Ken Ross, a member of a Vancouver drug gang. Tyler approached him at a club and asked what it would take to become a member. Ken told him he had a better proposition. They arranged to meet at a waterfront warehouse the following night. There, Tyler learned that Ken was skimming from the Vancouver gang, but now needed help from an outsider. They reached an agreement and started their skimming operation.

Still wanting to be part of a gang, Tyler joined a small gang in Squamish, just north of Vancouver. He'd approached one of their members, who introduced him to their leader. Tyler had no intention of skimming from them, as their drug business was still small, so any losses would be easy to spot.

Tyler and Ken had skimmed for months without a hitch. Then suddenly, Ken had called, warning him that his boss was on their tail. The next minute, some thug had tried to cut his throat, putting him on the run and forcing him to sleep in a stolen car on the side of some goddamned country road in the middle of nowhere.

He needed cash to disappear and intended to make Amy give it to him whether she liked it or not. If only the damned bitch would listen, she'd realize it would give her just what she wanted – never to see or hear from him again.

Tyler jerked awake at three in the morning. He swallowed a couple of amphetamines and got back on the road. An hour later, he turned west on Highway 3 and reached Vancouver's heavy workday traffic at dawn. Driving in the inside lane, his jacket zipped to the end of the stand collar and pulled up high, he moved with the traffic, scanning the cars around him, looking for someone tailing him.

* * *

Amy woke up at dawn on Friday morning, full of energy. After downing coffee and a fruit yogurt, she changed into her exercise clothes and jogged to the gym. Aerobics and a half-hour sparring session with her trainer followed.

Back home, she showered, got into black shorts, a black-and-white striped T-shirt and running shoes. She pulled her hair into a ponytail and put small silver rings in her ears. After looking around for a place to hide her laptop, in case someone would break in, she stuck it in the washing machine, then put her dirty laundry on top. Her toiletries bag, purse and wallet, book, and a change of underwear went into a daypack. Spare door keys went into a small, zipped pocket on her shorts.

She waved to Willa, already in the parking area, waiting to pull her old Toyota into Amy's space. Amy threw her dry bags into the back of her Kia, pulled out and parked to the side. She checked that her spare car key was secured in the magnetic box under the car, then went to help Willa unload.

"Rough night?" Amy glanced at Willa's pale face as she opened the back door and reached for her bags.

Willa looked up at Amy through slitted eyes, her glasses halfway down her nose. "Just came off a twelve-hour shift," she said in a raspy voice.

"Relax. I'll drive first. Go and lie down. I'll move your stuff."

Willa offered a weak smile. "Thanks."

With Willa napping beside her, Amy drove through a busy downtown Vancouver, between the giant cedars in Stanley Park, across the Lion's Gate Bridge and up a mountainside street to the Trans-Canada Highway.

Twenty minutes later, she turned onto the Sea-to-Sky Highway, which wound snugly along the edge of the Coast Mountains – evergreen thick forest which became snowcapped on peaks.

She glanced at her cousin, at her freckled cheeks flushed in sleep, her glasses on a slant. Wispy little thing, she thought, a woman in a girl's body. If it hadn't been for their auburn hair and green eyes, inherited from their fathers, no one would know they were related.

They had been close friends as children, living next door to each other in central Vancouver. But when Amy turned eleven, she and her family moved to Vancouver's West End. Their parents had different interests and only got together at Amy's parents' yearly summer BBQ, an event Amy steadfastly avoided. So the girls lost touch. They met again shortly after Amy and Tyler split up. Amy had gone to the Vancouver General Hospital for a checkup, and bumped into Willa, who was interning as a respiratory therapist.

Their childhood friendship slowly revived. Willa, at twenty-five, hadn't changed much. Amy, twenty-six, had changed after she met Tyler.

Willa stirred in her seat, sat up and stretched. "Ahhh, that feels better. Thanks Amy." She straightened her glasses and looked around. "Where are we?"

"Just south of Squamish."

"I'm so glad you decided to come along, Amy. Is Meg going to manage the salon all by herself?"

"She has a full schedule, but seemed fine with it. She's good, has varied experience. If Tresses keeps growing the way it is, I might ask her to become a partner."

"Do you think she'd like that?"

"I don't know. We'll see." Amy eyed a McDonald's as they passed through Squamish. "I'm getting hungry. What about you?"

"A bit." Willa studied the map. "If you're not too famished, we could stop in Pemberton, an hour and a half from here. I have an apple. I'll share it with you."

"That's fine. That would be a good spot to gas up before we go into the mountains."

Salivating at the thought of food, Amy scanned every sign as they neared Pemberton. A large scruffy billboard promising deli sandwiches in fading red letters made her turn off the highway. She parked at a slightly dilapidated house, around the corner from a line of pickup trucks. "Lunch," she announced, grinning as if she deserved a medal.

Willa examined the scrawny vine on the wall, clinging to white peeling paint. "It doesn't look like a place where food should be prepared."

"What's wrong with it?" Amy looked at the house. "I think it looks kind of quaint." She waved Willa closer. "Come on. Don't be so picky."

Loud talking and laughing stopped as they entered the diner. It smelled of barns and deep fryers. The only light came from two small windows, one at each end of the room.

Eyes adjusting to the light, they became aware of a group of men at two nearby tables, looking like they'd be cowboys or loggers, all looking their way. Willa tugged at Amy's T-shirt, whispered they should leave. Amy gave her a lopsided smile. "Don't be silly."

A big woman behind a counter wiped her pudgy hands on her apron and gazed at them through smudged glasses. "Can I help you?"

They ordered grilled ham and cheese sandwiches with iced tea and made their way to a table in the back. The noise level picked up again. Moments later, the heavy woman waddled over with iced tea in bucket-sized glasses and cutlery in paper napkins. She trundled off, saying their sandwiches would be ready in a minute.

When their orders arrived, Willa inspected the heaps of fries and pickles, saying, "Hey, where's the sandwich?"

"It's under there, somewhere," Amy said, starting in on her fries.

Willa scraped her fries to the side and stared at the greasy flat sandwich thus revealed. She looked up at Amy with a face full of dismay. "*Deli* sandwiches?"

Amy burst out laughing. "Hey, live a little. You haven't even tried it yet. The fries are good."

Willa cut a piece of the sandwich and examined it. "I wonder if the smell of this will linger long enough in my pores for the bears to pick up the scent. Oh, what the heck." She put it in her mouth. "I'm too hungry to care." She devoured the sandwich and started on the fries.

Amy shook her head. "How can you stay so skinny eating the way you do?"

"I don't know," Willa said with her mouth full. "Overactive metabolism?" She poured half a bottle of ketchup over the fries. "It's not my choice, you know. I'd die to be tall and slim and have curves like you."

"That kind of stuff isn't going to help you."

"I know. Maybe I'm going on adrenalin right now because I can't wait to get out on the water."

"You know, I've been thinking about that," Amy said. "When we did that tip-and-recovery course, we practiced with empty kayaks on smooth water. Our bags weigh more than we do. Can you see us trying to turn a heavy kayak upright in a strong wind? We'd be, like ..." Amy reached out to grab the ends of the table, knocking her ice tea all over her T-shirt. "Oh, *shit*."

Stifling giggles, they hurried to pay. Grins and growls from the men made Amy realize they were staring at her breasts through the wet cloth. She grabbed the T-shirt and held it away from her skin.

Once outside, she and Willa burst into laughter and ran to the car. Willa waited while Amy dug out a clean T-shirt from a bag. Then they hid behind a lilac hedge beside their car, where Amy could change unseen. She took the wet shirt off, then struggled to pull the clean one over her sticky skin.

"That's better," she said, then caught Willa staring at her. "What?"

Willa put a finger just below Amy's left collarbone. "What's that?"

Amy's face turned serious. "Nothing."

"Nothing? I work at the hospital. Remember? Looked like a burn mark to me, a pretty bad one at that. What's going on?"

Amy looked away. Tension crawled across her shoulders. She turned to Willa. "Listen, I don't want to talk about it. Not now. We're here to have a good time, so don't ask me, okay?"

"But, Amy …"

"No buts."

"Fine." Willa pursed her lips, started the car and pulled onto the highway.

Chapter 3

Tyler stayed off the main streets as he made his way through central Vancouver. It was almost eight o'clock by the time he reached Kitsilano. He turned onto Fourth Avenue and drove west. Seeing the 'Closed' sign in Tresses' window, he drove around the building, parked in an alley at the back and lit a cigarette. Just before eight-thirty, Amy's co-worker appeared, entering the salon through the back door.

Tyler scanned for Amy, an impatient frown on his lips. Was she late or home sick? His stomach ached. When had he last eaten? He pulled out of the alley and continued west on Fourth. He drove slowly, chain-smoking, checking the sidewalks and keeping an eye peeled for Amy's black Kia.

He parked on the street outside Amy's building and peered into the lobby through the glass door. The elevator had stopped on the fifth floor. Using his old passkey, he entered the empty lobby, taking the stairs to the third floor. After checking the hallway, he crossed to Amy's apartment, picked the lock with a bump key and slipped inside.

Amy wasn't there. He pushed the flashing button on the answering machine and listened to messages while he checked the fridge for something to eat. On the machine, a voice thanked Amy for her reservation, reminding her to check in at the Bowron Lodge Registration Center by ten on Saturday morning.

Tyler moved into the bedroom, rifled through the mess on Amy's desk and found a brochure on the Bowron Circuit Experience. Attached to it were several pages with pre-trip information, detailing rules and restrictions. Looking it over, he realized she must have left already. He'd just missed her. He folded the whole package, then put it in his pocket. Blood dripped as he kept searching the desktop. The gash in his jaw had opened up again. He spotted Amy's cell phone bill and stuffed it in his pocket as well.

His head felt woozy. He'd never liked the sight of blood. The musty, metallic odour of it sickened him. He staggered to the bathroom. Gazing in the mirror, he saw the white of bone between bleeding slabs of flesh. It made him gag. Taking off his jacket and bloodstained shirt, he found some hydrogen peroxide in the medicine cabinet and poured it over the wound. With pain spreading through his head like a raging fire, he held on to the vanity, rocking back and forth, sucking deep breaths through yellowed teeth.

He shook out two amphetamines. Scooping water with his bloody hand, he washed them down. When he couldn't find bandages, he rummaged through Amy's desk drawers and found Scotch tape. He tried to join the edges of the wound with the tape, but it refused to stick on his damp skin. Instead, he crisscrossed short lengths of it every which way until it looked like he had a jellyfish stuck to his face. He pocketed the disinfectant, put his shirt in a plastic bag and rinsed blood off his jacket collar.

Searching the closet for something to wear, he found a sweatshirt with a bunny on the front – the only thing big enough to fit him. He put it on, grabbed his jacket and prepared to leave. As he passed the phone he had an idea. He picked it up and called Tresses, knowing the number by heart.

"Tresses. Good morning. Meg speaking."

"Hi. I'd like to book an appointment for a haircut with Amy on Saturday."

"I'm sorry, Amy isn't working this week. Maybe I can ..."

Tyler hung up, wiped the receiver on the sweatshirt, put his jacket on, zipped it to the end of the stand collar and pulled the collar up high to cover his cheek. He peeked out into the hallway, grabbed the bag containing his bloodied shirt and left.

He reached his car without seeing anyone and drove off. Two blocks east, he spotted a phone booth at a gas station, pulled in and dialled Amy's cell number.

"Ya."

"Hi, where are you?"

* * *

Amy hung up, turned off her cell and put it away. Finding it impossible to hide her frustration, she turned and gazed out the side window, away from Willa. She *had* to get him to stop calling. But how?

* * *

Tyler dialled Amy's number again, but gave up when her voicemail kicked in. He knew she travelled with someone. She wouldn't drive that far alone. It could be the skinny bitch he'd seen her with a few times. He checked Amy's phone bill for frequently-used numbers, tried a couple, got no answer and decided to try again later.

* * *

"Who called?" Willa asked, pulling into a gas station.

"Nobody," Amy snapped.

Willa hesitated. "Okay. Check the oil while I fill up?"

"Sure." Amy popped the hood and got out. Pulling paper from a roll, she couldn't stop thinking her new life was now threatened by Tyler, who'd do his best to drag her back down.

Willa's cell rang. Amy reached in through the open window, picked it up and checked the caller ID.

"Amy!" Willa reached for it. "That's *my* phone."

"Don't answer it," Amy said, handing it to her. "It could be Tyler."

Willa checked the ID. "Is it him?"

"I don't know."

"Was it him earlier?"

"Yes."

"Why would he call me? Besides, he doesn't have my cell number."

"I wouldn't be too sure about that." Amy pulled out the oil stick, wiped and dipped it back in. She didn't like being pushed into revealing things she'd rather not talk about. "He's an energy vampire," she said, checking the stick and putting it back in. "I've tried to get away from him ever since we broke up. When I changed to an unlisted number, he had it three days later."

"Oh." Willa replaced the pump and tightened the fuel cap. "But why would he want to call me?"

"He's desperate for some reason." Amy closed the hood. "And he's sly."

"What do you mean sly?" Willa asked as they got back in the car.

"He sneaked up on me a few times – without a sound, like a frigging fog. When I noticed and stopped to talk to people on the sidewalk, he disappeared. Vamoose."

"That's creepy."

"Yeah."

Someone honked. "Oops." Willa started the car. "I'm taking up pump space." She pulled out and eased onto the highway. "So ... did that happen many times?"

"I don't know ... four, maybe five times. But the way he does it, like a jack-in-the-box, freaks me out. Anyway, he called again last night. Wanted a few thousand dollars. I told him he was out of his mind and hung up. Still he called a few minutes ago. He's intensely revengeful. He might try to reach me through you. I'm telling you, stay away from him."

"No problem. But you're scaring me."

"Well ... don't take his calls. Don't talk to him. What can he do?"

Willa sniffed. "Seems he has infinite resources. Listen, Amy, the man's stalking you. That's illegal."

"I'll find a way to stop it when I get back."

"Please tell me what's going on."

Amy cringed. She supposed Willa deserved some kind of explanation.

"Amy?"

"Will you just give me a minute?"

"Why do you sound so angry?"

"Sorry. It's just ... Let me think, all right?" Picking at her nails, Amy wondering where to start. She went back in her mind to when things started to go astray. "We were really happy for about a year," she began. "Then something went wrong with one of Tyler's investments." She told Willa what happened. "I started to wonder if I could trust him. Besides, I was worried about …" She stopped, not ready to tell Willa about the baby yet.

"What?"

Amy waved it off. "Nothing. Anyway, things got worse when he started to bring some new friends home. I thought they were sketchy and didn't want to be around them. We argued about it … One day, I saw Tyler searching through a drawer in my dresser. I kept a diamond necklace – a gift from my grandmother – hidden there. I didn't see him taking it, but the next day it was gone."

"For good?"

Amy nodded. "Yeah. That evening, he wanted to borrow money from me again. I got mad and asked if he'd lost my necklace gambling. Not very diplomatic, I know, but … anyway, he went crazy. He asked, *how* could I accuse him of gambling, *how* could I think he would steal my necklace. You should've heard him. He yelled obscene, demeaning things in my face like a lunatic! Then he started pushing and slapping me around."

Willa turned to Amy, looking horrified.

"Look at where you're going!" Amy warned.

Willa yanked her head back to the road ahead. "He hit you?"

"He slapped my face and pushed me … with a cigarette in his hand. I was wearing a tank top. His cigarette pushed into my bare shoulder." Amy covered her face with her hands at the memory. "Ohmygod. It hurt so much, I almost passed out."

"I can imagine."

Amy put her hands down and sat silent, looking into the past. "He backed off, staring at the burn, swearing it was an accident. Then he ran around in circles trying to figure out what to do. I couldn't stop crying. I wanted to go to the hospital. He wouldn't hear of it. He ran back and forth like a jackrabbit, washing the burn, getting bandages, bringing me water, painkillers … Oh, man …" She shook her head, staring at her feet.

"Did you go to a drugstore, at least?"

"No, not then. He brought out wine, spinning this spiel about being sorry, telling me how much he …. No, you don't want to hear it. But believe me, he gave an Oscar-worthy performance. I didn't know how to deal with it. I just sat there: my shoulder throbbing from the burn, my face stinging from his slaps." She looked away. "I should've left him then."

Willa touched her arm. Amy pulled away. "I'm fine." She took out a tissue and blew her nose. "I swallowed it all." Her chin quivered. "The painkillers, the booze, the acting. We made up in bed."

"Oh, Amy."

"Leave it alone."

Chapter 4

Tyler tossed the bag with his bloodied T-shirt into the woods as he drove north, heading for a broken-down cabin in the mountains that nobody went to anymore. He scanned the roadside for a payphone, cursing the telephone company for cutting him off for not paying on time. He had to get to a phone to call Mike Polanco, his gang leader in Squamish. Mike had connections, arranged false IDs, got people across borders.

Two nights before, Tyler had met with him at Aegis, their favourite hangout bar. Mike had heard rumours about the skimming. "I hear Tony Matzera is looking for you," he said. Matzera ran the gang Tyler and Ken had skimmed from.

"I need to disappear," Tyler said. "Will you help me?"

"For a price, yeah."

"All I have is my stash," Tyler said.

"How big?"

"A kilo. Coke."

"Bring that and $20,000. Cash."

Tyler agreed, knowing he couldn't bargain with Mike. This meant he'd need, at least, another $10,000 to add to the $12,000 cash he'd already gained from selling some of his cocaine. It would be too dangerous to sell more coke right now, so he plotted to top up on cash from Amy instead.

He planned to hide out at the cabin until the arrangements for his getaway had been made. Right now, he needed to know how long it would take, and how much time he had to get the money together. He stopped in Whistler Village and used the payphone in a bar.

"Are we still on?" he asked when Mike answered.

"You got the money?"

"Yeah."

"How much?"

"Twenty-thousand."

"And the coke?"

"Right here."

"Bring it here next Friday night at nine, and you can have the papers and the passport. Nine. Not a minute later."

Tyler got back on the highway. He had till Friday. That meant he had to get hold of Amy as soon as possible. Maybe he could catch up to her. He sped up.

* * *

Eyes sliding over the Coast Mountains scenery, Amy pondered over how she could have allowed herself to get into so much trouble. She knew how to manage a business well. Why was her private life in such a mess? Granted, she'd jumped into a relationship a bit too fast. There had been signs of trouble even before they were engaged, like the time Tyler had shown up on a date, high on drugs. She'd been too infatuated to see straight and chose to ignore it. But, at least, she'd learned something from that.

She looked at Willa, calmly driving the empty road as it climbed and twisted ahead, leaving nothing between them and eternity. "So here we are," she said, "just the two of us in a tin can, traversing colossal mountains on what used to be a logging road, and you look like you're enjoying it."

Willa smiled. "I am."

"I need a smoke before I take on this road."

"You don't have to take over. I love this kind of driving."

Amy let out a sigh of relief, leaned back and closed her eyes. "Thanks, Willa."

"We're nearing Lillooet," Willa said thirty minutes later, waking Amy.

"Already?" Amy looked out at mountains that had changed from cold greys to rusty brown and mustard yellow. "Who would've known you'd be such a racecar driver." She nudged Willa's thin arm. "The weight-lifting didn't do you any good, though."

"I'm stronger than you think." Willa flexed her bicep. "Feel it."

Amy gave it a squeeze. "Ha! Looks like a pimple. Feels like a pimple. A lot of help you'll be pulling a kayak."

The scenery kept changing. Land dotted with tumbleweeds and the occasional isolated conifer opened up. Mountains became rolling hills covered with bunchgrass, the road wider, sagebrush growing in the bunchgrass, slightly taller pine trees. The radio sprang to life as a new station came into range, playing oldies. Amy reached to change the station.

"Please leave it," Willa said. "I like it."

A few minutes later, Willa made a left at an interchange, then turned into a rest stop.

Amy looked at the map. "Where are we?"

"Heading north on 97 – Cariboo Highway. We'll be in

Williams Lake in less than two hours. Will you take over?"

"Sure, as long as I don't have to listen to oldies on the radio."

They switched places, with Amy driving north, singing along with Cyndi Lauper's 'Girls Just Want To Have Fun'. A moment later, Willa joined in. Soon they were laughing and swinging their shoulders to the beat.

After driving another hundred miles, they reached Williams Lake, pulled off the highway and, moments later, into the parking lot of a motel. When they were checking in, Willa nudged Amy, pointing to a poster on the wall. "They have a live band at the Surf N Turf restaurant down the road. Country music."

Amy groaned. She looked at Willa standing there with her please-indulge-me smile, and shrugged. "Why not."

It was after midnight when they walked back to the motel. "I'm sorry I snapped at you earlier," Amy said, staggering slightly. "Forgive me?"

"Of course." Willa hooked arms with Amy. "I'd be snippy too if I had someone hassling me on the phone."

"I'm a bit drunk," Amy said. "So I'm going to tell you one more thing, and then it's all out."

"Okay."

"Do you know why I was at the hospital that day when you and I met after all those years?"

"No, I thought you were visiting someone. Why were you there?"

"Something happened the day after Tyler burned my shoulder."

Willa gasped. "Did he hit you again?"

"Well, sort of ... I woke up the next morning with my shoulder throbbing. When I saw my bruised face, I knew I couldn't go to work for a few days. *Boy*, that made me mad. I stormed off to the den to show Tyler what he'd done."

"What did he say?"

"He looked shocked when he saw me. Yelled at me to get out, trying to push a big bag of white powder into a drawer."

"White powder? Are you saying it was drugs?"

"Wait … then he came after me, shoving me out of the room and into the living room. He kept shoving until I lost my balance and jammed my stomach into the corner of the dining table. I lay there doubled over in pain. He just went back to the den and slammed the door shut."

"What a brute! Your stomach … did you get hurt?"

"Well, I didn't know at first. I went to the bedroom with my heart banging like crazy, and my mind screaming: *Drugs!* I locked the bedroom door for the first time, ever, and stood there, scared to death that he'd break it down and come in to hit me again. Then I heard him leave. I got hold of a locksmith and had the lock changed."

"Did you call the police about the drugs?"

"Do you honestly think Tyler would take off, leaving the drugs?"

"I guess …"

"Anyway, just after the locksmith left, I noticed that my pants were wet. When I saw all the blood, I left a message on my parents' phone that I'd kicked Tyler out. Then I took a cab to the hospital. I was ten weeks pregnant and lost the baby that day. I had a D&C, rested for a few hours and went home. I'd been back for a checkup when you and I met."

Willa put her arms around Amy. "I'm so sorry."

"Me, too."

They started walking again. Tears rolled down Amy's cheeks

as she thought about loosing the baby, how depressed she'd been. She never opened the door to the den, couldn't look at the dining table and slept on the sofa every night. She finally sold the dining set and gave away the bed. She kept sleeping on the sofa for weeks before buying a new bed and a dining set with a round table. Another few weeks went by before she opened the door to the den. After repainting the walls in the den, she'd bought a white desk, an office chair, a colourful area rug and a plant.

"Did you report him for physical abuse?"

Willa's question startled Amy out of her thoughts. She stopped walking and stared at Willa for a moment, then buried her face in her hands. "No," she whispered.

"I don't understand …"

"We made up in *bed*, Willa. I was too *embarrassed* to tell anyone … In fact, I'm embarrassed *now* to be telling you."

Willa looked distressed.

Amy took her hands down and wiped her eyes. "I didn't think they'd put him in jail just for shoving me. He'd started on drugs. That's what changed him. He's a vengeful kind of guy. I didn't need him to come after me for reporting him. I just wanted to get away from him. Forever." She blew her nose.

"But … it's not working, is it?"

"It has to. It will. Don't worry."

"What did your parents say?"

Amy lowered her eyes. "I told them I had a miscarriage. They weren't surprised. Let's leave it at that."

Chapter 5

On Saturday morning, Amy woke with her head spinning. "Uhh … I'll never drink again." She squinted at the clock on the nightstand, then bolted out of bed. "Willa! Wake up! It's six-thirty." She stumbled to the bathroom and stood under the shower until Willa banged on the door.

They paid for their indulgence, dragging their tired bodies to the motel's breakfast room. They forced down eggs and bacon and drank two mugs of coffee each, until they felt awake and sober enough to drive.

Amy checked out while Willa finished packing. Willa noticed a missed call on her cell and pushed the callback button. She tensed up as a man's voice said his name was Tyler. She quickly turned the cell off, shoved it deep into her daypack and left.

Amy sat on the hood of her car, watching Willa approach. "Did you have the runs this morning, Willa?" she asked with a lopsided smile.

"Amy, please. I'm in no mood for jokes."

"Well, it took you long enough to get here, so I figured … you know."

Willa threw her daypack into the back seat. "Well, you figured wrong. Let's go."

Amy hopped off the hood and into the car. "You're sure you can drive now?"

"It's my turn." Willa started the car and moved onto the highway. She drove with her body close to the steering wheel, her eyes staring ahead like a freaked-out Pekingese. A few minutes later, Amy told her to stop. Willa didn't seem to hear her. Finally, Amy yelled "*Willa!*" in her ear.

Willa flinched. "Yes?"

"Aren't you going a bit far with this thing about my turn, your turn? You're cross-eyed, for Christ's sake. I'm in danger here. Let *me* drive."

Willa blinked and slowed to a stop. She turned a grey face to Amy. "You're in better shape than I am?"

Amy grunted. "Let's just say I've partied more. Move over."

Amy drove with all windows down, listening to a rock station, trying to ignore her headache and raw throat. She'd finished her last cigarette after breakfast, promising herself that she'd never smoke again.

"*Jeez!*" she yelled as a rusty old Dodge flew past her, making her swerve onto the shoulder before gaining control. She watched the car disappear in the distance. "That guy must be driving 200 clicks."

"What's that?" Willa asked half asleep.

"Some speed freak almost scared me off the road. Relax. He's probably in Alaska by now."

* * *

Tyler slowed down wondering if it was Amy's Kia he'd just passed. She'd be going through Quesnel, a few minutes up the road. He should stop there and check it out. He speeded up again. Five minutes later, he entered Quesnel, pulled into a mini mall on a corner and parked near the highway. He grabbed his binoculars, got out of the car to get a clear view from behind it, adjusted the distance and waited. As the Kia neared, he looked straight into Amy's eyes with his raised binoculars trained on her window. "Gotcha."

He jumped back in his car and pulled out on the highway as the third car behind the Kia. He'd caught a glimpse of a girl sitting beside Amy. This wasn't the right time. He'd get his chance. Nothing could stop him now. Amy could have given him the money when he'd asked nicely. Now she had no choice.

* * *

Amy drove straight past Quesnel with all its cigarette-selling stores, then turned east toward Barkerville. Fifteen miles farther east, she pulled onto the last leg of the drive, a dusty, bumpy dirt road leading to Bowron Lake Park. She rolled the windows up and turned on the air conditioner. It blew hot air instead of cold. She opened the windows again. A pickup truck in front of her stirred up a cloud of dust that made its way into her eyes and mouth.

Why didn't I buy cigarettes in Quesnel?

She glanced at Willa who slept through the rough ride. *How can she sleep like that?* Amy touched her arm.

Willa sat up and rubbed her eyes. "Are we there?"

"How much longer do we have on this godforsaken road?"

Willa yawned and stretched. "Forty-five minutes, something like that. Why is it so hot in here?"

"The air conditioner isn't working."

"Oh."

* * *

Tyler watched Amy turn left onto a dirt road and followed. There were no other cars between them now. The sand and dust stirred up by Amy's car hung in the air far behind her, making it hard for him to see the road. He slowed down a bit, but not too much, needing to keep her in sight to know that she hadn't turned somewhere. Soon he could barely see the road through the streaks of dust moved around by the windshield wipers. He pressed the washer switch. The water made it worse – his wipers were too old to move it around. When he drove with his head out the window, he could see her car now and then as the road twisted. Suddenly, he saw her turn left. He fell back some more. When he reached the road Amy had taken, he saw a large campground on the left with people milling around. He kept going straight ahead.

Chapter 6

When Amy pulled into the Bowron Lake campground, she was covered in grit, dying for a cigarette. Willa rolled down her window, reached over and beeped the horn, waving to a group of people at a picnic table by the water. "Part of our gang," she said. "Everyone's here now except Max and Kaley."

Her friends waved back, picked up their backpacks and made their way toward the car.

Amy had just parked when a dust-covered VW Beetle with luggage sprouting from the windows pulled into the parking lot.

"Oh, here are Max and Kaley now," Willa jumped out. "Come and say hello."

As Amy walked up to them, a stocky guy with short hair and glasses and his blonde girlfriend, small enough to fit into his pocket, climbed from the car and hugged Willa.

Willa reached for Amy. "This is my cousin, Amy."

Handshakes and smiles all around.

"And here's the rest of the gang." The group from the picnic table caught up with them. Willa introduced her friend and fellow intern, Chad, a tall gangly man with longish blonde hair and knobby knees. He introduced his girlfriend, Kim, a perky redhead with freckles everywhere, even on her ears.

Max motioned to two tall men with caramel-coloured skin and black hair standing off to the side. "And there's Ben and his younger brother, Paul," he said.

Probably of East Indian descent, Amy guessed as she shook hands with Paul, a little soft around the edges. Ben, beside him, leaner with blue eyes and strong angular features, obviously spent more time at the gym. He nodded. Amy returned the nod, thinking he wasn't the shaking kind, wondering where he got his blue eyes from.

They all went to the registration centre and signed in. They were asked to leave their car keys at the centre and dry bags on the ground beside their cars.

"Kaley just got her real-estate licence," Willa said to Amy when they unloaded the Kia. "She's very excited about it. Max is a defence lawyer."

"He looks too young for that," Amy noted.

"I know. He's a bit of an oddball, but he's very bright."

Amy walked down to the beach and washed the dust from her face and arms. Heading back, she saw a short-haired woman in a brown T-shirt, cargo shorts and leather hiking boots approach the group. "I see you're all here," she said in a strong voice. "I'm Helen, your guide."

After the introductions, Helen smiled at the group. "We'll start with orientation, and then we'll have lunch." She motioned to the lodge entrance. "This way. Follow me." She moved toward the lodge with brisk strides.

Amy clicked her heels and saluted. Willa turned away, stifling a snicker. A large map on a wall in the orientation room depicted a chain of interconnecting lakes and rivers. Viewed from above, they formed a giant rectangle, enclosing a large, jagged-edged landmass between them.

Helen pointed to the northwest corner of the rectangle. "This is where we are now." She moved her pointer horizontally. "Today, we'll paddle east on Kibbee Lake to the end of Indianpoint Lake and set up our first camp there. Tomorrow, we'll start paddling the long Isaac Lake and set up camp, over here." She pointed at a spot on the rectangle's right side. "On day three, we'll paddle the rest of Isaac Lake to the southeast corner …" She went through the whole route, tracing it with her pointer, "and on our last day, we'll paddle Bowron River and Bowron Lake back to where we are now."

"How far is that?" Paul asked.

"The full circuit is 116 kilometers long, or 72 miles," Helen said.

"Sounds like a long stretch to cover in only six and a half days."

Helen smiled. "It's doable."

"Will there be other people around?" Kim asked.

"Yes," Helen said. "There will be other groups, but you might not see them. We space the groups to allow everyone to have as much privacy as possible. On rare occasions, you might see or hear a powerboat. Those are manned by park rangers. No other motors are permitted on the water. The rangers patrol the lakes every day, checking wildlife, watching for fire hazards, keeping the park safe."

* * *

Tyler continued on the dirt road leading behind the resort, past stacks of lumber and discarded garden machinery, scanning for an obscure place to park unseen. The road ended at a large storage shed. He noticed a field of chest-high grasses behind the shed and drove into the weeds alongside the shed, turned behind it and pulled deep into the grasses and stopped.

Leaning back in the seat, he grinned at the luck of the draw. He couldn't have found a more perfect hiding place. As he relaxed, he became aware of a pulsing pain in his jaw and checked the rear-view mirror. His stomach heaved at the sight. The bandage had come off, and the gaping wound, filled with sand and dust, made him look like a zombie. Faint and shaking, he scrambled for his pills, downed a couple and sat with closed eyes, waiting for them to take effect.

After rinsing the dust out of the wound with disinfectant, he checked his backpack for things he'd need to bring: syringe, dope, map, binoculars, tarp, water, jerky, duct tape, rope, flashlight knife, gun. Before leaving, he scanned the surroundings, grabbed his jacket and quietly slipped outside. Moving away from the car, he glanced back. The high grasses and the dust rendered the car almost invisible. A spiteful smirk flashed across his face as he disappeared into the forest.

Chapter 7

After the orientation, the kayakers went into the dining room to have lunch. "Enjoy the meal," Helen said. "It'll be awhile before you have gourmet food again."

Amy stared at the breaded piece of fish on her plate. Not her favourite food. She looked up at Willa. "Gourmet? What are we getting from now on?"

"Don't worry. Chad told me we'll get simple, healthy meals. Some fresh food, some pre-cooked and frozen, some canned."

Amy finishing her food and pulled her cell from her bag to check for messages. "Cell phones don't work here," Chad said.

Max, sitting beside Amy looked at the phone. "What's with the vintage phone, Amy?" he said. "How old is that?"

Amy grinned. "I got it seven years ago. It works great and it suits me. I only use it for making calls and checking messages. Less distraction." She put it back in her bag and told Willa she'd make a quick call to Meg before they were leaving. She went to use the phone at the registration desk. "Hi boss," she said, when Meg picked up. "How's it going?"

"Hi Amy, things are going great here. I'm a bit backed up today, but you know, it's Saturday. So where are you now?"

Amy was in the middle of telling her when a shrill whistle jerked her attention toward the entrance door.

Helen took her fingers out of her mouth and pointed to a van outside. "Your transportation is here to take you and your gear to the weigh station. Let's move."

"What's that?" Meg asked.

"Our guide," Amy said. "She's a boot camp wannabe."

Meg chuckled. "Well, off to the battle station."

At the weigh station, assigned kayaks and two-wheeled carts were waiting in a line. "When you load your kayaks, keep a warm jacket handy and leave some space for food," Helen said. "We all have to carry an equal weight of food, liquids and tools."

Amy watched Helen loading a canoe. She was just about to say something when Helen looked up at her. "It's lighter and easier when you're paddling alone," she said.

"Aha."

After loading and making sure the kayaks were properly tied to the wheeled carts, the group lined up at the trailhead.

"It's been a dry summer, so the water level is low," Helen said. "We have to portage the first three miles, about five K. Then we'll have a short paddle on Kibbee Lake, portage another three K and then have a final paddle to our first campsite on Indianpoint Lake."

"Don't worry," she added, seeing their stunned faces, "It's mainly downhill."

Amy looked over at the beginning of the trail, which sloped steeply uphill. "That doesn't look downhill to me."

"Don't worry about a few slopes along the way," Helen said. "We'll all help."

"Right." *I need a smoke.*

Ben and Paul, first in line, practically ran up the hill with their kayak. A moment later, Ben came back, offering Amy and Willa a hand.

"Thanks," Amy said. "But we can do it ourselves."

Ben nodded and stepped aside.

Amy turned to Willa. "Ready?"

"Sure am."

As they struggled to get their kayak up the hill, Amy felt the odd push and suspected Ben hadn't taken the hint. At the top, she quickly turned around to make sure, but saw only Willa with an innocent look on her face.

Amy pointed to her. "I know that look. He helped, didn't he?"

Willa turned around. "Who?"

* * *

From his hiding place in the forest behind the weigh station, Tyler was getting drowsy as he listened to the guide shouting her boring instructions. He closed his eyes.

* * *

The group filed down the trail to the sound of carefree chatter and laughter until the load got the better of them and the sounds of conversation faded. By the time they reached Kibbee Lake, their legs were shaking, faces burning and T-shirts soaked with sweat.

"Let's take a break, have some food before we continue," Helen said.

Relieved, they let go of the pull-straps and watched Helen set out packages of crackers, individually-wrapped cheese slices and a few strips of jerky. "There you go," she said. "There's juice in the cooler. Bon appétit."

Amy looked at the food. "I see what you meant with your comment about gourmet food."

"Well, you could try sending out some smoke signals," Helen quipped. "Maybe a gourmet chief will come to your rescue."

Ben laughed.

Amy took a juice from the cooler, grabbed a jerky and walked off.

Helen shrugged. "I guess she's used to bigger and better," she said, sitting down on a log beside Ben with her food.

"I think she just quit smoking," Willa said, joining them on the log.

"Oh, I see," Helen said. "That explains it. I went through that hell a year ago. I'm glad you told me."

A few minutes later, Helen got up and put the food away. She stuck two fingers in her mouth and whistled. "Gather over here, please."

Helen showed them how to tie their wheeled carts onto the kayaks, and one by one, the group members put into the water. After a short paddle and another portage, they put in at Indianpoint Lake.

As they travelled farther east, heavy clouds moved in bringing rain. Within minutes, the air turned grey and a cold breeze came up from the southeast. As sudden gusts of wind whipped up the water, the kayakers quickly secured their paddles under the hatch straps, got into their jackets, then retrieved their paddles and braced themselves for waves coming from all directions.

"Get closer to the shore!" Helen shouted.

They struggled to inch forward in the strong wind – hoods up, heads down. Waves splashed over their kayaks and water seeped in under skirts designed to keep it out, soaking their shorts and chilling their bottoms and legs. Checking the shoreline, they didn't seem to be moving forward at all.

* * *

Tyler woke up to howling winds pulling at the tarp around him. He peeked out at a grey sky and drizzling rain. A family of four came out of one of the guest cabins along the waterfront, hurried across the yard and disappeared into the main lodge. He looked at the time. Five o'clock. They were probably serving dinner. The resort area lay quiet. He knew from the brochure that groups were spaced, leaving several hours between them, so from now it should be quiet until the next morning.

He hadn't seen any paddles in the canoes lined up on the beach by the water, but guests had left their paddles on the porch at one of the cabins. He inched his way there and soundlessly removed one. Moments later a green canoe was lifted off the beach onto the back of a dark figure quickly moving into the forest, past the deserted weigh station, up the hill and out of sight.

Tyler reached the first lake, checked his map, wrapped the tarp around himself and started to paddle along the left shore.

Chapter 8

"Head for that first tongue of land!" Helen pointed with her paddle.

A few minutes later, the rain stopped as swiftly as it had begun, and shortly after that the wind died down. It was as if it all had been an illusion. When the group slid to a stop on the sandy beach of their first campsite, they remained in their kayaks, wind-whipped and weary, waiting for the painful knots in their arms and shoulders to loosen up before unloading.

Willa crawled from her kayak and sat down on the beach. Amy looked at her face, drained of colour. "How are you doing?"

"Think if we'd capsized," Willa said, her voice small and shaky. "We could've drowned."

"It's fine now, so stop scaring yourself."

* * *

Tyler moved steadily over the water, enjoying the feel of a canoe again. He'd learned how to paddle long before his parents threw him out of the house for stealing from them. Cheap bastards. They had money to burn and wouldn't help him out in a squeeze. They'd had a bit of a scuffle, he'd pushed his mother down a set of stairs. It was only half a stair, five steps. She barely had a bruise, but his father threatened to notify the police.

Fuck'em.

The rain and wind had stopped by the time he found the landing for the second portage. He had a smoke, checked the map again, then quickly made his way through the dense forest to the next lake. He started the longer paddle, moving closer to shore as the sky turned darker. Soon, the nagging uncertainty of being on course in the darkness left him exhausted and agitated. The only thing that kept him going was his quest for money, which he intended to make Amy pay. This time he wouldn't ask – he'd take her for all she had.

Suddenly he heard voices and slowed down. Moving forward with silent strokes he scanned for movement. A moment later, he saw a glimmer of light between the trees on his left.

He'd found the bitch.

* * *

The group set up camp, still a bit shell-shocked from the storm and happy to be on solid ground. "The outhouse is in the forest behind us." Helen pointed. "Follow that path and you'll see it. Don't venture beyond it in the dark, though. There's a ledge a few meters behind it that's hard to see. It slopes steeply onto sharp rocks on that side of this beach."

Chad and Max had a fire going by the time they sat down to eat. Willa couldn't get warm and ran off to the tent to get her jacket. After dinner, everyone sat around the fire, talking about the day, pretending to sip on Helen's version of coffee: instant powder mixed with leftover water from the boiled potatoes.

"It's good for you," Helen insisted. "And it gives the coffee a delicate flavour."

Willa took a sip and nodded to Amy. "It's not bad, you know."

Amy stared into the murky liquid. "Hmmm."

* * *

Tyler hid the canoe in the shrubbery near the edge of the beach, slipped his backpack on and quietly skulked through the brush into the woods behind the campsite. Suddenly the ground gave way under his left foot. Flailing, he managed to grab hold of a small tree and regain his balance. He checked the ground with his flashlight and froze – one more step, and he would have fallen down a steep bank onto sharp rocks below.

At the sound of someone approaching, he quickly turned the light off and crouched in the thicket. Feeling the ground, he found a rock as big as his fist and seized it. He relaxed when he realized he was hiding behind an outhouse, but the smell made him gag. When the person left, he moved into the woods and found a spot from where he had a clear view of the group. He wrapped himself in the tarp and settled in for a long wait. Amy always went to the john in the middle of the night. This would be his next chance to snatch her away. He had the syringe ready. She wouldn't know what hit her.

Eyes adjusted to the light from the campfire, Tyler watched as a girl got up and walked toward him. He'd seen her before somewhere. She ducked into a tent nearby. A moment later she came out carrying a jacket. Tyler grinned as he recognized the skinny bitch he'd seen with Amy.

When she returned to her friends, he slipped into the tent, searched through the daypacks, found Amy's wallet, pocketed her bankcard and slipped back out.

Chewing on a jerky, Tyler checked who went to the john before retiring for the night. Someone extinguished the campfire, and shortly after, all talking stopped. As soon as his eyes adjusted to the nightlight, he trained them on Amy's tent, looking for movements. If she didn't show before two, he'd have to leave – it would be too risky to stay longer; he needed the night to get her to his car and leave unseen. He fished out a couple of pills and swallowed them. He'd been dosing more frequently lately. But these were strenuous circumstances.

At close to two, Tyler saw a weak light, heard someone approaching. He slid out from under the tarp and got ready to pounce, but quickly dropped behind a bush when he saw that it was a man. The man stopped and looked searchingly in his direction. Before the man knew it, he'd been felled to the ground, knocked unconscious with a rock.

Tyler knew he had to split in a hurry. The guy was going to be missed. Soon this place would be crawling with cops. Mad with fury over another failure to nab Amy, Tyler dragged the man to the steep bank and pushed him over onto the rocky beach. He quickly retrieved his belongings and slithered off into the forest like a menacing snake.

Chapter 9

On Sunday morning Amy woke early. She grabbed her jacket, slipped quietly out of the tent and walked to the beach. Veiled by clouds, the mountains appeared distant beneath the pale grey sky, the air moist and cool. The lake lay hidden beneath a silvery mist, out of which came the sad cry of a solitary loon.

Amy felt safe there, distanced from bad news. The strenuous paddling the day before had finally steered her mind away from the city, its worries and dangers. The physical challenge stimulated her. She'd never felt so alive.

She jumped as someone screamed for help. She got up and ran to the campsite where everyone came stumbling out of their tents, looking toward the outhouse. Helen was almost there with Ben in hot pursuit. When the rest of the group caught up with them, Helen asked them to stay at the top of the bank. She pointed to Willa. "You're a nurse, right?"

"I'm a respiratory therapist," Willa said. "I'll do my best to help."

"Come with us," Helen said.

Grabbing on to roots, Ben, Helen and Willa made their way down the bank to the rocky beach where Chad lay on the ground with his head in Kim's lap. Kim was crying, begging them to help. Ben gently led her aside to let Willa tend to Chad.

"He's conscious," Willa said. "A cut on his head is bleeding. I need compresses." A few minutes later she added, "He has bruises, but no broken bones. His breathing is regular, but he's weak and confused; signs of hypothermia."

"Thanks Willa. I'll get on the two-way radio," Helen said. "Paul, come and fetch the first aid kit."

Ben asked the rest of the group waiting on top of the bank to bring blankets, sleeping bags, anything warm.

Willa tended to Chad, attached layers of compresses over the cut on his head, and checked his pulse, mouth and breathing. They covered him in sleeping bags and wrapped a padded jacket around his head, then moved in close to him for additional warmth.

"Help's on the way," Helen announced as she approached. "Kim, can we talk?"

Kim looked back at Chad. "Okay," she said reluctantly.

As the two of them talked, Ben asked Chad if he knew what happened. "A b … bear … black bear," Chad stuttered weakly.

"Thanks, Chad." Ben patted his shoulder. "Help's coming. Just try to relax."

Amy and Kaley helped Kim dismantle the tent. "I'm so scared, I'm shaking," Kim said as she packed her and Chad's belongings. "He isn't sure, but he thinks he surprised a bear. All he knows is he was whacked off his feet, slammed his head into something and passed out. He could've been killed. I hope he's going to be okay. I'm so worried."

"I know," Kaley said. "Do you want me to come with you?"

"Oh, no. You guys carry on. Once the paramedics get here, I'll be fine."

"We'll all be anxious to know how he's doing. Promise to call the lodge as soon as you've talked to his doctor."

"I will."

Helen came up to Amy. "The ranger is here to pick up Kim and Chad's kayak," she said. "Can you show me which one it is?"

"Sure," Amy said.

"Hell of a way to start a holiday," Helen said as they made their way across the campsite to the sandy part of the beach. "I don't understand how this could happen. We keep track of where the bears are, and none are supposed to be in this area right now."

"That's interesting," Amy said, "because Willa told me she couldn't tell if he'd been hit by a bear, that the tears in his clothes didn't look like claw marks to her."

Helen looked thoughtful. "I just can't think of what else it could be. Well ... I'm sure we'll hear about it if there's any doubt about what happened. By the way, are you and Willa related?"

"Yes. Cousins."

"Where do you live?"

"In Vancouver." Amy pointed. "There it is. The one with the green stripe along the top."

Helen stuck two fingers in her mouth and whistled to get the ranger's attention, pointed to the kayak. He nodded and started to back up to it.

"I hear the zodiac," Helen said. "Let's go back and see how they're doing." She kept her hand on Amy's shoulder as they walked back to the others. Once there, she gave it a squeeze. "Thanks for your help."

"No problem."

A large zodiac carrying medical personnel had pulled up on

the rocks near Chad. The medics were checking him, while asking Kim what happened.

"He woke up at three in the morning with stomach cramps," Kim said in a shaky voice. "He headed out to the outhouse, and I went back to sleep. When I woke up at five, he wasn't back yet, so I went to check on him. I knocked on the door, whispered his name. At first I didn't hear anything. Then I heard moaning behind the outhouse, so I hurried around there. Luckily it was dawn, so I could see the ledge or I would've fallen down, too … Is he going to be okay?"

"It looks pretty good," one of the medics said. They removed the sleeping bags and jacket, lifted Chad onto a stretcher, wrapped him in blankets and moved him into the zodiac. Then they helped Kim get in and sit down.

"I'll call the lodge," she called out to her friends as the zodiac pulled out.

The sun stayed with the kayakers most of the day as they paddled the first part of Isaac Lake. Knowing the group was anxious to know how Chad was doing, Helen used the two-way radio at the campsite to find out. Kim had left a message. The doctor examining Chad hadn't found anything more serious than cuts and bruises, but because of the hit to his head, decided to keep him overnight for observation.

The group set up camp in an upbeat mood. As they waited for Helen's chili to warm up, they sipped on wine – compliments of Max – and toasted to Chad for being out of danger.

Willa nudged Amy. "I'm proud of you," she whispered. "No smokes for two days."

Amy felt a twinge of guilt. "I've been irritable, haven't I?"

Willa shrugged. "On and off."

"Sorry. I don't mean to be."

"It's all right. I hear it's tough to quit."

"Yeah, but still, I'll work on it."

After dinner, they cleaned up and settled in around the campfire. Max sat with his arm around Kaley, whispering in her ear, kissing her cheek. Amy felt a strange sadness as she watched them. Suddenly a painful memory invaded her mind, cramping her stomach. She needed to be alone.

Bidding the others goodnight, she headed for the trail. She stopped outside the spill of light from the campfire to let her eyes adjust to the meager glow of a crescent moon, then made a beeline for the beach. She saw a kayak on its side and lay down on the wet sand behind it.

Almost four months had gone by since she'd lost the baby. Why couldn't she wipe the image from her mind – of her mother trying to hide her relief at news of the miscarriage? Her words were scratched into Amy's soul and repeated like a broken record: "Well, it's no big surprise to me, the way you two carried on. It's probably just as well as you decided to throw the baby's father out. You should've waited to start a family until you'd become more mature, that's what I think."

Amy thought back to her childhood, growing up in Vancouver's ritzy Kitsilano area, watching her father on the phone, giving directions and telling people what to do. Her mother used to say he could sell ice to Eskimos. Her parents barely knew she existed. The two of them were always going places. Amy adored them, looked up at them as people she'd die to get close to, but didn't know how to. She worshipped her mother; thought her to be the most beautiful woman in the world.

A sharp rock turned in Amy's chest, making yet another etching on her inside as a vision from her childhood appeared.

She was four. Begging her mother to stay with her, even though she could see how much it annoyed her. Her mother would show her displeasure by turning her back and stop talking altogether. Amy could still feel how devastating that felt. Afraid to lose her mother's love, she then started to tell her she was sorry, beg her to forgive her. Her mother wouldn't respond, wouldn't look at her, just let her cry and beg for what seemed like hours. She always held off until Amy's voice became so raspy, and her words so wracked by sobs and hiccups, she couldn't hear what she said. Her mother would become impatient then, and would reluctantly agree to forgive her.

That happened so often, it became Amy's strongest memory from her early childhood. Feeling miserable, she took it out on her nannies. Many came and went. She was the kid from hell.

By the age of thirteen, she'd become a head turner. Things changed. It seemed as if her parents suddenly discovered her. They started to meddle in everything she did. They insisted she wear dresses instead of jeans, interfered with her choice of friends, and referred to anyone with darker skin as "those people".

At that point, Amy didn't want their attention, tried to keep her distance, but they always found a way to haul her back, seeing that as a sign of their love and compassion. And that's how they had continued to this day.

Tears started running; Amy let them come.

A sudden sound snapped her from her grief. Someone was coming down the path. When the sound of footsteps grew more distant Amy sat up, peeped over the kayak and saw Ben walking down the beach.

She relaxed when she realized he hadn't seen her, and lay down out of sight, snug to the belly of the kayak. She tried to focus on something else. Soon, the cold dampness of the sand penetrated the back of her sweat suit. She rolled over, crawled to the bow and peeped around it. *Where did he go?*

The sound of a throat being cleared made her freeze. *Oh, no.* She must be quite a sight on her hands and knees with her wet butt in the air. She sat down and turned, looking at Ben's face, barely visible in the weak moonlight. "What are you doing here?"

"Came down for a bit of solitude, and look what I found in the dark."

Amy looked away. She knew he was trying to be funny, but felt so weighed down she couldn't smile. "I should get back." She held on to the side of the kayak and started to get up. The kayak tilted and her hand slid. Ben grabbed it to steady her.

"Thanks," she whispered, looking down.

Ben moved closer. "Are you all right?"

"I just needed to be alone for a moment."

"I'm sorry."

"It's not your fault. Don't worry about it." She pulled her hand out of his and wiped her face on her sleeve. "I … Never mind." She turned and walked away. She'd just crawled inside the tent when she heard Willa say goodnight to Ben.

"I've had my fill of jokes," Willa said when she came inside and changed. "I guess you and Ben had enough too, eh? What did you two talk about?"

"Not much."

"Oh yeah?" Willa poked her head out of her pyjama top, waggling her eyebrows.

"Willa, give it a rest."

Chapter 10

Tyler sat in the ramshackle cabin, spooning cold soup from a can. He didn't use the woodstove, fearing the smoke might attract unwanted attention. He knew he was dirty, smelly, even looking like a derelict with his hair and beard growing wild, but none of that mattered right now. As long as he kept his pill popping to a minimum, he could keep his head clear and focus on his next step. He didn't have time for another screw-up.

He tossed the empty can into a cardboard box on the floor, wiped the food from his beard with a sleeve, then pulled the Bowron Lake package and a pen from his pocket.

He circled the phone number on the back of the brochure, thinking he had two more days to get the money together for Mike Polanco. His greasy hair straggled on the table as he bent over to study the Bowron Park Rules and Restrictions, thinking up a new plan.

* * *

As the group paddled south on Isaac Lake on Monday morning, glacial melt-water from the Cariboo Mountains chilled the air, making them reach for warmer clothes. A swift wind whipped the water into froth, forcing them closer to shore. Ten minutes later, it was calm again. And so it went. The wind surprised them every time, as did the intervening calm spells. Finally, after paddling ten miles, they reached the new campsite.

"Why didn't anyone tell us about the insane weather in this place?" Kaley said. "It's more moody than Grandma's potbellied pig."

"I shouldn't have quit that aerobics class," Willa said. "Thanks for doing most of the work, Amy."

Amy rolled her shoulders. "Don't mention it. I loved the workout."

"Could use some help with the grill," Helen said, walking by. "We're having steaks tonight."

"Steaks?"

Exhaustion forgotten, everyone hurried off to set up camp and start a fire.

Soon after dinner, Willa stumbled off to bed, saying she couldn't stay awake. Amy poured herself a cup of coffee and sat down on a log by the fire, contemplating going to bed as well.

Ben sat down beside her and looked around at the group. "When Paul and I accepted Max's invitation to come on this trip, we didn't know what we were in for," he said. "It's different from anything we've done before. So far, it's been a lot of fun, bear attacks aside."

"Same here," Amy said. "It's just by coincidence, and Willa's unflagging determination, that I'm here at all."

"I suggest a toast to Willa, then." Ben grinned and raised his mug.

Amy looked at him from under her bangs, thinking that would've been okay without the ambiguous grin.

Max stood up. "I'm going for a walk on the beach before I turn in. Anyone else?"

Everyone got up, kicked their shoes off and strolled down the moonlit beach.

"Mmm," Amy said dreamily as she wiggled her toes through the soft, cool sand.

"What are you smiling at?" Ben asked, suddenly at her side again.

"I was just thinking about how nice it would be to have a sandbox behind my chair at work."

Ben looked confused.

"I'm a hairdresser. I stand a lot … behind chairs."

He smiled. "Ah-ha. Now I get it."

Max called, "Let's go for a dip." He pulled his T-shirt off and ran into the water, daring the others to join him. Ben and Paul followed, throwing themselves in the water before they realized it was icy cold. They raced back to the beach, shouting and cursing while the rest of the group kept walking, ignoring them.

"How about this place?" Helen said, siding up to Amy, pointing to the sky. "Brighter stars, private beach. Beats anything they can offer you in the city, eh? You should have brought your boyfriend."

"Hah," Amy said. "That'll be the day."

"Oh yeah?" Helen reached up and touched Amy's hair. "I love your hair. It's so soft."

"Thank you." *What's up with her?* Amy could feel Helen staring and turned to see if she wanted something. Helen looked into her eyes with a radiant smile. Amy looked away, feeling uncomfortable. *Where is everybody?*

The guys behind them raced around on the beach trying to warm up from their cold dip. Willa and Kaley walked way ahead, stargazing.

Helen leaned into Amy. "You're a good kayaker," she said, placing her hand on Amy's arm, stroking her bicep. "And strong. You must be working out."

Jeez. Amy glanced at Helen again, still looking at her with that silly smile. *She's hitting on me.* She'd never been in a situation like that before. Didn't know what to say. She wanted to tell her she wasn't interested like that, but didn't think she could phrase it the same as she would to a man. She liked Helen and didn't want to hurt her.

Right then, she saw Willa and Kaley turn and walk toward them. "I suppose it's time to go back," she said, relieved.

Amy woke up at dawn, dressed and crawled out of the tent. The air smelled of fall. Towels fluttered on lines, and leaves slapped each other in a light wind as she made her way to the beach. She saw Paul wading back from a swim, reaching for a towel on a log.

"You're up early," she said and sat down on the sand.

Paul smiled, wrapped the towel around his shoulders and sat down beside her. "That dip sure beats having a shower."

"Too cold for me. I hear you're going to medical school."

"Not yet. I will be in a couple of weeks from now."

"What made you decide to become a doctor?"

Paul shrugged. "A toss between being a cop or a doctor really."

"Why is that?"

Paul picked up a handful of sand. "Our father, a police sergeant, was killed in a crossfire. I hated that helpless feeling – that I couldn't stop it or fix it, you know. If that makes any sense."

"I think it does. I'm sorry about your dad."

"Yeah." Paul sat in silence sifting sand from hand to hand.

"Would you like to talk about it?"

"Maybe some other time." He brushed sand off his hands. "Should we go and have something to eat?"

* * *

At dusk, Tyler tucked his hair into a ski hat, pulled the jacket collar up to cover the wound, checked that he had the Bowron brochure in his pocket and headed for the nearest town. He entered a phone booth at a gas station and made a call to the Bowron Lake Lodge. He introduced himself as Sergeant Bellamy of the Vancouver Police Department and requested their assistance in having one of their vacationers return to Vancouver as soon as possible, stressing it was an emergency situation, that they needed to talk to her about a case they couldn't discuss over the phone. The ranger taking the call said he would contact the person and deliver the message early the next morning. Tyler thanked him and they hung up.

Knowing that anyone looking for him would be looking for his car, Tyler drove around town, looking for a car to steal. When he spotted one in an almost deserted shopping mall parking lot, he left his car at an empty construction site nearby, walked over to the other car, hot-wired it and drove off. Next, he stopped at a gas station, paid cash at the pump and filled up. He bought a hamburger and a drink at a drive-through and headed for the cabin. He finished the burger, threw the wrappings out the window and let out a loud belch. So far, everything was going according to plan. He could almost taste the tequila.

Back at the cabin, he checked on the coke he kept hidden and counted the money in his money belt. It wouldn't be long now until he had enough cash for Mike. This time, he'd been doing it right. He pocketed a knife, checked his gun and popped a couple of pills. He'd earned it.

Chapter 11

At the end of Isaac Lake, the kayakers made camp in a grassy area at the base of a narrow peninsula that stretched halfway across the lake. The water was warm and calm near the campsite. Farther out, the current picked up speed, swirled around the land's tip and rushed down a chute into rapids below, at the beginning of Isaac River.

After a swim, Amy went to sit on a grassy knoll by the edge of the chute. She leaned back on a tree and closed her eyes, soothed by the sound of rushing water and the warmth of the afternoon sun.

She started as Ben said, "There you are." He and Paul sat down beside her. Paul studied the chute, said, "Can't wait to go down this one in the morning."

Ben nodded, taking in the churning water. "It'll take a bit of maneuvering."

Amy screwed a finger in her ear, as if to clear it. "Did I hear you right? What are you talking about?"

Ben burst out laughing.

Amy glanced at him. *He has an awesome smile.*

"He thinks I'm kidding," Paul said to Amy.

Ben slapped Paul on the back. "Have a nice trip."

Max walked up, waving a Frisbee. "Anyone want to play?"

Paul jumped up. "Sure thing."

Ben turned to Amy. "I'm thinking of going for a walk along the riverbed. Do some exploring. Do you want to come along?"

"No, I'm quite content here, thanks." Amy saw the disappointed look on his face. "Well, okay. As long as I don't have to get down there in a kayak."

"No need to." Ben slid down the sandy bank to the bottom, turned and stepped up on a boulder. "Put your legs over the edge."

Amy did, and Ben reached for her ankles. "Slide down a bit, and I'll catch you."

"You'd better." She started to slide.

He caught her, lowered her to the ground and stepped down from the boulder. He took her hand to steady her as they crossed the wet stones beside the chute. Farther down the riverbed, where the going got easier, she slipped her hand out of his – wouldn't want him to get any ideas.

The sound of the rapids softened behind them. Rounding a bend, they stopped dead. Fifteen meters ahead, a grizzly stood up on two legs by the water's edge, sniffing the air and looking their way.

Ben swung Amy behind him and told her to back away slowly. With her fingers digging into his sides, he held his arms out to appear larger. Inching back and avoiding eye contact, he mumbled soft words she couldn't hear. Suddenly the bear dropped down on all fours – and charged. Amy screamed, convinced this was the end of her life. Seconds later, the bear skidded to a halt only three meters in front of them, veered off and ran into the forest.

Amy was shaking, too petrified to speak. Ben put his arms around her, telling her not to worry. As he guided her back to the chute, Amy kept glancing over her shoulder, fearing the bear would come charging after them. Ben lifted her onto his shoulders. Max and Paul saw her head appear over the edge and reached down to help her up.

Paul looked down at Ben and grinned. "Now let's watch Ben getting out of this hole."

Ben glared at him, glanced back toward the trees and gestured impatiently for help. Paul followed his gaze, but saw nothing. Still, he and Max hauled Ben up right away.

"What were you looking for?" Paul asked as Ben brushed himself off.

Ben went over to Amy, "Are you all right?"

"I'm fine," Amy managed. "But that must be the mother of all riverbed strolls."

"What's going on?" Helen asked as she approached.

Ben told her what happened.

Helen's face darkened. "We're in the wilderness," she said. "You know I'm counting on you all to stick together and not venture off on your own."

Ben scratched his head, looking embarrassed. "You're right. My fault. Won't happen again."

"All right … anyway, I'm surprised. Bears have very good hearing and usually avoid people. Were you talking?"

Ben shook his head. "It was too noisy to talk that close to the chute. We were busy trying to keep our balance on the wet rocks and didn't pay attention."

Helen looked up at the trees for a moment. "Well, there's a bit of wind this way. He didn't smell you. Sounds like you surprised him, and he made a bluff charge. I don't think he'll be back, but I want you all to stay together on designated trails from now on."

"Why didn't you use your gun?" Max asked. "You could have scared him off with a shot in the air."

Ben gave him an annoyed glance. "Guns aren't allowed in the park."

Everyone looked confused, wondering what they were talking about. Ben glared at Max for a moment, then said, "My day job is detective."

"Now the secret is out," Paul mumbled.

Ben looked at Amy's questioning face, and offered a resigned nod.

"Are you a private detective?" she asked.

"Police detective."

"And a bodyguard. Lucky for me."

"I shouldn't have asked you …"

"Then I wouldn't have had that experience," she said with a lopsided grin, slapped his back and left with Willa to get into warmer clothing.

"Dinner will be ready in twenty minutes," Helen announced. She caught up to Amy and Willa and walked with them, her arm around Amy's shoulders. "That must have been a real shocker," she said.

Amy nodded. "No kidding. It was terrifying."

"Are you sure you're all right?"

"Yes, I'm fine."

"I'll come and help you with the dinner in a minute," Willa said to Helen.

When they were inside their tent, Willa stared accusingly at Amy. "Why did you guys wander off? You could have been mauled to death."

Amy sat down and gazed at her with an analytical eye. "You need a drink," she decided.

"That's for sure." Willa's eyes widened. "You mean you brought something?"

Amy pulled a mickey of scotch from one of her dry bags. "Thought it might come in handy."

"Scotch and wilderness kayaking. All right." Willa held her mug out. "Let's confuse my brilliant mind."

Amy poured a small amount into their mugs. "So …" Willa said, sipping her drink. "It seems like Ben is courting you."

"Courting? You sound like my grandmother."

Willa laughed. "I've been hanging around my dad too much lately. He's forever working on our family tree. When he talks about his grandparents, he uses words like that."

"How far back is he?"

"About 280 years. He's dying to see if any of his ancestors came from the Vikings, so he has a long way to go yet. Anyway, what do you think of Ben?"

"Well," Amy squirmed. "I think you're right about him being interested. He's a nice guy, but I'm not ready to get involved."

"I understand. You might have another problem, though. Paul thinks Helen's hitting on you, too."

Amy grunted. "I'd started to wonder. Apparently I'm a popular girl on this trip."

Willa gave her a quick hug. "Well, you're like a sister to me."

Amy gave her a bewildered look. *How do you respond to that?* "All right," she said. "That's good. Thank you. I think." She waved a hand. "But you have to stop drinking. You get too mushy. Let's go and eat."

Chapter 12

"We'll have a different experience today," Helen said on Wednesday morning. "We'll be kayaking part of the Cariboo River. The river is about a hundred meters wide, so you'll have room to move around and enjoy the experience."

"What do you mean 'the experience'?" Kaley asked.

"Once we get to the open river, things start to move faster …"

"How fast are we talking?" Willa interrupted, pushing her glasses up.

"At about the same speed as when you're paddling hard," Helen said. "There will be some ripples …"

"Ripples?" Kaley cut in, looking toward the chute.

"Those are not ripples," Helen said. "Those are rapids on Isaac River, and we're portaging around them. Ripples are like tiny waves ruffling the surface of the water. The idea is to relax, to let the river pull you along. That said, I'd like you to follow a few rules. I'll paddle in front at a safe speed. The rest of you stay behind me at all times. After about twenty minutes, we'll exit the river and veer into a channel that will take us to Lanezi Lake. Before that, you'll see me moving to the right side of the river.

You need to follow, quickly. Soon after that, you'll see a large yellow-and-black warning sign, telling you a waterfall is ahead. Just paddle in line behind me, near the riverbank, and it'll be an easy turn into the channel. The water there is calm and safe, so we can stop for a break."

"Sounds like we'll be close to the waterfall," Kaley said.

"The sign is well ahead of the fall. We'll have plenty of time to leave the river. Just follow me."

"Sounds like fun," Max said.

"Yeah," Amy said. She turned to Willa. "And you can rest your arms the whole time."

Willa tightened her lips. "Sounds a bit scary to me."

"One more thing," Helen said. "You might see a log, tree roots, or a low-hanging tree sticking out from the riverbank. We call them sweepers. Stay clear of them, and you'll be fine."

The group portaged past the chute and launched their kayaks in a sheltered area of the river. Forming a line behind Helen, they set out on calm water glittering in the morning sun. Rounding a bend, their kayaks were pulled along by the current. Everyone whooped in appreciation.

Amy put her paddle down and used the foot pedals controlling the rudder to steer. She leaned back in her seat and let the sun kiss her face. Willa, in front of her, held her paddle like a tightrope walker. "Willa, relax," she said. "Enjoy the ride."

"This feels like flying through major turbulence," Willa said. "I hate that."

"Major? Aren't you exaggerating just a teensy little bit?"

"Well … I guess." Willa lowered the paddle. "But we're moving so fast. Are you paddling?"

"No. I'm just steering to stay away from sweepers."

Helen, moving down the middle of the river, looked back at

the rest of the group now and then as they played in the current, tried to paddle against it, zigzag across it, make quick turns.

A few minutes later, Helen started to move over to the right side and waved to the rest of the group to follow. Everyone pulled in behind her, except Max and Kaley, busy playing around in the current in the middle of the river.

Helen yelled at them to slow down and move over to the right. Max saw her stabbing a finger repeatedly to a spot on her right side, and nodded.

Amy spotted the big yellow warning sign and pointed it out to Willa.

"Ohmygod." Willa looked at Max and Kaley struggling to veer right and slow down at the same time.

Helen told the rest of the group to fight the current and hang back to allow Max and Kaley to get into the channel first. Everyone struggled to paddle backward, anxiously watching.

When Max and Kaley finally reached the right side, just in front of Helen, they gave it all and pushed into the channel opening, almost capsizing as the back of their kayak bounced off the swampy channel bank, then righted itself. They were safe.

Relieved, the rest of the group followed. Everyone sat in the channel for a while, collecting themselves, grateful that no one had been hurt.

"I'm sorry, guys," Max said.

Helen grunted behind clenched teeth and looked at the group with an impatient frown. "You guys hired me to take you out into the wilderness as a guide. You better pay attention when I warn you about something, or you'll put us all in danger."

"Sorry, Helen," Kaley said, tears welling.

"All right," Helen snapped. "Enough apologizing. You're both safe, and that's what counts. Let's move on."

The group paddled the rest of the channel in silence. Their mood started to change as they moved onto Lanezi Lake, surrounded by spectacular mountains. After a short stop for lunch, they got back on the water and soon entered the shallow Sandy Lake on the southwest corner of the circuit. They dragged their kayaks over a few sandbanks and reached their next campsite in the late afternoon, overheated and exhausted. After setting up camp, they had a quick dinner before going for a twilight swim.

The seven of them rolled around in the shallow lake, moaning in pleasure as the warm water soothed their muscles and washed away their tension.

Helen was ducking up and down like a dolphin in the water, every now and then surfacing next to Amy. Amy saw her friends' amused looks and knew she had to do something – had to figure out how to make it clear to Helen that they wouldn't be a couple.

When she saw Helen waiting for her to get out of the water, Amy dried herself off, wrapped the towel around her neck and went up to her. "Helen, it's not you," she said in a kind voice. "I'm just not wired that way."

Helen gave her a disappointed grin. "What a shame."

They walked together to the tent area and said goodnight. Relieved, there had been no hard feelings, Amy snuggled up in her sleeping bag and drifted off to the sounds of Willa's soft breathing, wolves howling and owls hooting.

Chapter 13

Amy stirred in her sleeping bag. Someone was tapping on the tent.

"Amy, it's Helen," she whispered.

Amy blinked and opened her eyes. "Yes?"

"Will you come out, please?"

Now what? Amy sat up, grabbed her jacket from under a pile of clothes and crawled from the tent. Helen, barely visible in the early dawn, beckoned Amy away from the tent area.

Amy slipped into her jacket and checked the time. Five-thirty. She walked up to Helen, rubbing her eyes. "What's going on?"

"The ranger just motored down here from the lodge," Helen said in a hushed tone, pointing toward the beach where a uniformed man stood waiting beside his powerboat. "He wants to talk to you."

Amy tensed up. "Why?"

"I don't know. He has a message for you. Just talk to him. I'll come with you."

A message? Amy walked down the path, trying to ignore a feeling of foreboding.

"Hi, my name is Jim," the ranger greeted her. "Jim Maxwell.

Are you Amy Robinson?"

"Yes."

"I took a call from your local police last night. Your apartment has been broken into, and they want to see you. It sounded urgent."

Amy's heart sped up. "I don't get it. Someone broke into my place? I don't own anything worth stealing. What's the hurry?"

"I wouldn't know, ma'am. I just know they insisted you get back to the city right away."

"You mean now?"

"Yes." He cleared his throat. "I'm very sorry, ma'am."

There must be a mistake. "What could have happened to my apartment that can't wait two days? I don't think I have to go if I don't want to. Am I right?"

"Yes ... I guess," Jim admitted reluctantly. "But they said it was an emergency situation and they needed to talk to you about a case they couldn't discuss over the phone."

Amy's stomach cramped. It wasn't his fault. Something bad must have happened. "Oh, all right. What's the number to the police? Who should I ask for?"

"A Sergeant Bellamy, ma'am. I'll give you the number when we get to the lodge."

"Can't I just call him from here?"

"You can call from the lodge. There's no transmission out here."

"How far is it to the lodge?"

"About thirty kilometres." He motioned to his boat. "An hour, at least, with that motor. Well ... anytime you're ready."

Amy turned to Helen. "I'll check with the police when I get to the lodge. If I'm lucky, I'll be back before you guys finish breakfast."

"Sorry, Amy. I'd love to see you back here, believe me, but that's not going to happen. There are very strict rules here. The rangers are way too busy to be a taxi service. They're allowed to pick up and deliver a person in an emergency only." Helen put her arm around Amy's shoulders. "Let's go talk to Willa and get your things together."

Amy struggled to hide her frustration. "And what about her? We have a double kayak. She can't paddle it alone."

"Not a problem, said Helen. "I'll join her in the double and leave my canoe here to be picked up later."

"But it's only Thursday morning," Amy moaned. "I have two more days. Willa will freak."

"She'll be fine. We'll take good care of her."

"I need to talk to the others. Say goodbye."

"Amy, I don't see the point in alarming them. I'm sure they'll get in touch with you as soon as they're back in the city. Also, Jim needs to get going."

Inside the tent, Willa's sleep-fogged mind struggled to grasp what Amy was telling her. "Wait a minute. We only have two more days. Can't they wait?"

"Apparently not." Amy changed into jeans and a long-sleeved top. She put her pyjamas, toiletries bag, water bottle, book, a couple of T-shirts and a sweat suit in her daypack. The rest of her clothes went into a dry bag.

"You're going to drive all that way alone? I'll come with you."

Amy threw towels and her other books into another bag. "I don't want you to cut your holiday short just because I have to be in Vancouver a couple of days earlier. I'd feel bad about that."

"Yeah, but …"

"I wouldn't be surprised if it was Tyler who broke into my apartment, and I don't want to subject you to that either. So you finish the trip, and I'll get this mess cleared up, okay? You can catch a ride home with Ben and Paul, then we'll get together in a few days."

"You'll take the Trans-Canada Highway I hope."

"You betcha. I'll leave the roller coaster driving to you." Amy packed her sleeping bag.

"It's a shorter route, but still, don't try to make it in one day."

"I won't drive ten hours in one go, all stressed out and mad." Amy checked her daypack to make sure she had her purse and wallet there. "I'll send a message as soon as I've checked into a motel – probably sometime in the afternoon. And another one tomorrow when I'm back in Vancouver. Will that make you feel better?"

"Yes. So, what do I say to the others?"

Amy plopped on the ground. "I just hate to leave." She twisted her hair and secured it with a clip on top of her head. "I really like your friends. And this trip has been amazing. Tell everyone that from me. And tell them I'd like to get together sometime."

"I will. I'm sure everyone feels the same. They're your friends too now."

"Yes." Amy's face softened. "I guess you're right."

"What about Ben?"

"What about him? He's a friend now, too, isn't he?" Amy looked around in the tent. "I think that's it. Will you help me with my stuff?"

They brought the gear to the beach. The ranger was busy pushing his powerboat away from the shoreline. When the water reached halfway up his rubber boots, he lowered an anchor and waded back to shore.

"The lake is shallower than normal this summer. I have to make sure we can get out after we're loaded." He picked up Amy's gear. "You better roll up your pants," he added. "I'm not carrying you."

"I promised Willa to call," Amy said to Helen. "I plan to check into a motel for the night. I'll call the park people from there to let them know I'm fine."

"Okay. Unless we hear something to the contrary, we'll presume that's the case."

"Sounds good."

Helen told Jim about Amy's forthcoming call.

"I'll let the office know to expect it," he said.

Amy pulled Willa into a quick hug. "Take care, buddy. See you in a few days." She rolled up her pants, picked up her shoes and waded to the boat. She waved until Helen and Willa were out of sight, then watched the landscape rush by, thinking it would all be gone in an hour. She wanted to wake up to find that leaving was just a bad dream.

Chapter 14

As Willa and Helen watched the boat vanish in the distance, they heard people stirring at the campsite. "We should let the others know," Helen said.

Ben was stretching as they walked into the tent area. His arms froze in the air as he examined their faces. "What's wrong?"

"Just let me get my coffee," Helen said.

"Willa?"

"Relax," Helen said. "I'll explain." She poured coffee and settled on a log. "Amy had to cut the trip short," she said when the others had gathered. "She's on her way back to the city." Helen told them what happened while they prepared their breakfast. "She's checking into a motel this afternoon and will call the lodge to let us know she's fine."

Something nagged at the back of Ben's mind. Amy being called back to the city didn't sit well with him. But he didn't have enough information about what really happened. After breakfast, he asked Helen if he could talk to her in private.

"Sure," she said. "Help me load the kitchen stuff into the kayak. I'll be paddling with Willa from here."

"Maybe it's just me being a suspicious investigator," Ben

said as they carried tools and cooler to the beach, "but there's something odd about the way Amy was told to leave like that."

"You think?" Helen looked uncertain.

"It is to me. Chad's accident the first night seemed a bit hazy, and now this ..." He stroked his chin in thought, then shook his head. "I don't know."

"There's another two-way radio at the next camp site," Helen said. "If there's a problem, we'll find out then."

Ben tightened his lips. "Yeah. I guess I'll have to wait and see."

When he got back to the tent area, Ben went up to Willa. "How are you doing?"

"A bit worried I guess."

"Would you like a ride back to the city with me and Paul?"

"That would be great, thanks."

* * *

Ranger Jim docked his boat on the sandy beach of the Bowron campsite, unloaded Helen's canoe they'd picked up on the way, then helped carry Amy's bags to her car. She had a big breakfast at the lodge, retrieved her car key from the office, said goodbye to the park people and pulled out.

When she stopped for coffee in Quesnel, she called her mother to find out if she knew about the break-in.

"Yes, I do," she said. "When I came to check on your plants yesterday, I couldn't get in. The key didn't work. I notified the superintendent. He said someone had broken the lock, and called the police. The police went through every room and then inquired about you. I told them where you were, and offered to check with the resort to make sure. The resort people told me you and Willa were fine, which I told the police. They said they'd get in touch with you when you got back."

"When I got back? But I'm on my way home right now. The ranger said the police wanted me to come back to the city right away."

"That's not what they told me."

Amy groaned. She was missing two days of kayaking because of some stupid mistake. She sat for a moment holding back tears of disappointment. "Well, there isn't much I can do about it now. I should be home before noon tomorrow."

"All right, dear. Your super changed the lock. The new key will be in your mailbox."

After hanging up, Amy called Tresses. "Hi, Meg. How are things?"

"Amy! Good to hear your voice. Everything's going great. How's the trip?"

"It's been amazing. I just wanted you to know that I'll be home a day earlier than expected. If you need me on Saturday, let me know. All right?"

"I don't expect to, but if I do, I'll call you."

Driving south, Amy wracked her brain over what could have happened. Why did the police tell her mother they'd get in touch with her when she got back? Had they changed their minds about wanting her back right away?

She rolled her shoulders to relieve tension, but this time it didn't work. She'd never wanted a cigarette more.

Chapter 15

Tyler knew he had to station himself north of where Highway 99 intersected with Cariboo Highway in order to be sure to catch sight of Amy driving south. On Thursday morning at nine, he pulled onto a dirt road off the Cariboo Highway just north of the town of Clinton. He drove up the road a bit to check it out. Weeds growing in the gravel told him it wasn't used very often. He turned the car around to face the highway, then pulled to the side and into the shade of a large, wild-growing mountain ash. He took a leak, then settled down to check the light south-going traffic. With only one lane in each direction on the only road south, he was sure to spot Amy driving by on her way home.

He'd found some helpful information on the rules and restriction pages attached to the brochure he'd picked up at Amy's apartment. They didn't have a shuttle service, so if she left the group, she wouldn't be able to get back to them. With that in mind, he'd made it quite clear to the park ranger that the police wanted her home right away. There was always a risk she'd ignore the callback, but knowing her, he didn't think she would.

The bitch is trapped, he thought, crossing his hands behind his head and leaning back. If everything worked according to plan, she'd be passing within the next two to three hours. He'd left enough leeway to make sure not to miss her. If it didn't work, he had a backup plan. One way or the other, he'd have her in time for the payoff. "Ahhh," he grinned, "the thrill of the chase."

A few trucks and less than twenty cars had passed in the first ten minutes. An hour later, Tyler caught himself nodding off. Alarmed, he got out of the car and trudged around in the brush, chain-smoking, until he felt wired enough to stay awake, then got back in the car.

* * *

Amy stopped for an early lunch at a small café in Williams Lake. She ate, listening to the waitress and the patrons bantering back and forth and laughing. Only a few days ago, she and Willa had been there, carefree and excited about the kayaking trip. She'd wanted it to be a new beginning and had started to feel that it might work, but now … *No*. She had to stop feeling sorry for herself.

She paid and left. Restless from sitting for too long, she decided to take a walk along the lake before continuing her drive. Soon, she speeded up and started to jog. Thirty minutes later, she got back in the car, sweaty, but refreshed and feeling optimistic. Driving south, she decided she'd get into running more, enter a local fundraiser, like a race for kids maybe. There were plenty of neglected kids in her city.

Two hours later on the quiet highway she started to feel drowsy. How could she be at barely three in the afternoon? Granted, she'd been roused at five-thirty, as well as being uptight and dispirited most of the day, but still.

* * *

Tyler was getting nervous. Amy should've been there by now. He got out of his car and moved into the thicket near the highway to get a closer look at the people driving by. She couldn't have snuck past when he nodded off – that would've been too early.

He impatiently tore his sweatshirt loose from thorns of a blackberry bush, making other branches sway and attach themselves to his pants. He looked down for a moment – and almost missed Amy as she passed. With an infuriated roar, he burst free of the thorns and chased back to his car. He waited for another car to pass, then followed.

He relaxed as they drove south through the town, even smirked at the thought that very soon now, they'd be at the undeveloped stretch where he planned to squeeze her off the highway.

* * *

Amy had seen that the town of Clinton would be coming up next. Remembering reading about it in school as being a historical town of some sort, she'd decided to check it out. After all, she was still on a vacation and could use a break.

When she drove into Clinton and saw a nice-looking motel by the highway with a restaurant next-door, she pulled in.

* * *

Tyler stiffened and hit the brakes. "What the hell?" He watched as Amy pulled into a motel parking lot near the end of town. As he slowly drove by, he saw her enter the office. What was she doing? Meeting up with someone?

He pulled off the highway where he had a view of the parking lot and waited. A few minutes later, Amy came out, picked up a bag from her car and walked up a set of stairs at the halfway point. The bitch was fucking it up for him. The thought of having to hang out and wait made him so sick with rage, he got out of the car to charge after her before he came to his senses, getting back behind the wheel.

He forced himself to calm down. He needed to think. He couldn't just sit in the car for hours in a small town like this. It wouldn't be safe for him. He'd have to find a way to camouflage his car and himself and start making new plans regarding Amy – without losing sight of her.

Chapter 16

Amy entered her room on the second floor and went to fill the bathtub. After a long bath, she crawled between the sheets, soon falling asleep. An hour later, she woke up feeling rested and decided to go for a walk down the strip.

Dropping into an old country store, she found herself absorbed by a history she hadn't paid much attention to in school. Pictures of people, wagons and old roadhouses brought her back to the mid 1800s. Clinton had been a stop along the Gold Rush Trail – seventy miles from its start in Lillooet, called Mile 0. Amy took a few moments to read the success and defeat, joy and hardship written on the faces of the people in the photos. It felt good to think of something else for a while.

After leaving the store, Amy took a brisk walk around town. On her way back to the motel, she dropped into the restaurant next-door and ordered ribs, salad and soda water with lemon for take-out. She paid and was told she could pick it up at the motel front desk in forty-five minutes.

Back in her room, she called the Bowron Lodge and left a message for her friends. The thought of them made her feel like she'd been transported to another dimension, from a place of peace to a frightening domain. She lay on the bed, wondering how their day had been and what they were doing at that moment. When she closed her eyes, she could see them in their kayaks and hear their laughter. She'd give anything to have canned pea soup with them instead of barbecued ribs alone in a hotel room.

The dinner arrived, and she enjoyed it, though it would have been better if shared with a nice guy, like Ben, her grizzly bear protector. She pressed lemon into the soda water, took a sip and grimaced. It was lukewarm. She put it aside. Soon a headache was looming. She took an aspirin and changed into her pyjamas. Not sleepy yet, she tried watching a movie, but couldn't concentrate, too worried about her impending meeting with the police.

She took a sip of the soda water and shuddered. She had to get some ice. Pulling on a guest robe, she grabbed the key and a bucket and made her way down the hallway, hoping none of the other guests would see her.

She hurried back with the ice. As she unlocked the door, she heard a noise behind her. Before she had a chance to turn round, she found herself flying through the air, landing facedown by the foot of the bed. The door slammed shut. Someone leaned heavily on her back, pressing her mouth into the carpet so she couldn't scream. She started to gag. A few seconds later, her dinner shot out through the side of her mouth.

"*Fuck!*" yelled the man on her back.

Tyler?

She was roughly rolled over and thrown on the bed. Tyler's face stared down at her, his features distorted by disgust. He pinned her down and wiped her face with the sheet.

She hardly recognized him with his shoulder-length hair, all tangled and greasy, his dirty unshaven face with a fresh, ugly wound on the left side of his jaw. It sickened her to look at it.

"You came alone," he said with a smirk. "Good girl."

Amy turned her head to get away from his stale, smoke-filled breath.

"And right on time."

What? Amy's mind raced back and forth in confusion. He'd been waiting for her?

"Are you expecting your friend to join you?"

Amy cringed as his unwashed hair touched her face. "You stink."

"Fuck you. *Answer*, dammit!"

Amy coughed in disgust, struggling to keep her head to one side. "Why would I expect anyone? What are you talking about? All I know is the police in Vancouver wanted to talk to me right away, so I left."

"Where's your cell phone?"

Amy motioned to the daypack on the floor beside the dresser.

Tyler sat up, pulling Amy with him, twisting her arm back as he reached for the bag.

"*Ow!* You're hurting me."

"Shut up!"

Amy was shocked at the change in him. He'd been abusive before, but this went beyond that. She watched him rummage through the bag and pull out her cell phone and keys. He dropped her door and mail keys back into the bag, but pocketed her cell phone and car key.

"What are you doing?"

"Shut up."

When he dropped the bag to the floor, the bunny sweatshirt under his unzipped jacket caught her attention. *It looks like mine.*

Why is he wearing it? Then it hit her. *He* called the park people.

"Why are you here?" she asked. "If you want money, just take my wallet and leave."

"Shut the fuck up!" Tyler pushed her down, leaning on her as he moved the telephone onto the bed beside him. "You're going to call the front desk and tell them to bring your bill to the room, so you can sign it."

"Why?"

"Because we're going on a trip, and I can't have the cops after you for skipping on the bill."

"I'm not going anywhere."

"Yes, you are." He held the receiver up. "Ready?"

"If you think you'll get away with this, you're crazy."

Tyler's eyes narrowed to slits. "You don't want to know how crazy I am." He waved the receiver impatiently. "I don't give a fuck about how you word it, just tell them."

Amy clenched her jaw. *We'll see about that.* She wasn't going to leave without a fight ... she'd alert the front desk. "All right, give me the phone."

He let out a sarcastic snort, dialled the front desk and jammed the receiver to her ear.

Easy. Stay calm. Waiting for the clerk to pick up, Amy took a deep, silent breath.

"What the hell?" Tyler cut the signal and grabbed her throat, cutting off her intended scream. He flicked a knife in her face.

"Don't," Amy managed to say. "I'll *tell* them."

Tyler's hand unclamped her throat. He scooped up the phone and waited impatiently for Amy to stop gasping.

He must need me for something, or he would have killed me by now.

"Listen." He pointed the knife at her. "I'm on the run. I have no intention for you slowing me down, so don't fuck with me.

Don't ask questions. Just do what I tell you, and neither of us will get killed." Leaning hard on her, he dialled the number again and jammed the receiver to her ear without waiting for a response. He placed his own ear next to hers.

Amy froze as the cold flat of his knife touched her throat. Her heart raced. She couldn't think.

"Front desk," the clerk's voice answered.

"Umm ... my name ... this is Amy Robinson in two ... in *room* 203," she said in a small voice. "Umm ..."

"Ma'am, are you okay?"

Tyler's hand pressed over Amy's mouth. She shook her head. He took his hand away.

"Miss Robinson ... hello ... are you there?"

"Sorry, uh ..." Amy swallowed. "I'm not feeling well ... I have stomach flu. Could you bring my bill to my room, so I can sign it now and leave when I feel better?"

"Oh ... sure. I'm here on my own right now, but I can bring it up when my boss comes back. Should be less than an hour. Will that be okay?"

"Yes ... thank you."

"You're sure you're okay? I mean, it wasn't the food ..."

"No ... uh ... it started before. I shouldn't have eaten anything. I'll be fine. I just need to rest a few hours."

"I understand." The clerk sounded relieved.

Tyler cut the connection and put the telephone out of Amy's reach. "When he gets here, tell him to slip the bill under the door. I'll slip it back out after you've signed it."

Amy looked away. Couldn't stand the sight of him.

Tyler shook her. "Did you hear me?"

"*Yes!* Get off me."

Tyler loosened his grip. Amy screamed and thrashed around,

trying to burst free. He quickly trapped her arms, flipped her around and threw himself on top.

Amy screamed into the pillow.

Chapter 17

As the kayaking group paddled the length of Spectacle Lake, Willa missed having Amy behind her, scolding and teasing. The group was more quiet than usual, but as the day wore on, their spirits lifted and chatter and laughter echoed across the water as they reached their new campsite.

After dinner, they sat around the fire and reminisced while Kaley kept asking them to smile for her camera. Willa felt a bit sad about this being their last night and didn't feel much like smiling. She got up and walked to the beach. She was surprised to see Ben there, sitting on a log, tossing rocks into the lake. She sat down beside him. "Are you missing someone?" she said.

Ben nodded.

"Me, too."

* * *

Amy couldn't breathe. The weight of Tyler pressing her head into the pillow drained her of air. "If you want to breathe," he hissed, "you better shut up."

She struggled to nod.

He spun her over and glanced at her gasping for air while he reached inside her bag, took out a T-shirt, then cut it in half with his knife. He flipped her over again, used one half of the shirt to tie her hands behind her back, then spun her over once more. Amy's scream died in her throat as he used the other half to gag her.

I won't let him get away with this, she told herself. *I'm still alive. I just have to wait for him to screw up. And he always screws up.*

Tyler took his jacket off and threw it on the bed. He pulled Amy with him to the bathroom and pushed her down on the floor between the sink and the bathtub.

She watched him go through her toiletries bag and take out an elastic band, a brush and a razor. *Why is he getting cleaned up? Where are we going?*

Tyler washed his face and neck, grabbed a towel from a rack above Amy, wiped his skin dry, then dropped the towel on top of her. Disgusted, she shook it off and kicked it away. She looked at the large grey area in the middle of the white towel, thinking if he actually wanted to get clean, he'd need a sandblaster.

After washing his hair, Tyler brushed it back into a tight ponytail. Examining his nicotine-stained teeth and red, puffy gums in the mirror, he used Amy's toothbrush to brush his teeth and tongue. He dabbed the wound with hydrogen peroxide, wiped his shoes clean with a hand towel, then dragged Amy back to the bedroom and shoved her into an armchair. "Stay." He fell into another chair and waited, checking his watch every few minutes, rolling an unlit cigarette between his fingers and smelling it. At ten-thirty there was a knock on the door. Tyler pulled Amy from the chair and stepped behind her, pressing the knife to her throat.

"Ma'am," a male voice called through the door, "I have the bill for you to sign."

Amy's heart raced.

Tyler loosened the gag. "Talk or die," he whispered.

"S-slip it under the door, please," she said.

"Huh?"

"I'm not dressed." Amy started to take a deep breath.

"Ma'am, are you okay?"

Tyler suddenly clasped his hand over Amy's mouth and drove his fist into her midriff, forcing the air out. "You prefer to die, don't you?"

Amy shook her head.

"Ma'am?"

Tyler removed his hand.

"Yes," Amy croaked and took a couple a quick breaths. "I'm okay." She swallowed. "Stomach flu is no fun."

"Yeah, no kidding," the man agreed as Tyler tightened the gag. "Well, here it is."

An envelope appeared under the door. Tyler dragged it into the room with his boot, picked it up, took out the bill and put it on the dresser. He untied Amy's hands, twisted her left arm back and put a pen in her right hand. Amy signed the bill. Tyler put it in the envelope and slipped it back out.

"Thanks," said the voice outside. "Hope you feel better soon."

Tyler listened as the man walked down the hallway and bounded down the stairs, then pulled Amy to the bed. "Sit down." He scooped up her jeans and T-shirt and threw them at her. "Get dressed."

With trembling hands, Amy pulled her jeans on over the pyjamas, telling herself not to panic. They were still in the motel, and there must be people around. She picked up her running shoes, her eyes on the base of a floor lamp near the window. She fumbled with the shoelaces. *Break the glass.*

She screamed through the gag as Tyler's foot bore down on hers. He tied her hands back, pulled the laces off the running shoes and used them to tie her feet together.

Amy's brain ground to a halt. She watched him drop the toiletries bag into her daypack and take a quick look around the room.

"Now that I have your attention," he said, hovering over her, "you should know there are some very nasty guys coming after me. If they find me, I'm dead. I need to disappear. I've arranged for it, but I need cash, and you're going to give it to me. All of it. And when you do, I'll be gone, and you'll never hear from me again. That's a promise. So I don't want any more trouble from you. Got it?"

Amy's brain slowly started up again. A promise? Was there a hope in hell he'd keep it?

"I asked you a question."

Amy nodded.

"Good. How much do you have?" He loosened the gag. "No point in lying."

Amy moved her lips around to unstick them from her gum. "I don't know exactly," she said, "but I have just over nine thousand in my business account. Hardly any – maybe three hundred – in my personal account."

Tyler sat quiet for a moment. "Who else might notice your business account's been emptied?"

"No one. Nobody else has access to it. And the bank ... I guess they might want to check with me about a large withdrawal, but I mean, I could be on a business trip and need money."

"Okay. I'll let you leave when I have the money."

"I can't wait to give you the money and never see you again."

"Makes two of us. But you give me any grief, I won't let you go, and both of us will probably get shot."

Ohmygod.

"Did you get that?"

She nodded.

Tyler tightened the gag. He picked up the remote and sat down in a chair. "We'll leave when there's no one around."

"Where are we going?" Amy sputtered through the gag.

Tyler ignored her. He turned the lights off, flipped channels and settled on a Van Damme movie.

Amy pulled at the tie around her wrists to the sound of Van Damme smashing his fist into someone. When the nail on her longest finger broke off, she gave up and lay listening to the rain pummeling the window behind the drapes.

Suddenly Tyler got up and switched off the TV. He turned on a small lamp and picked up a hand towel from the bathroom. Amy watched as he moved around the room in her bunny sweatshirt, wiping fingerprints from the remote control, telephone and doorknob, thinking, if this situation wasn't so terrifying it might almost be comical.

Tyler peeped out from behind the drapes. "The lights are out in the other rooms," he said as he put his jacket on and zipped it up. He untied Amy's legs, put the laces in his pocket, grabbed her arm and pulled her to her feet. "Time to go."

He draped Amy's jacket over her shoulders. Reaching under the jacket, he grabbed her thumb and pulled it back until she folded over in pain. He eased up on the pressure, allowing her to straighten up a bit, grabbed her bag and turned off the light. After checking the hallway in both directions, he stepped out with Amy in tow. Every time she tried to slow down, he tightened the pressure on her thumb until her legs buckled.

At the top of the stairs, he suddenly lifted her up. Amy twisted and kicked at his legs, trying to make him fall as he ran down the steps with her in a vice-like grip. When they reached the bottom, he scanned the parking lot and motel windows, then put her down.

Brandishing the knife, he walked her across the lot, passing her car. Amy could only pray that someone would see them. But she saw no signs of life in the darkness. The faint glow inside the office across the drive looked like a nightlight. There were only three other cars in the lot, all parked at the far end. He led her to the last one, pushed her face down onto the back seat, quickly tied her feet together, bent her knees to shut the door, got in behind the wheel and drove off.

Chapter 18

Darkness surrounded them. Tyler lit another cigarette. All Amy could see through the smoke was his silhouette in profile, illuminated by the dashboard lights and the digital clock showing 1:34 a.m. They had been driving for more than an hour, but she didn't know in what direction. She listened to the sound of the engine, the spatter of rain on metal and the incessant whooshing of the windshield wipers, trying to ignore her gnawing fear and the pain in her shoulders.

Tyler slowed to turn off the highway. Amy slid back and forth on the seat as he rounded sharp curves at high speed. Suddenly he cursed and stomped the brakes. Amy flew off the seat, crashing to the floor. Tyler backed up and made a quick turn. Amy fought for air as she lay jammed between the front and back seats, her face on the carpet. Tyler glanced back, reached over and pulled the gag down. As the car bounced over bumps in the road, crud from the floor-mat flew into her mouth. "I'm getting sick," she gasped.

"Now what?"

"Please …"

"What the hell …"

Tyler stomped the brakes again, came around and untied the laces around Amy's feet. He pulled her up on the seat and jerked her upright. "Stop whining or I'll throw you in the trunk."

Amy glowered at him. *Creep*.

"Bitch." Tyler kicked the door shut and got back behind the wheel.

Amy took deep breaths, trying to stop whatever was left in her stomach from surfacing. Cold sweat ran down her forehead into her eyes, making them sting. She blinked and stared out as the headlights sliced through the night, revealing a narrow dirt road edged with dense conifers. They must be miles from any bank.

"Where are we going?"

Tyler ignored her.

"I thought you wanted money. What is this?"

"Shut up."

The dirt road became a trail. Tyler slowed down. The car rocked wildly, crashing over tree roots and boulders. Amy stared straight ahead at the forest closing in on them. It felt as if the long tree branches reached out for her as they brushed against the windows.

The scratch of branches stopped when they drove into a small clearing. Tyler pulled up in front of an old cabin, barely visible in the thick underbrush. He pocketed the car key, picked up a flashlight and stepped from the car, leaving the headlights on.

Amy's heart sped up as he disappeared into the cabin. What was he doing in an isolated shoebox in the middle of nowhere?

A moment later, Tyler came back, picked up Amy's bag and grabbed her arm. "Let's go."

She shook his hand off, got out of the car and reluctantly followed him. She stopped by the door and grimaced at the pungent odour coming from the cabin. "I'm not going in there."

Tyler shrugged.

Amy glanced back. She could barely discern the forest beyond the car. The rain had stopped. Maybe she could hide out there until dawn. She started to back up, but stopped as she pictured herself rushing through the dark with her hands tied back. She wouldn't get far.

Tyler sneered. "If you'd rather keep the cougars company, go ahead." He dropped her bag to the floor, lit a match and reached to light a candle stump stuck to the middle of a table.

She hadn't thought about the cougars.

Tyler brushed past her on his way to turn off the headlights. When he returned, the trees behind him were no longer distinguishable. Amy stepped back to the threshold and watched him scan the room with a flashlight. The beam moved past two chairs, settling on a wooden crate with a kerosene lamp on top. As he brought the lamp to the table, cobwebs trailed like veils behind it. Soot rose when he lit the wick, staining the glass on its way to the top and dispersing its carbon into the room. He moved to the back of the cabin and disappeared through a doorway.

Amy's eyes slowly adjusted to the light from the candle and the kerosene lamp. She shuddered at the scenery. The only window in the room was covered with a dirty towel nailed to the upper window frame. The grimy Formica tabletop had been used as an ashtray. Dirty dishes, canned food, half a bottle of water and a few slices of mouldy bread sat atop a rusty woodstove behind the table. On the floor, caked with dirt and mouse droppings, lay a sagging, soiled mattress with a sleeping bag on top. Pieces of clothing hung from nails on the wall. Calendar pictures of naked women had been tacked to the walls and used as dartboards.

Two of the darts were knives.

Knives!

Amy took a step inside. If she could pull one out with her teeth, she could drop it behind the mattress to use later. She moved closer to the wall.

Tyler came back into the room. His eyes flew from hers to the wall, and in an instant, he had the knives in his hand. He motioned toward the door behind him. "The john's back there."

Amy tightened her lips. "I'd rather go in the woods."

"Okay, princess, whatever."

"Is this where you live now?"

"For the moment, yeah."

Amy glanced at his right hand, still holding the knives.

"Sit down," he ordered.

"Where?"

"Umm …" He looked around, then went over to the crate and picked up two tubular steel chairs with peeling vinyl seats. He put one chair down beside her, brought the other chair to the opposite side of the table and sat down. He opened a pack of Marlboros, pulled one out and held it up with a questioning look.

The knives were gone. She shook her head. "I quit."

"Good for you." He lit the cigarette.

Amy glanced at the crate, then at the mattress.

"Now, let's talk," Tyler said, blowing smoke in her face. "It'll be light soon. We have some planning to do."

Amy felt like screaming. She wanted to hit him – sitting there looking superior, laying down the rules, pushing her around like a piece of dirt.

Don't, she cautioned herself. *He thrives on hostility. It'll only make things worse*. As she looked down, fighting to keep her anger at bay, a feeling of exhaustion slowly replaced the anger. *What's the point?* Her shoulders slumped. "I can't take this anymore," she said. "I'm scared. I'm tired. I'm cold. My shoulders hurt. My wrists hurt, my whole body hurts. I can't think."

Tyler leaned back in his chair and glared at her with a slack, suspicious face. A moment later, he dropped his cigarette to the floor and stepped on it. "I'm tired of the noise," he said and came around and untied Amy's hands. He pulled her with him to his car and pushed her into the back seat. "Sleep it off," he growled and slammed the door shut.

She watched him pass into the faint light seeping from the cabin. He disappeared inside, leaving the door ajar. She looked out at the forest, but saw only blackness beyond the first row of tree trunks. She might not run into a cougar, but what if she slipped into a crevice? Deciding to wait until the first sign of dawn, she curled up on the seat.

Soon the stale, smoke-filled air in the car was making her sick. She sat up and opened the door just a bit. The light came on. She quickly closed the door, peeking out at the cabin to see if Tyler noticed.

He appeared at the threshold and stood there until the light in the car went out. He disappeared for a second, then returned with a chair. Placing it by the open door, he sat down and stared at her.

Amy locked all doors and leaned back in the seat, mad at herself for alerting him. She looked out the window at Tyler smoking another cigarette. He leaned back in his chair, crossed his legs and looked up at the black sky as if enjoying the night.

Shivering cold even with the pyjamas under her clothes, she buttoned up her jacket, then waited for what seemed like a lifetime before looking out again. He hadn't moved. He didn't look tired. *He's probably on speed*.

Feeling weary, she lay down on the seat. *No*. She sat up. She mustn't fall asleep.

Chapter 19

Amy jumped as Tyler banged on the car in the morning. "Open up!"

She inched herself up on the seat, dazed and stiff. She was still in hell.

"Open up!" Tyler yelled again.

"You have a key."

"Not on me."

She unlocked the door, taking note of his hollow-eyed and weary appearance. He reached in for her. She pulled back. "Don't touch me."

He waited until she got out, then followed closely as she walked up to the door and stopped.

"Do you want me to carry you over the threshold?" he taunted.

She wanted to spit in his face, but made herself go inside and sit down.

"Are you still using the Royal Bank?" he asked, taking the other seat.

Amy nodded.

"Take out nine thousand and leave the rest."

"I'll have to go into the bank then. They won't let me withdraw that much cash from the bank machine."

"I know that." Tyler's lips tightened. His eyes burned into hers as he slid his elbow across the table and pointed a finger in her face. "And if you double-cross me – one wrong word, any kind of sign – we'll be out of there before they know it. Then you are my enemy. My life might be over, but dammit, yours will be, too. Do you know what I'm saying?"

Amy looked into his red-rimmed, unblinking eyes. "I hear you," she said. "I won't trick you. I wouldn't risk my life for nine thousand dollars. I'll be the best actor you've ever seen. I'll be *happy* to give you the money."

"Good." Tyler sat back in his chair. "One other thing. These guys are killers. Make no mistake, they want me. If they find out that you know me, they'll come after you to find me. You think *I'm* dangerous? Think again. I wouldn't tell one living soul about any of this."

"I won't. It'll be my pleasure to never see you or talk about you ever again."

"You keep telling yourself that. When are your parents expecting you?"

"Why?"

"Don't ask questions. Just answer."

"Today. Around noon."

"How are you going to explain that you'll be late? I can't have them calling the cops to find you."

"I'll think of something. I just want to go home safely. I won't do anything to jeopardize that."

Tyler snapped his fingers. "Let's get back to my question."

"Did you break into my apartment?"

"Yeah, I holed up there for a bit." Tyler fingered his wound. "I needed to take care of this."

Amy couldn't look at it. It made her nauseated.

He pointed to Amy. "That's another little secret between us. Now, answer my question. What are you going to tell your folks?"

"Let me think." She couldn't believe she was conspiring with Tyler to fool her parents. She picked at her nails, thinking, maybe she could say she'd gone to visit someone. Suddenly she thought of her friend in Kamloops. "My parents know that my best friend from high school moved to Kamloops. I can tell them that I took a detour and won't be back in Vancouver until ... when ... midnight?"

"You can be, if everything works out the way I want."

"What do you mean everything?"

"When you get the money, you put it in your wallet and then we leave the bank. When I ask for the money, you give it to me. Then I'll let you go. Clear enough?"

"As soon as I hand you the money?" She could see herself throwing the money at him in the bank and screaming.

"I said, *after* we leave the bank."

Tension prickled across her shoulders. *He's evasive. But I have to go along, buy time.* "All right. I'll call and tell them I'll be home around midnight." She held her hand out. "Give me my cell."

"Pff." Tyler looked amused. "Forget it."

"Why?"

"You don't need it. We're using a payphone."

"But I'll need it later."

"So do I." Tyler smirked. "Cell phones without GPS are hard to come by." He scooped a water bottle from the woodstove and held it out to Amy. "Want some?"

She shook her head no, almost folding over as her stomach cramped. *Relax.* She lowered her shoulders, thinking she'd get her chance at the bank. "Can I have my bag?"

"What for?"

"I'll need my bankcard."

Tyler pulled it out of his pocket and tossed it to her.

Amy picked it up, confused. "When did you take this?"

"None of your business."

"Why did you take it?"

"For safekeeping." He picked up Amy's bag, looked inside, took out her hairbrush and kicked the bag over to Amy.

She took out her water bottle and drank slowly, watching Tyler pour most of his water over his hair and remake his ponytail. She'd never use that brush again. She pulled her sweat suit top out of the bag. "I smell barf under my T-shirt. I need to change."

Tyler squinted at his watch. "Okay. Hurry up."

He didn't make a move to look away so Amy turned her back, hesitated for a moment, then pulled her T-shirt off, unbuttoned her soiled pyjama top and quickly exchanged it for the clean top. "I'm done."

Tyler slapped the table. "Let's go."

"I need to pee."

He motioned to the door. "Pick a tree."

Amy squatted behind a wide tree stump while Tyler waited by his car, blocking the license plate. She'd barely pulled her jeans up when he came and grabbed her arm. He led her to the car and pushed her into the back seat. "Lie down and keep quiet." He slammed the door, slipped behind the wheel and pulled out.

Chapter 20

Willa squeezed her last dry bag into the kayak hatch and tightened the straps over the lid. "It's hard to believe it's Friday already," she said to Helen beside her, pumping lake water through a filter for everyone's water bottles. "Part of me doesn't want it to end, and another can't wait to get on the phone with Amy."

Helen straightened up and wiped her forehead on a sleeve. "Yeah, I can understand that. I got a kick out of her. She tries to be such a tough-ass."

"Amy? I don't think she means to. She's got a wicked sense of humour, that's all."

"I suppose. Hop in." Helen called out for everyone to get going, then pushed off and headed for the entrance to Bowron River.

* * *

As they drove through the forest, Amy watched the branches brushing the windows. They didn't seem as sinister in daylight. Tyler turned left onto the curvy road, then right onto a paved one. They were going east. Amy made a mental note of it and rehearsed what to say to her mother and the bank teller. Leaving the woods behind, she looked out at rolling hills, struggling to stay awake. Soon the lack of sleep took its toll, and she drifted off.

She woke up when Tyler slowed down, then pulled into a gas station. She checked her watch. They'd been driving for less than two hours. Tyler stopped beside a phone booth and told Amy to get ready. He followed her inside the booth, standing beside her as she dialled. No one answered. Tyler's finger rested lightly on the receiver hook, ready to hang up while Amy left the rehearsed message.

Back in the car, he locked the doors and told Amy to duck down on the seat. As he drove to the bank, Amy pictured herself alerting the bank teller. She felt a bit jittery about it, but confident it would work. Did Tyler really believe she would play along and not alert the bank people? And once she'd done that, how did he plan to get out of the situation? Start chasing her around with the knife?

Tyler pulled into an empty lot behind the bank and parked. Amy sat up and looked around for a name of the town they were in. She didn't see one.

Tyler turned and fixed his eyes on hers. "There's one more thing you should know. If you make a wrong move at the bank, utter one wrong word, I'll push this button, sending a message to one of my gang buddies." He held up her cell phone with a Vancouver number keyed in. "He's in the area of Fifteenth and Yew, only meters from your parents, waiting for a signal from me to go after them. He's not a nice man. Actually, he's a psycho who can't wait to hurt them."

Amy stared at the number keyed in on the display. Her heart banged so hard in her chest, it made her cough. *Take it easy. Don't freak out.* She would have to do it his way.

Tyler tossed her the shoelaces and her hairbrush. "Tie your shoes and brush your hair."

She threw the brush back, ran her fingers through her hair, tied her runners and buttoned her jacket. She watched Tyler wipe his shoes with the hand towel from the motel, zip his jacket all the way to the end of the stand collar, concealing the jaw wound.

The most repulsive thing of all, is that others will probably think he looks handsome. She went ice cold as she saw him slip a gun into his right sleeve. *Where did that come from?*

"Leave the bag. Bring your purse. Let's go."

Holding her close, pressing the hard steel of his gun to her side, he marched her toward the bank. As they approached, they saw two tellers busy with customers. No one else was in sight.

Then, one of the customers walked out.

"Don't fuck up." Tyler flicked Amy's cell in front of her eyes. With a fake smile, he held the door, following her in.

Both tellers looked up at them as they approached. One of them nodded to her. "Can I help you?"

Amy told herself that this was just another time at the bank and recalled how she'd normally act: just walk over to the teller with a relaxed face, nod and say hello. Amy handed over her bankcard and calmly asked for a withdrawal of nine thousand dollars from her business chequing account.

She entered her pin number, and while the teller looked up her accounts, Amy glanced at Tyler, standing off a bit to the side, looking relaxed and patient. She knew he could hear every word she said.

"You wish to withdraw nine thousand dollars from your business account?" The teller asked.

"Yes." Amy nodded. "That's correct."

"Your home branch is?"

"In Vancouver. Fourth Avenue West."

"Thank you. Just a moment, please." The teller walked over to a glassed-in room labeled Business Transactions and conferred with a lady there. A moment later, she came back. "All set." She smiled and started the transaction.

The teller asked Amy to enter her pin number again and what denomination she wanted.

"$100 bills, please."

"Just give me a moment," she said. "I'll get the cash."

It was done in a heartbeat. Amy left the bank in a trance, feeling the teller's eyes in her back. Her legs were shaking as she walked back to the car with Tyler's gun pressed to her side.

He pushed her into the back seat, got in and locked the doors. Without a word, he held his hand out. Amy took the wad of bills from her purse and handed them over. He jammed them into his pocket. "Good work." He took two apples from the glove compartment and tossed one to Amy.

She threw it back, shaking with anger. She wanted to rip his hair out.

"Lie down," Tyler said and took a bite from his apple.

Amy's eyes widened in shock. "What? You said you'd let me go after I gave you the money."

"Here? Do you think I'm stupid?"

"Where, then?"

"Lie down. I'll tell you when and where to get out."

"You expect me to believe anything you say after this?"

"I don't give a shit what you believe."

Amy lay down and stared in bewilderment at the landscape through pouring rain. She had no idea of where they were. An hour later, they turned off the highway. They were back on that curvy road.

"Why are we going to that sewer?" Amy asked, sitting up. "I don't want to be there on my own."

"You want the comfort of my company?"

"You're sick." She looked at him. Parts of his hair had come undone from his ponytail. Dark stubble had already started to show. *Once a thug ...*

Tyler drove into the clearing, made a complete circle and slowly drove back up the bumpy trail a bit. He stopped where the long tree branches cradled part of the car and turned the engine off. "I'm getting something," he said. "You stay." He hurried off through the rain and disappeared behind the cabin. A moment later he came back carrying a black bag. He put it in the trunk, jumped into the car and told Amy to get out.

She grabbed her daypack, and the moment she got out, Tyler took off, tires splattering mud all over her.

The branches closed the car door. An instant later, they closed up in front of Amy like curtains at a stage play. Again, there had been no time to check the car's plate number.

"*I hate you!*" she screamed, throwing her daypack on the ground.

Chapter 21

The kayaking group paddled the narrow Bowron River as it curved through marshland with grasses so high, all they could see beyond it was sky. A blue heron startled them as it squawked and took flight nearby. They watched it glide away on widespread wings.

Ahead, Max stopped in a curve and signalled for everyone to be quiet. "Moose ahead," he mouthed.

They all crowded close and stretched to see. There, less than five meters in front of them, a large cow moose stood in water up to her belly, blocking their passage. They watched her plunge her head and neck underwater. A few seconds later, she raised her head with a mouthful of aquatic grasses. She munched on them for a while, then went back in for more. And so it went.

When she finally climbed up on the riverbank, the group, eager to get going, charged forward. Suddenly, they scrambled to back up. The cow moose had stopped at the edge of the bank and emptied her bladder in a heavy gush that splashed high and wide. "*Jeezus!*" Max screamed, recoiling in disgust as the brunt of the liquid splashed over him, and the others rocked with laughter.

"You did that on purpose!" he yelled, as the moose walked calmly into the marsh.

"You always blame the females," Kaley said.

Around the next curve, the river ended as Bowron Lake opened up before them, smooth and glittering in the midday sun. In the far distance, at the water's edge, they could just make out the red and white of the resort lodge building.

An hour later, they arrived at the resort and relinquished their kayaks and wheeled carts to the personnel. After taking group pictures with five different cameras, they went inside the lodge to have their first really good meal in a week. There, they finally found out that Amy had called on Thursday evening from a motel in Clinton, saying all was well.

Relieved, Willa loaded her gear into Ben's car, thanked Helen and waved as they headed back into the real world, feeling paradise fall behind them.

* * *

Amy stood in the drizzling rain, hyperventilating in frustration, staring at her daypack as if it were a foreign object. She turned to eye the cabin. She didn't want to go in there, but it didn't look like the rain would stop anytime soon. She needed to find something to keep her dry.

After taking a few breaths of bloody determination, she scooped up her daypack and stormed across the clearing into the cabin. She cried out and froze when a rat scuttled past her. She stood for a moment, listening for movement. But all she heard was rain rapping the cabin roof. She relaxed a bit and started looking around for something she might use as a poker.

Her eyes fell on the darts sticking out from the calendar pictures on the wall. She pulled two of them out and used them to lift the cover off the crate. Begging to find something rainproof, she dug through the stale, mouldy contents, but found nothing useful. She checked the tattered garments hanging off nails on the walls, hoping to find a raincoat, but found only spiders, scrambling away.

Moving outside, she looked through the rubbish around the cabin. Her heart skipped in relief when she saw a scummy-looking tarp draped over a pile of firewood at the back. Shaking it off to dislodge water and bugs, she wrapped it around herself.

Slogging through the mud, dragging her daypack behind her, she searched for a way out, a major road.

* * *

Tyler pulled onto the highway and headed west for his meeting with Mike Polanco. He couldn't help feeling apprehensive – he'd only been a member of Mike's gang for a few months and didn't know if he could trust him.

But then he couldn't trust anyone now. His only chance to escape certain death was Mike – a real son of a bitch.

An hour later, Tyler turned off onto a deserted logging road. Stopping at a spot where his car couldn't be seen from the highway, he listened to the messages on Amy's cell to make sure that no one had noticed her absence, then settled down for a few hours' rest.

* * *

Shivering with cold, Amy reached the paved road where Tyler had turned right in the morning. She pulled the tarp closer, crossed the highway and walked east.

She didn't quite know why, but even in this remote area, it felt safer to be on the highway. Tyler was out of her life. That must be it.

The rain faded to a light drizzle. She lifted her face to the sky, letting the rain wash the mud away, then quickened her pace, hoping to reach a farm or find some kind of shelter before darkness fell.

An hour later, only three cars had driven past. She'd ignored them, and they'd returned the favour. But now her legs were getting tired and her daypack had practically fallen apart. When she stopped to secure it, she heard the sound of an engine. An old pickup truck loaded with hay slowed as it neared her. A husky-looking woman peered down through the open window. "Hey, what happened to you?" she asked.

"My boyfriend kicked me out of his car."

"Same thing happened to me." The woman reached over, pushing the passenger door open. "Name's Winny. Hop in. I'll give you a lift."

"I need to get to Clinton."

"No problem. I'm headed a few miles north of there."

Amy introduced herself, rolled up the tarp and climbed in. As Winny pulled out, Amy looked down at her shoes and daypack. Both were toast. She felt lucky that Winny had come along when she did.

"If you're hungry, there's an apple in the glove compartment."

"Thanks." Amy reached to take the apple out, but saw how dirty her hands were and stuck them out the window instead. When the rain had washed away the mud, she pulled them back in. She'd meant to wipe them off on her jeans, but they, too, were covered in mud, so she sat there with her hands hovering in midair, not sure of what to do next.

Winny chuckled. "Here," she held out a paper towel, "that stuff's hard on the digestion."

Amy flicked her a grateful smile, wiped her hands, grabbed the apple and dug in. It was gone in seconds.

"When did you eat last?" Winny asked.

"Midday yesterday," Amy said, not counting the dinner she had thrown up.

"Then have another apple."

"Thanks." Amy smiled and went for it. She ate slower this time, watching the landscape slide past, praying her car was still at the motel. If Tyler took it, how would she get home?

Winny chatted about her small farm in Chasm and her four kids, not one of whom wanted to farm the land. Amy enjoyed listening to her stories. It surprised her that two hours had gone by when they turned north on Cariboo Highway.

"We'll be in Clinton in fifteen minutes," Winny said.

Amy sent her a grateful smile. "I'm really lucky you came along."

They stopped outside the motel in Clinton and Amy cheered when she saw her Kia in the parking lot. She took her purse out of the daypack. "I'm afraid I don't have …"

"Put that back," Winny said. "I was headed this way anyway."

Amy shook her hand. "Thank you very much."

"Appreciate the company."

"Can you burn that thing?" Amy motioned to the tarp as she climbed out of the cab.

"I'll find some use for it. And don't take any more shit from that boyfriend."

"Don't you worry."

Winny waved and drove off.

Amy crossed the street, took out the spare key from the box under the car and slipped behind the wheel. She drove off with one eye on the mirror, hoping no one from the motel would come running after her.

She stopped at a fast-food restaurant, picked a change of clothes and hiking boots from a dry bag in the trunk and went inside. A woman, waiting for her turn outside the washroom, moved away from Amy as if she were a skunk.

When Amy finally got in, she flinched at the sight of herself in the mirror. *Is that me?* The blotchy face, puffy red eyes and tangled hair reminded her of mouse droppings, dirt and misery. Stripping off her muddy clothes, she stuffed everything into the daypack and washed herself under the tap. She dressed in clean clothes and boots, dropped her muddy running shoes in the garbage bin and left.

* * *

Tyler blinked awake in his car at seven. Time to leave. He wanted to get to the bar in Squamish early, so he could scout the grounds before Mike showed up.

He pulled his ski hat down to his eyebrows, wound the scarf around his neck and drove down the logging road with the lights off. When there were no cars in sight, he flicked on the lights and pulled out on the highway.

At seven-thirty, he used Amy's cell phone to call the bar and ask for Mike. The bartender taking the call said he could barely hear him.

"I'll call back," Tyler said.

As soon as he had better reception, he called the bar again.

"Sounds like you're in the mountains," Mike said when he came on the line.

"I'm in town," Tyler lied. "My battery is gonna quit on me any second. Just want to make sure the meeting is on, and you have the passport."

"Everything's under control. So, if you're in town, what's stopping you from coming here right now?"

"I have a couple of things to take care of, but I'll be there at nine."

"If you say so."

"Got to go." Tyler hung up.

Chapter 22

Amy drove to Vancouver in a daze, her hands glued to the steering wheel, trying to concentrate on staying in the right lane and driving as close to the speed limit as possible.

She arrived at her apartment building at ten-thirty and pulled into a guest parking space. She pulled out her door keys from her purse, realizing that Tyler didn't take them from her because he'd destroyed her lock. She used the passkey to enter the lobby. Praying that her chatty neighbours were in bed, she hurried through the lobby and retrieved the new door key from the mailbox.

The moment she entered her apartment, she dropped the daypack to the floor and leaned back on the door. "I made it," she whispered, almost dizzy with relief, then stumbled through the dark to the bedroom and crashed on her bed like a Douglas fir in a windstorm.

* * *

Tyler kept a careful eye on the traffic as he drove west. A few cars had passed him and vanished in the distance. Nothing seemed out of the ordinary.

At dusk, a car appeared behind him, seemingly out of nowhere. It backed off a moment later, keeping its distance. Tyler tried to make out the face of the driver, but the car fell farther back, making it impossible. Soon, Tyler couldn't see its lights at all.

It had turned dark when a car with the lights off suddenly drove up beside him and tried to force him off the road. "What the hell?" Tyler tried to escape, but the other car was faster, forcing him farther and farther to the side, until he ran into a thicket and stopped. The other car pulled in behind him.

Tyler slipped the gun into his sleeve and waited for a door to open, expecting to see Tony Matzera's thugs.

Instead, Mike stepped from the car. The double-crossing sonofabitch was going to muscle him!

Mike waved for him to get out.

"What the fuck is this?" Tyler asked as he got out, moving toward Mike. "You told me to meet …"

"Don't move," Mike snapped, pulling a gun. "Show me the money. Thirty grand."

"We said twenty."

"Twenty grand will hide you from Matzera. You want to hide from Borelli, Matzera's boss. That'll cost you thirty."

"Who the fuck … Okay. Hey, come on, put the piece away. I'll give you everything I have. Twenty-two thousand. Search me, search the car. You won't find more than that."

"Where is it?"

"Pockets, money belt."

"Take it out. Nice and slow. Put it on the ground and back off."

Tyler did.

"Turn around and lie down on your stomach. Arms over your

head."

"Don't get excited," Tyler said as he turned and let his gun slide into his hand. "I won't argue about the money. There's no need for this bullshit. I thought we had a deal. What about the junk?"

"Arms over your head!" Mike yelled.

Tyler swung around and fired. The shot hit Mike in the arm. Mike's gun went flying. He rushed at Tyler, slamming into him and trying to pry the gun from his grip. Mike could only use one arm, but being bigger than Tyler, he began to overpower him. Mike pulled a knife.

Chapter 23

Ben, Paul and Willa decided to stay over in Williams Lake. "I suppose Amy's back in the city by now," Ben said, as they checked into the motel where Amy and Willa had stayed on the way up north.

"Yes, she should be. I'll call her when I get to my room."

Amy didn't answer her cell or home phone. Willa left a message on the home phone, saying she'd call again in the morning. After a quick shower, she met up with Ben and Paul. She told them about the message she'd left.

"Why don't you try again later tonight?"

"Sure." Willa smiled to herself. *He's getting involved.*

The three of them went to a nearby seafood restaurant. The place was buzzing and almost full. A singer wound down on the stage, drawing scattered applause. Ben's eyes devoured the menu.

"I'll pay for the food," he said, "so don't hold back." He passed the wine list to Paul. "You students can pay for the wine."

They ordered steak, sweet potato fries, Caesar salad and a bottle of red wine. After a week on camp food, the dinner tasted almost too good for words.

"Ben," Willa said. "What would make the police call someone back from a trip like ours. Wouldn't it be because of something serious?"

Ben nodded. "Yes, it would have to be."

"Yeah," Willa said, a faraway look in her eyes. She wished she could ask him if drugs would do it.

Ben reached over to squeeze her hand lightly. "Enjoy your dinner and don't worry."

Willa nodded with a thin smile.

"Does Amy have family nearby?" Paul asked.

"Yes, her parents live just a few blocks away. Actually, I should try calling them, too."

Paul made a toast to good food, good wine and good friends. He even toasted to the singer, now back up on the stage.

By the time they were back at the motel, Willa decided it was way too late in the night to call Amy and went straight to bed.

On Saturday morning, she tried Amy again. No answer. She left another message on her home phone, saying she'd call back around seven, and that Amy had better answer, or she'd break in the door herself. Then she phoned her Aunt Louise, asking if she'd talked to Amy.

"Yes, I certainly have," she said. "And I must say she baffles me. First, she calls to tell me she's coming home early because of the break-in at her apartment. Then yesterday, she called and left a message saying she'd met an old friend on the way home, so she decided to spend a few hours in Kamloops. Suddenly, it didn't seem so urgent to get home anymore."

"Did she tell you what time she'd be home?"

"She said no later than midnight. And that she'd call back later today."

Willa told Ben and Paul about Amy's side trip when she joined them in the motel breakfast room. "So … she's probably at home, sleeping in," she concluded. "I left a message."

"Hmm," Ben said, stroking his chin, looking thoughtful.

* * *

Amy heard the phone ringing and groped for her cell on the bedside table, until she remembered that Tyler had taken it. She turned over and blinked. Her eyeballs felt sandy. There seemed to be a war raging in her head. She massaged her temples. Scenes from the previous day bubbled up through layers of sludge clogging her brain. It occurred to her that she should pick up the phone. But the answering machine took over, and Willa's voice made some sort of threat about breaking her door in.

Amy shook two painkillers out of a bottle in the bedside drawer, washing them down with stale water from a glass left on the table since before her holiday. A few minutes later, she rolled gingerly out of bed and shuffled to the living room to check her other messages.

The police had left a number to call. Meg welcomed her back, said she'd be fine on her own on Saturday and looked forward to seeing her in the shop on Monday. Several messages were from her mother, asking for a call. Amy thought back to their conversation the morning she'd left Bowron Park. Her mother had said the police would get in touch with her when she returned from the trip. She'd better call them to make sure it really was Tyler who called the resort, and not the police.

She phoned, introduced herself and told the officer she'd been called back from a trip, then she asked to speak with Sergeant Bellamy. The officer informed her they didn't have a Sergeant Bellamy there. He asked her to wait while he checked her file.

Amy's heartbeat picked up as she waited. The hand clasping the receiver felt damp. She gazed down at her shoes. She slept with her shoes on?

The officer came back on the line. "It seems there's been a misunderstanding," he said. "There's no reference to a callback request in the report. It *does* recommend that you come in and answer a few questions on your return."

Amy relaxed. "Sorry, I must have heard it wrong."

"No problem. Can you come in this morning around ten?"

"Yes. Sure."

After hanging up, Amy kicked her shoes off, brought them to the front hall and almost tripped over the daypack on the floor. She shuddered at the sight of it, wished she could just burn it.

Back in the living room, her eyes settled on the bookcase for a moment before her mind registered that the shelves were empty. She stared at the messy heap of her favourite books on the floor, then turned and ran to the laundry room. She pulled the dirty laundry from the washer and let out a sigh of relief. Her laptop was still there. She took it out and clutched it to her chest.

She checked the rest of the apartment. Cupboards in the kitchen were in complete disarray. Jars and cans stood open on the counter. Some of her clothes lay on the closet floor. The contents of her chest of drawers had been rifled through, papers on her desk shuffled around.

He'd been everywhere. She ran her fingers through her hair in frustration, fingers catching in the tangles.

She undressed, got in the shower and scrubbed her body like never before. Looking for her hairbrush afterward, she remembered Tyler using it, that she'd thrown it away. Recalling him using her toothbrush and shaver as well, she went and pulled her muddy jeans out, then dropped the daypack with everything in it into a plastic garbage bag, tied it shut and left it by the door. She watched it for a moment, wishing it would self-destruct, then went to get dressed.

Her stomach barked from neglect, reminding her that she'd only had two apples in the last twenty-four hours. Her heart softened at the thought of Winny, the woman in the hay truck, her own personal angel.

She ate toast with jam and drank two mugs of coffee to clear her head, but it only gave her the jitters. After making an afternoon appointment with a locksmith to install a deadbolt, she put her laundry in the washing machine and left for the police station. On her way, she shoved the garbage bag down the chute by the elevator and closed the door tight. *There, gone.*

She shivered in her light jacket as she made her way to the station. The air was unusually chilly for mid-September. She felt apprehensive about the meeting. No matter how hard she tried to convince herself that her troubles were over, deep inside she had her doubts. She'd wiped every trace of Tyler from her apartment, but his threat remained. Just a slip of her tongue, and she might be forced to tell the police about him. Then, how long would it be before those thugs looking for him would find her?

At the station, a policeman with white hair, a long nose, and a face like weathered buckskin shook Amy's hand, introduced himself in a deep voice as Detective Dave Krucik. He pointed to a chair and asked her to take a seat. Amy tried to ignore the tension growing in her body as he glanced through a file on his desk. After a moment he looked up, saying they'd been summoned to her apartment by the building superintendent and had made a search. "Did you find anything missing on your return?" he asked.

"I checked this morning, and it all seemed to be there."

Krucik made a few notes.

"Not that I have a lot to check, mind you," she added.

He glanced back at her. "Hmmm."

"Can you think of anyone specific who could have broken in?"

Amy picked some invisible lint off her pants, pretending to think about it. She shook her head. "No." Her ears were getting hot. *I should've left my hair down.*

Krucik looked up from the report. "Are you sure about that?" he asked with a hawkish gaze.

Alarmed, Amy stopped fidgeting with her hands, looked up at his weathered face and saw doubt. She was screwing up. *Say something.* "I'm sorry, officer, but I've never been inside a police station before, and I've never been questioned by a policeman. It's making me a bit nervous."

He fingered a birthmark on his forehead for a moment as if thinking it over. "All right," he said and returned to the report. "The reason for our concern about your well-being is blood was found in the apartment."

"Blood?" Amy stared at him. "Where? I didn't see any."

Krucik consulted the report and read out loud: "Drops of blood on several envelopes on a desk in the bedroom, drops of blood on the floor from the bedroom to the bathroom, a large smudge on the side of the bathroom vanity, a puddle of blood on the floor under the smudge."

"Oh."

"Fingerprints were lifted from around the apartment," he continued. "If you don't mind, we'd like to get your prints as well, for elimination."

"Sure. I don't mind."

He asked questions about the time and date of her departure, who knew she'd be away, who'd been in the apartment since she'd moved in, who might have a key, and on and on. Amy answered confidently, watching as he dutifully jotted it all down.

Finally, he put the pen aside. "That should be enough information for now. A copy of the report will be mailed to you."

Amy was fingerprinted and left.

She walked out of the station like a robot, stiff and guilt-laden for withholding information, feeling the officer's eyes burning holes in her back.

Back home, she headed straight for the bathroom, pulled the shower curtain to the far side of the tub and stared at the large smear below the countertop and the puddle on the floor. "For God's sake!" She thought she'd cleaned up after him for good.

She put the cleaned wash in the dryer, stuffed towels, the shower curtain and the bathmat into the washer, then brought cleaners, rags and rubber gloves to the bathroom. After cleaning the spots off the floor, she scrubbed the bathroom as if possessed, nearly wearing the paint off the vanity.

She stopped when her fingers poked through the gloves' fingertips. Trashing gloves and rags, she moved to the bedroom, collected the red-spotted envelopes and threw them away. *There.* She'd cleaned him out.

She had tidied up the rest of the apartment by the time the locksmith arrived. While he installed the deadbolt, she checked her bank accounts. She had enough in her personal savings to manage for a month, but nothing in her business account, thanks to Tyler. She'd have to put utility costs, the deadbolt and Meg's salary on credit. Good thing she'd stocked up at the salon before she left.

Meg. Amy picked at her nails, thinking of her biggest asset to the business. She didn't want to lose her perfect co-worker. But how could she afford an employee now without taking out another loan, or even worse, asking her father for an extension on his loan?

All of a sudden she remembered playing with the idea of making Meg a partner. If Meg would go along with that, it could save the business. A partner would be as interested in the business as she was. She'd feel more secure.

But what about Meg? Would she want it? Could she afford it? Amy wanted to talk to her right away, but knew this wasn't the right time. She needed to feel more balanced or she'd scare her off.

She paid the locksmith, wrote a restrained grocery list and left to go shopping. On her way, she stopped by the super's apartment to give him a spare key to the deadbolt.

Chapter 24

Feeling he'd be safer in a more remote part of BC, Tyler drove north, listening to the news on the radio. He was surprised to hear they'd found Mike and his car already. At least, Mike hadn't been identified yet.

Tyler was tired after driving all night and his arm throbbed with pain. He shook a few painkillers out of a bottle, chewed and swallowed. They'd had a hell of a fight, leaving Tyler with some pretty bad cuts, but Mike had lost in the end. In the darkness of the night, Tyler had placed Mike's body in the trunk of his car and driven it to what looked like a perfect dumping spot. He'd pushed it over the edge into a deep crevice and listened to it crashing to the bottom. When it caught on fire, Tyler sprinted back to his car and started to drive north.

He felt lucky to get out of that. Mike had probably never intended to give him the passport anyway. At least, now he had all his stash left and more cash than ever. He could find a place to stay in rural BC. Sooner or later something lucrative would show up.

* * *

Willa's parents came out to meet them as Ben drove up the driveway. "Welcome!" A small, round woman with sandy curls wrapped her arms around Willa. "It's so good to have you back."

"Ben, Paul," Willa said. "Meet my mom, Carol, and my dad, James."

A tall man with auburn greying hair kissed Willa's cheek, then shook hands with Ben and Paul. "Thank you for bringing Willa home."

"Our pleasure."

After unloading Willa's gear, Ben and Willa exchanged phone numbers, promising to keep in touch.

* * *

Amy could smell the warm barbecued chicken as she rode the elevator up to her floor. The aroma almost drove her mad. She wanted to tear it apart and eat it like a savage, right there on the floor.

She hurried to put the groceries away, then brought the chicken, a small Greek salad and a glass of milk to the dining table. With her hands stiff from the scrubbing, the eating proved slow going, but she relished every bite. Looking around the room, she felt happy to have reclaimed her home. This time for good. *It better be.*

Her phone rang. It was Willa. "Hi, Amy. I just got back. I heard about the detour. When did you get back?"

"Late last night."

"So … what happened?"

Amy told her about the mess in her apartment, the deadbolt and that she'd talked to the police. "They'd found blood in the bathroom."

"I *knew* it had to be something like that," Willa said. "Ben told me they wouldn't call a person back from a trip unless something serious had happened. Was it a lot of blood?"

"Enough to worry them, I suppose. Enough with the interrogation. Did you have a nice ride home?"

"We did. Actually, Ben asked a few questions about you."

"Oh yeah? What questions?"

"A few, leading to his main question: 'Is she single?' Do you want his number?"

Amy couldn't help feeling a bit intrigued. "I … well, sure." She wrote it down. "Does he expect me to call him?"

"I wouldn't know about that, but he wanted you to have it just in case. I'm telling you, he has a crush on you."

"He's a great guy. I feel he's a friend, but that's all. Willa, I do have to go to bed."

"I know. I'll call you tomorrow."

After hanging up with Willa, Amy forced herself to pick up the phone and dial her mother. "Hello, Mother. I'm back."

"Oh, so you finally remembered you have a mother."

"I had a busy day." Amy told her the same things she'd told Willa.

"Blood? I didn't see any blood."

"At the side of the bathroom vanity, hidden behind the shower curtain. They fingerprinted me and I left."

"What? Your prints are in the police records now? We need to check with them about that."

"Oh, please. It's my business, not yours." *I'm 25 and still answering to my mother.* "They're elimination prints. To compare with the fingerprints they took from the apartment."

"Dear God."

"Listen, I have to go to bed."

"Come for dinner tomorrow."

"I can't," Amy lied. "I'm expecting a guest."

"Who's coming, if I may ask?"

"A special friend. I've got to go. I'll call you next week."

* * *

Tyler blinked, then jerked. *"Holy shit!"* He checked the rear view mirror and quickly swerved back to the right side of the road. He'd dozed off. Shaken, he pulled onto the shoulder. It was only early afternoon, but he'd been on the road for fifteen hours. He shook out two pills and swallowed. He still had a few things to do before checking in somewhere for the night. A few minutes later, he continued his drive.

He stopped in at a Thrift store in the outskirts of Dawson Creek and bought horned-rimmed specs with plain glass lenses, a baseball cap, jeans, sweatshirts, boots, a cotton scarf and a jacket. After making a stop at a drugstore to fill up on hydrogen peroxide, he bought a hot dog from a street vendor and continued driving, scanning for a place to stay. He continued to Pouce Coupe, where he found a mediocre-looking motel that looked 'safe'. The guy behind the desk barely looked up when he checked in.

The room reeked of chlorine and tobacco fumes. He dropped his bags on the floor, plunked down on the bed and turned the TV on. Smoking and eating the hot dog, he watched the news. Nothing new about Mike.

He went to have a shower, his first in weeks. His sweatshirt, covered in dirt and blood, was stuck to his arm. He slowly peeled it off and winced as blood welled up from two deep cuts. He grabbed a towel, clamped down on the cuts and stepped into the shower.

After cleaning himself, he cut the new scarf into strips and bandaged his arm, stemming the flow. He checked the wound on his chin. It had started to heal, but his beard, still too short to cover it, was making it look more obvious. He used the shaver to make his thick, dark eyebrows less prominent, studied his face in the mirror and grimaced. He looked like hell.

He thought about the many people that were after him. He should let Amy know he was still around, just as a reminder to keep her mouth shut.

He rinsed the blood from the tub, stuffed the old clothes and bloodied towels in the shopping bag, got dressed, then drove to a gas station. There, he stuffed the bag in a garbage can, then used a payphone to call Amy.

"Hi," he said when she answered. He smiled as he heard her gasp. "Yes, I'm still around, so don't get too comfy. Just so we're on the same page about the thugs chasing me and possibly you, I'm talking about hard-core killers from Vancouver, not small-town wannabes. So if you talk, those thugs will come after both of us, yes, but then you'll have both them and me coming after you. Do you hear what I'm saying?"

He listened to Amy swallowing in the background, satisfied by her distress.

"I keep my word," she said, her voice shaking. "Something you don't know the meaning of."

"I'm keeping an eye on you," he said, and hung up.

* * *

Amy slammed the phone down and stood for a moment, staring

at it in bewilderment before stumbling back to bed on shaky legs. She lay in the dark, distressed about this new turn of events. She'd thought to bury recent events once Tyler left, but something must have happened. He was still around, threatening her.

And there'd been something new in his tone of voice this time. He sounded as if he enjoyed it – like some lunatic getting his kicks from scaring her. She found it hard to believe that he would kill her – he'd had plenty of opportunities to do that at the cabin.

So he liked to scare her. Too bad, she wouldn't give him the satisfaction of knowing how scared she was. She'd find a way to carry on with her life and forget he existed.

Chapter 25

On Sunday morning, Amy had a quick breakfast and went to the gym. When she got home, she had a message from Willa. She dialled her number. "What's up?"

"Ben called. He wanted to know if you had any problems with the police when you spoke to them."

Amy tensed up. "Thanks Willa, but why didn't he ask me?"

"Because I didn't know if you wanted me to give him your number."

"Oh, yeah. Thanks, Willa. Sorry. Uh … I'll get back to him about that myself."

"Okay."

Amy found the note with Ben's number and dialled.

"Hello, Amy." Ben's voice sounded like a silken murmur.

"You're still in bed? I thought you were up with the birds."

"Only when I'm having fun. I work tonight, so I'm trying to build up some spare sleep. So tell me, what did they tell you at the station?"

"Well, the officer I met with said they hadn't asked for me to come back, that there must have been a misunderstanding." Amy explained the gist of the conversation as well as about being fingerprinted.

"Sorry you had to go through all that," Ben said. "I'll try to find out what went on. "Who did you talk to?"

"Umm … I have a problem with his name. He had white hair and a long nose …"

"That must've been Dave Krucik. We call him Hawkeye because he looks like a hawk when he stares at you over that nose."

"Yeah, he really did!"

"By the way, did something happen to your cell phone? We tried to reach you a few times."

"Yeah, I lost it," Amy lied, cringing with guilt. She hated Tyler all the more for putting her in this position. "I don't know where, but it must have been after I ran into an old school friend at a gas station at the Cache Creek highway junction. She wanted to show me her new place in Kamloops, so I decided to take a quick detour. I didn't even think about my cell until I got home."

"I see."

Amy felt almost sick with guilt. "I should let you go back to sleep."

"I've had enough sleep. Listen, can I take you out for dinner tomorrow night?"

"Thank you, but no. Ben, it has nothing to do with you. It's just that I'm not into dating right now."

"Fair enough, but instead of a date, how about we just hang out? I enjoy your company. You need to eat, don't you? How about we go for tapas at the Bin?"

Amy hesitated. "Sure. Tapas sounds good."

"Pick you up at seven-thirty? Eight?"

"You know where I live?"

"No, but I'm hoping you'll tell me."

Amy let out an amused snort. "All right." She gave him her address. "Make it eight."

After the call, she sat with the receiver in her lap for a moment before hanging up. Her conscience was eating away at her. In the past day and a half, she'd lied to the police, Willa and Ben. She thought about Meg. She'd probably be next.

She felt wary about beginning a friendship with Ben. She thought about cancelling dinner and cutting ties with him. It didn't seem like a good idea to pal around with a cop in her precarious situation. On the other hand, the way things were going with Tyler, she might need a cop friend, especially Ben who seemed the protective type.

Before leaving for work on Monday morning, Amy called Meg and found out they were both fully booked, and then some. The partnership discussion would have to wait until Tuesday.

Blocking out any thought about Tyler, Amy walked to work, thinking about the evening with Ben, still worried that a friendly dinner with a detective could prove to be her downfall; that he'd see right through her.

When she arrived at the salon, she went straight to Meg and gave her a hug. "I can't thank you enough for taking such good care of the business, Meg. Don't ever leave me."

"Thanks." Meg smiled. "I don't plan to."

As they took a short break in the afternoon, Meg asked Amy if she'd heard about the accident in the Coast Mountains.

Amy shook her head. "I've had my hands full since I got back from the trip. Haven't had much time to watch TV. What happened?"

"A car went off Highway 99 and crashed down the mountain to the bottom, into a blazing mess. The rescue team didn't find anyone inside the car or in the area around it, but they found remnants of a body in the trunk."

"That's creepy. Did it happen yesterday?"

"No, before that. A logger found the car on Saturday morning."

"Where on 99?"

"Somewhere north of Whistler."

"Hmm."

As the day wore on, Amy began to look forward to the dinner with Ben. She even felt some comfort at the prospect of having him as a friend.

"Meg, can you come in fifteen minutes earlier tomorrow morning?" Amy asked as they closed up for the evening. "I'd like to talk to you about something."

"Sure thing."

Once home, Amy had a shower, got into jeans, a black T-shirt and ballet flats, trying hard to make it look like she didn't care. She went out on the balcony to see if Ben had arrived. Traffic was slumbering after the evening rush. In the distance, high construction cranes stood like majestic herons against the darkening sky. Amy shivered and turned to go inside. Her eyes fastened on the sand-filled can on the floor, home to a lone cigarette butt. She wouldn't need that anymore. She swept it up and threw it in the garbage.

The phone rang. It was Willa. "Hi Amy, I just wanted to tell you that I talked to Chad today. He's still a bit fuzzy about what happened in Bowron Park, but he'll be back at work next week."

"That's wonderful news," Amy said. "Thanks for letting me know."

"By the way, did you talk to Ben?"

"Yes ... well ... I'm about to. We're going for tapas."

"Aha!"

The intercom buzzed. "Here he is now." *Saved by the bell*. "Call ya later." Amy hung up and hurried to the intercom, telling Ben she'd be right down.

Her heart took a little skip when she saw him waiting by his car, all dressed up in a dark suit and tie. She'd only seen him in jeans, or shorts and a T-shirt. *Wow!*

"You didn't have to change," she said, suddenly feeling underdressed.

"I didn't." He held the passenger door open.

"What's with the suit? Don't you wear a uniform?"

"Sometimes."

"Do you always dress like that when you go out for tapas?"

Ben laughed, palms up. "I confess. I didn't finish work in time to go home and change."

"So which Bin are we going to?"

"The one on Broadway, okay?"

"Good choice."

They ordered four tapas and beer. Ben told Amy they were sorry she missed out on the trip. It appeared to be a screw-up, someone got their wires crossed, and there was no match to the prints lifted in her apartment.

Relieved, Amy relaxed. "Tell me about the last two days," she said as they ate.

"Everyone missed you."

"That's nice to hear. Now tell me what *I* missed."

"We had a couple of sunny, uneventful days, with one exception: a moose pissed on Max." When Ben told the story, Amy burst out laughing. Ben sat back, watching her, smiling.

"What?" she asked when she noticed.

Ben shook his head. "Nothing. How's your food?"

"Amazing. So tell me, what do detectives do when they're not chasing crooks."

"Nothing very exciting I'm afraid. Apart from hockey and hiking, I like to run, listen to music, mainly blues and jazz. Ray Charles. Miles Davis. I like to read thrillers, some nonfiction. Also I'm trying to impress the shit out of my superiors." He smiled. "I'd like to be the chief of police one day. There. Now you know more about me than my mother does."

"I meant to ask about that – where were you born?"

"You sure have a lot of questions. Generally, I'm the one doing the interrogation."

"Well, you look kind of exotic with your black hair and blue eyes. Don't people ask you about that?"

"Sometimes. Let me see. I've lived in Vancouver all my life. I never met my grandparents, but I've seen pictures of them. My tall, dark-skinned grandfather, born in India, married my grandmother, a lady small enough to fit under his arm, when he worked on an engineering project in Thailand. They had two boys: my father and another who died at birth.

"My dad went to England to study engineering, found it wasn't for him, so he moved to Vancouver and became a police officer. There, he met my mother, a social worker born and raised in Sweden. They fell in love and got married – frowned upon by some – and here we are."

"Fascinating," Amy said, thinking of her own parents, still in the Dark Ages. "I don't know much about my grandparents, but my uncle, Willa's father, is into genealogy research, big time, so I'm sure I'll hear all about it one day."

"So now that you know everything about me, tell me a bit about yourself."

"Some other time." She hoped that didn't come off as rude.

"All right. How about we go for coffee on the weekend?"

Amy looked at him from under her bangs. "I told you I'm not ready for dating."

Ben cocked his head to the side and gazed at her. "Can't we meet once in a while for coffee without calling it dating?"

Amy looked at him with a lopsided smile. "You might be a hell of a detective, but that sounded like a come-on to me."

Ben looked sheepish. "I'm not doing very well, am I?" He shook his head. "Cops spend too much time with other cops – mostly male." He looked down at the floor, stroking his chin. "All right." He looked back at Amy. "Here it goes. I'm having a good time tonight. I want to spend more time with you – call it what you want – but I like you."

Amy felt her resolve crumble. "You're doing just fine, officer. Okay … Coffee. Sunday afternoon at two."

* * *

Tyler felt the need to move. Three nights in the same motel was asking for trouble. He needed to get someplace where nobody gave a shit. Some secluded hiding spot to hang for a week or two – a place where he could hide his stash rather than driving around with it in the car. The cops and the gangs would think he'd left the area. Then it would be easier to sneak out.

He thought of a place he hadn't been to for a long time, a good place to hide out. He didn't remember exactly how to get there but knew he could find it once he was in the area. But first, he should change his looks. He picked up the knife and the bottle of peroxide and went to the bathroom.

Chapter 26

When Amy arrived at the salon on Tuesday morning, Meg was already there, pouring coffee into two mugs. She handed one to Amy. "Is there a problem?" she asked in a worried voice.

"No, nothing like that." Amy motioned to the seating area. "Let's get comfortable. I'd like to get your opinion on something." They went and sat down. "Do you remember before I left for my trip, I told you I felt lucky to have found you?"

"Yes," Meg said, looking at her cup.

"And you said you liked it here."

Meg looked up. "Well, I do."

"Have you ever thought about partnering up with someone in the business? Being your own boss at a salon, sharing the costs of the business, like rent, heat, phone, equipment, tools?"

"Yes." Meg sat up, her face radiating expectation.

"So have I. Now I'd like you to know that I think you and I would make a great team. So if you by any chance feel the same way, please let me know. Okay?"

"Yesss!" Meg bounced in her chair, splashing coffee on her pants. "Oops." She grabbed a rag and wiped them, saying, "I do feel the same way. I've felt the same ever since I started working for you. This is great! When can we start? I mean ... whenever you want to. I know an accountant who can get us started with the preliminaries as well as a lawyer who can help with anything legal."

Amy laughed at her exuberance. "You've been thinking about this longer than I have. All right. We'll start by meeting with the accountant then, so will you set it up?"

"You bet."

Relieved, Amy began to feel her life might turn around, that from now on, things would get better.

* * *

Tyler left the motel in the morning and drove south. He kept looking at himself in the rear-view mirror, amazed at the difference a bit of trimming and bleach could make to dark eyebrows and a bushy moustache. Soon it would cover the scar on his jaw. He lifted his cap and grinned – the blonde shag and the horn-rimmed glasses made him look like some painter artist.

He'd been driving for about three hours when he spotted two police cars on the road ahead. It looked like they were handling an accident. Tyler detoured and hung out behind a mini mart, waiting for the cops to go away. Two hours later they finally left and he could pull back out on the highway.

Driving through the city of Prince George, he saw a strip mall with a grocery store and a beer store and dropped in there. As he was unloading his groceries and beer in the car, a couple approached him, asking for directions. Tyler shook his head, said he didn't know and got into the car. In his rush to leave, he drove off in the wrong direction and got lost. He backtracked and drove around, trying to find the highway, or at least the strip mall, getting increasingly agitated as he made more wrong turns. He had no idea where he was. He had to calm down. He backtracked again and finally found the strip mall. Going in a different direction this time, he finally got out on the highway. He washed down two speed pills with coke and drove south, downing fistfuls of chips and listening to the evening news. Mike had been identified.

* * *

When Amy came home from work, she had a call from her mother, asking her to come for dinner on Friday.

"I'm not sure I can make it," Amy hedged.

"I don't want to hear any more excuses. I think you're avoiding us."

"No, I'm not," Amy lied. "I'm backed up at work because of my trip."

"Don't punish us for that."

"All right, all right. I'll be happy to come for dinner on Friday, as long as you don't mind me getting there late, say seven-thirty at the earliest. And I'm not ready to talk about my private life, so please don't milk me about it."

"Fine," her mother snapped. "See you on Friday."

Amy hung up, frustrated with herself for always resisting her mother. *Grow up!* She heated a leftover casserole, brought her dinner to the living room and turned on the TV news. They were reporting the story of the crash. The dead man in the trunk had just been identified as Mike Polanco, the owner of the car and leader of a Squamish drug gang. Three gang members had been located and brought in for questioning. One gang member was still at large. Amy wondered if Ben was working on that case. She turned the TV off and got ready for bed, thinking about their dinner out. She'd enjoyed it. Ben had seemed honest when he talked about them being friends and going out once in a while. But she'd made mistakes before. She didn't want to be taken in by another seducer, or by her own need to be loved.

* * *

Tyler was getting too tired to drive and started to scan for a place to pull off the highway for the night. Motels were out of the question at this point – none of them would be safe for him. Just south of Quesnel, he saw a closed-down car repair shop, pulled in behind it and went to sleep.

* * *

Amy had breakfast watching the Wednesday morning news. "There's been a breakthrough in the Highway 99 murder investigation," a newswoman announced. "This morning, the RCMP in Squamish announced that the last gang member, a suspect in the case, has been identified. His name is Tyler Corman."

Amy choked on her toast, spewing bits and pieces all over the table. She turned and stared at the screen in wide-eyed panic as the newswoman continued: "The suspect is still at large, and the police are asking anyone who has any information about Tyler Corman to call this number." A phone number appeared on the screen. "All information will be treated as confidential."

It's a common name. It doesn't have to mean it's the Tyler Corman I know. But deep inside she knew it must be him. He'd been on that highway last Friday afternoon. He'd told her he was still around when he called on Saturday night, threatening to take her down if she talked. But if he'd killed the leader of his gang in Squamish, wouldn't he be running from the other members of *that* gang? Why had he talked about running from a gang from Vancouver?

"This wasn't part of my life," she whispered aloud to convince herself.

When she arrived at the salon, Meg bounced over to her, looking excited. "I just talked to Mary Thompson, the accountant. She'd like to see us next week some time, preferably Monday or Thursday afternoon or evening if we can make it."

Amy tried to give her a genuine smile. "Great. Thanks, Meg. Monday after work would be great. I'll have the paperwork ready by then."

* * *

Tyler woke up in the morning, stiff from cold, his stomach aching from lack of food. He started the car and turned up the heat, then went to take a piss. Back in the car, he pulled a loaf of bread from a grocery bag and chewed on it, listening to the news. Suddenly he heard his name mentioned. Someone had identified him. Cursing, he flung the loaf onto the passenger seat and hightailed out of there. He needed to find that cabin in a hurry.

In a lonely area, about twenty kilometres south of Quesnel, the car slowed. He was running out of gas. Cursing, he looked for an inconspicuous place to ditch the car before it would stop altogether. He saw an old barn near a cornfield, pulled to the side of the road, then pushed the car down a slope over to the side of the barn. He stuffed a few groceries and as many cans of beer as he could fit into his backpack and started to walk back to Quesnel, leaning over under the weight, trying to look like a backpacker.

Thinking it was high time to warn Amy, he decided to use her cell. He went through his pockets, but couldn't find it. He searched through his backpack, but still couldn't find it. He must have left it in the car or dropped it at the motel when he rushed to leave in the morning. He'd left a trail.

More agitated than ever, he kept walking toward Quesnel. He arrived four hours later, found a payphone and called Amy. Her machine took over. He left a message warning her about describing him, then went to find a secluded area where he could rest and have something to eat without being seen. In the afternoon he set out to find a car to steal. It was dark before he finally found a good one. He drove off, planning to get as far from the city as possible, but it had been a hard day, so when he saw a secluded place to pull in for the night, he decided to take an early break. He settled down, had a few beers, a couple of pills and passed out.

* * *

Amy barely remembered how she got through the day. She hurried home after work, desperate for solitude. Back in her apartment she collapsed on the sofa, too exhausted to move. If only the police would find Tyler, there'd be no reason for the other thugs to come after her. But, knowing Tyler, he wouldn't make it easy for anyone to recognize him.

For anyone but me.

She jumped when her phone rang. She waited for the machine

to take over. A few minutes later, she checked her messages. The last one had an unknown number. She clicked to listen. "Don't even *think* about describing me," Tyler hissed, and signed off.

Amy backed away from the phone, staring at it as if he'd seep out of the receiver like a homicidal genie. This wasn't working. She couldn't handle it anymore. She covered her face with her hands. *I'm falling apart.* Maybe if she could get him to go away, be locked up, things would work. She didn't want to feel this way forever. As her fears won, she scrambled to find Ben's number.

Chapter 27

"Amy, what's wrong?" Ben said when he heard her voice.

"I need your help."

"Where are you?"

"At home. Can you come please?"

"I'll be there in ten minutes."

At the sound of the intercom, Amy hurried to buzz Ben in. She waited by the open door as he stepped out of the elevator and hurried over to her.

"Come in," she said, then went to sit on the sofa.

"What's going on?" Ben asked, following her.

Amy took a deep breath and looked up at him. "Are you investigating the Highway 99 murder?"

"Actually, the VPD is cooperating with the Squamish RCMP on that case, since the missing suspect lives in Vancouver. Why?"

Amy looked away. She was tired – tired of lying and scared of telling the truth, but she couldn't see her way out of it. "I can't do this anymore."

"Do what? What are you talking about?"

Amy pulled tissues from a box on the coffee table, wiping her eyes and nose. "I was engaged to Tyler Corman."

Ben looked startled for a moment. "Go on."

"I broke up with him when I suspected he'd become involved with drugs. I don't know to what extent, but once I saw him handle a bag of white powder." She stopped for a moment. "I shouldn't tell you or anyone else about this, but …"

"Amy please, I'm lost." Ben looked worried. "What are you trying to tell me?"

"Tyler is the one who broke into my apartment. Some thugs chasing him had cut a long, deep gash in his jaw, and he needed to hide, somewhere to clean up. I guess his T-shirt was soaked in blood, so he took a sweatshirt from my closet – the only oversized shirt there. I'd bought it for a costume party."

"Have you talked to him? How do you know all this?"

Twisting the tissues in her lap, Amy told Ben about her relationship with Tyler: the abuse, the burn, the miscarriage, the breakup and his continuing harassment afterward. She told him that Tyler had called the resort, not the police, and that he'd ambushed her in the motel room on her way to Vancouver before taking her to a cabin at knifepoint.

"He had my bunny sweatshirt on. I questioned him about it. That's how I know."

"But why didn't you tell that to the officer at the station?"

"I couldn't. Tyler kept me in the cabin until it was time to go to the bank the next morning. He extorted money from me to pay for someone's help in his disappearing act. He took my cell phone and held it up to show me a Vancouver number already keyed in. He said if I told anyone in the bank, he'd call a waiting gang member to go after my parents. He knew their address." She covered her face with her hands. "It made me feel so helpless. I hated to do it, but I didn't have a choice. And now he's wanted for murder."

"You're right. You didn't have a choice. I understand the pressure you're under ..."

"But I'm scared, Ben. He said that if I told anyone I'd given him money, the Vancouver thugs chasing him would find out and come after me." She looked away. "I'm so sorry I lied to you before."

Ben slid closer. "Amy, listen. You've downloaded a shitload of guilt over something that isn't your fault. I know how guys like him think, how they manipulate others. Believe me, it's not your fault. Do you understand that?"

"I guess ... I want to, but ..."

"Don't guess. Believe it." Ben put his hand under her chin, turning her tearful face to him. "It's not your fault. Okay?"

"Okay ... but I might be the only one who can identify him – the way he looks nowadays." Amy reached over and pushed replay on her house phone. "I just got this message."

After listening to Tyler's threat, Ben called his office phone. When his machine picked up, he pushed the message to record and put his phone close to the speaker to get two recordings. He asked Amy not to erase the message.

"I won't. Ben, I don't understand what's going on anymore. Who is he running from? It doesn't sound like it's from his own gang members, the way he keeps threatening me about Vancouver thugs. If I describe him, and those thugs recognize him, both Tyler and the thugs will come after me."

"That would be very foolish of them. If a drawing is released, the department will keep whatever information given to us under wraps until we have Tyler and any other suspect behind bars. We would station an unmarked police car outside your apartment and business. Someone will follow you at all times. We might have to put you in protective custody if you're threatened again, but only until all suspects have been arrested."

"It's just that I don't trust Tyler. He shoots people. Do you think he cares if it's a cop?"

Ben's eyes narrowed. "I'd like to see him try to get past me. Do you know where his parents live?"

"No. He never told me, only that they live somewhere in the eastern part of BC."

"We'll find them."

Amy reached out and touched Ben's hand. "I'm so relieved you're on the case."

He flashed a hesitant smile. "Well, I'm not sure I should stay on the case anymore."

"What are you talking about?"

"Amy, now I'm going to tell you something. You must have noticed that I like you ... a lot. I already did in Bowron Park. But," he held up a hand, "as I promised, I'll settle with just staying friends. The dilemma is, if my boss finds out about my feelings for you, I'll be off the case because I'm personally involved. But I need to stay close, to make sure they go the extra mile."

He likes me a lot? Why didn't she mind? Was it because she needed his help? "Umm ... thank you," she said hesitantly. "I don't know what to say to that, but I do know that I'm happy that you're on the case."

Ben smiled. "Good enough. I'll take it."

"But, if you don't tell, how would your boss find out?"

"He's a very smart man. When things heat up, few people can hide anything from him, believe me."

"What are we going to do then?"

"Technically I should have called him the moment you started to tell me. And he would have assigned a different officer to take your statement."

"Why don't we do that?"

"Do what?"

"Tell another officer. I can call the station in the morning and tell them what I told you. I don't have to tell them that I told anyone else. Wouldn't that work?"

It took Ben a moment to catch up. "Are you sure?"

Amy nodded. "Yes. It's important to both of us."

"Then that's perfect. Tell them everything you know. They'll ask questions about Tyler, his parents, his friends. They'll ask you to describe him to a composite sketch artist. They'll want to check your phone records …"

"But …" Amy stared at him, hand over mouth. "Your number will show up. I used my house phone when I called you on Sunday, and then again tonight."

"You're right. I'll just have to make sure I'm the one who looks through the phone records." Ben wrote something on his notepad, tore off the page and handed it to Amy. "That's the public number for our squad. It's the same number as you saw on the news. Explain to whoever picks up the phone and ask who you should talk to."

"Okay." Amy put the note by the phone.

"As a short-term solution to the phone record situation, I'll give you the number to my private cell phone, so you can get hold of me if you need to. Use a payphone when you do, until you get a new cell phone. Just leave a message, and I'll get back to you by way of Willa."

"By Willa?" Amy looked unsure. "She might seem a bit naïve, but she's smarter than you think. I don't want her to get any ideas about us. She wants to see us getting together, talks about it openly. Before you know it, your boss will hear about it."

"I'll talk to her. She'll understand. Trust me."

Amy hesitated. "Okay. I trust you." She took out a small notebook from her shoulder bag and opened it to M. "Okay, mister Malik, what's the number?"

Ben gazed at her as she wrote it down. "You've been through hell and back without me having the slightest idea," he said, softly. "It must have been hard to tell me all that."

Amy thought about it. "I actually feel better now. Probably needed to get it off my mind."

Ben had just left when Amy had a call from Willa. "I just heard on the news the name of the guy the police are looking for is Tyler Corman. Tell me it's not the same …"

Amy went cold. She hadn't thought about what her parents and Willa would think when they heard the name. "I don't know for sure," she said, "But it could be. I just found out myself. I've decided to tell the police about him, so I can't say anything more about it because of their investigation. Promise not to say anything to anyone until I tell you. Please."

"I won't. Are you in trouble?"

"No, I don't think so. But I don't want people to start speculating about something just because of a name. It's very important that you don't say anything about me. If anyone asks you, just tell them you have no idea. After all, it could be another Tyler Corman. It's a common name. Just for now, okay?"

"I promise. Be careful, Amy. And call me."

After she hung up, Amy went to bed, shaken by how easily things could go wrong just by deciding not to tell someone something. She turned out the lights and tried to relax. Clutching her sheet in the dark, she thought of the call she had to make to the police in the morning, already feeling nervous about it. She cringed at the thought of all the lies she'd told the first officer, lies that could be used in court if it came to that. She had to tell them everything and didn't think she could do that over the phone.

Chapter 28

In his apartment, a few city blocks away, Ben couldn't sleep, couldn't stop thinking about Amy. He should remove himself from the case. If he didn't, and Sergeant Harrison, the lead investigator of the crime unit, learned of his feelings for her, he could be out of a job.

But he couldn't do it. He didn't think any of the others on the squad would be as motivated as he was, and he couldn't risk that. He didn't like to see Amy so distressed, and yet he'd gone along with her suggestion that she'd call the station and repeat things that were obviously painful to her. But he couldn't see any other way. He wrote a note to remind himself about Amy's phone records. If anyone else checked them, his relationship with Amy would be out in the open and he'd be off the case, at best.

* * *

On Thursday morning, Amy left a message for Meg that she had a meeting in the morning and might be a bit late. Then she called the station and asked to talk to someone about Tyler Corman. A moment later, she was transferred to Detective Stephanie

Collins. "Thank you for calling," she said. "I understand you might have some information for us."

Amy told her she'd like to speak to her in private. Not on the phone.

"We can do so here if you like," the detective said.

Fifteen minutes later, Amy arrived at the police-station counter, giving her name to the desk sergeant. Shortly after, a tall woman in a dark suit with a black bob and black-rimmed glasses approached her. "Hi, I'm Stephanie Collins," she said, flashing a beautiful smile, "Thanks for coming in." She led Amy into a small office. "Excuse the mess." She closed the door and pointed to a chair in front of a cluttered desk. "Coffee?"

"No, thank you."

Detective Collins sat down behind the desk, took out a pad from a drawer and looked up at Amy over her glasses. "Any time you're ready."

"Umm … actually, I came here last Saturday to talk to a police officer about a break-in at my apartment. What I told him has a lot to do with what I have to tell you now, so … you might want to get that file."

"What's the officer's name?"

"I'm not sure. It was something like … Cruise?"

"Krucik?"

"That's it."

"He isn't here this morning." Collins pushed her glasses up on her nose and checked her calendar. "September ninth," she mumbled and scribbled something on the pad. "I'll be right back." She hurried out the door.

Amy waited, picking at her nails, wondering why it took her so long.

Collins came back, smiling, holding up a file. "I've got

Hawkeye's report," she said. "Give me a minute. I'll have a quick look at it."

Amy was about to say something about Krucik's nickname, but stopped herself, realizing that would be a give-away. Her heartbeat sped up as she watched Collins read the report full of lies.

"All right." Collins moved her glasses down on her nose and looked up at Amy. "Do you mind if I record your statement?"

"No."

Collins recorded date and case details, then asked in a business tone, "What do you have for us?"

Amy looked into her big brown eyes. "I was engaged to Tyler Corman, the man you're looking for," she said. She took a deep breath. "I lied to Officer Krucik because Tyler scared me to death. The day before that," she pointed to the report, "he'd ambushed me in my motel room and threatened me with a knife. He made me withdraw all my money from the bank at gunpoint, and told me he'd 'sic' some crazy gang member on my parents if I didn't cooperate. He said the thugs chasing him would come after me if I told anyone what happened." She crossed her arms. "I was *afraid* to tell the truth."

Collins nodded. "Most of us would've lied under similar circumstances. Now I'd like you to start from the beginning and tell me everything you can remember about all of that."

Amy nodded and waited for her pulse to slow down. Her hands were clammy. She thought back to the morning the ranger arrived at the campsite and began her story there.

"Do you know any of the people he hung out with?" Collins asked when Amy finished.

"Well, the last couple of weeks before we broke up, he started to bring new friends to our place," Amy said. "I didn't like them, they acted like street punks, so I asked him to stop inviting them. We argued about that."

"Do you have their names?"

"Yes." Amy gave the names of three men and one woman.

"Do you have Tyler Corman's phone number?"

"He didn't have a phone. At least, I never saw one. That's probably why he took mine. But I remember the number he had when we lived together, if that helps."

"Yes, it would. And yours too, please."

Amy gave her the numbers.

"We'll need to look at your cell phone records. Who's your service provider?"

Amy gave her the information.

"Do you have a photo of Tyler Corman that we can use to help identify him?"

"No. Sorry. I had a few, but I burned them all when he left."

"All right." Collins turned the recorder off. "Thank you, Amelia." She reached across the desk. "Let me shake your hand. It takes a brave woman to step forward after all that. We need one more thing from you. Can you describe Tyler Corman's face to a forensic artist?"

"I think so. Now?"

"As soon as he's available. He'll want to interview you, get to know you a bit to make it easier for him to interpret and illustrate your information. It could take a few hours."

"I have clients waiting at the salon."

"Can they be rescheduled if necessary?"

Amy squirmed. "I suppose … My co-worker doesn't know any of this. I came clean to you, but I'm not sure I'm ready to tell her what's going on, yet."

Collins looked thoughtful for a moment. "Just a minute," she said, picked up the phone and dialled. "Hi Steve. Stephanie here. We need a composite. How soon are you available?"

"At noon?" Collins looked at the time, then turned to Amy. "Can you be back here in three and a half hours?"

Amy nodded, thinking at least she could do her morning customers.

Collins went back on the phone. "Great. Thanks, Steve."

"All right, Amy. Noon is good. We'll be waiting for you."

Amy left the station with mixed feelings. Telling the truth made her feel light enough to take flight, but the thought of what would happen when the drawing of Tyler's face appeared on the news gave her an icy shiver.

"Hi Bev." Amy waved to her customer, who'd just arrived for her usual trim, when she walked into the salon. "Please take a seat. I'll be with you in a sec."

Meg told Amy she had booked the meeting with Mary Thompson on Monday evening at seven-thirty.

"Excellent," Amy said. "Meg, I hate to do this to you, but something's come up and I need to take the afternoon off. The reason I came home earlier from the kayaking trip was because of a break-in at my apartment. I have to go to the police station and give them some information. I'll tell you more about it later, but right now I need to know if you can take on any of my afternoon appointments. I'll reschedule the others."

Meg scanned her appointment list. "I can take one haircut and reschedule one or two of the others."

"You're a lifesaver. Thanks, Meg. Please don't say anything about this to anyone for now."

"My lips are zipped."

Waiting for Bev, Amy called and left a message on Willa's

phone that she'd call again in the afternoon.

Amy washed Bev's hair, then went to get her a cup of coffee. Bev had settled in her chair with a *People* magazine when Amy came back. She looked up, smiled a thank you, then got lost in the magazine. Grateful for having a quiet customer at this time, Amy pondered over what to tell Willa about Ben. She shouldn't have said anything about the tapas. Now she'd have to do some damage control before Willa went viral with some imagined love story and possibly got Ben into trouble. She also needed to make sure that Willa knew she'd turned to Detective Collins with her story about Tyler, and not to Ben.

Chapter 29

"Attention, team." The buzz of voices in the command centre hushed. The homicide squad gathered around Sergeant Harrison, his face lined and serious under a mop of grey hair. "A young woman, Amelia Robinson, has come forward with information about Tyler Corman," he said in a dark, raspy voice. "Detective Collins will fill you in on the details."

Ben was relieved to hear that Stephanie Collins had taken Amy's call. Of all the detectives on the squad, he trusted her the most. They'd teamed up on several cases. She was a good cop and particularly skilled at working with women. They'd had a relationship a couple of years back, an infatuation that had changed into a strong friendship. The sex had been good, so once in a while they'd got back in bed together, but not since Ben returned from his kayaking holiday.

After listening to Collins' report, the team discussed the situation. Ben insisted they assign a car for Amy Robinson's protection.

A twelve-year veteran of homicide, Roger Wilson, called Curly because of his bald head, disagreed. "What's your hurry? There's no immediate danger."

"I think there is," Ben pushed on. "Both Tyler and the men chasing him might see the composite drawing we're about to release to media. She'll have people coming after her from two directions."

"We'll decide on that when we have a composite to show," Harrison said. "Our first priority is to find the parents and to locate Corman's friends." He pointed to Collins. "Make sure Squamish gets your report right away."

Reasoning that Harrison might find out that he knew Amy, Ben decided to tell him. "I happen to know Amelia – or Amy as her friends called her – from a group holiday I went on recently," he said. "She was there with her cousin, Willa Robinson."

"Do you have any information other than what we've heard this morning?" Harrison asked.

"No, I don't, but if we should need it, everyone exchanged contact information."

"Very well. Carry on."

On the way back to their desks, Detective Ian Burke caught up with Ben.

Ian and Ben had become close friends during a law enforcement training course the year before. But when Ian and his wife lost their firstborn to SIDS a few months back, Ian became distant with everyone, including Ben. He stopped joking around and began to drink. He often called in sick on Mondays – or came in late, red-eyed and smelling of old whisky. Ben had tried to talk to him about it, but Ian brushed his concern off and increased his consumption of throat lozenges and mouth spray.

"What a coincidence," Ian said.

"What?"

"That you were on the same trip as that Robinson chick."

Ben shrugged. "I guess. Coincidences happen."

"Uh-huh."

Ben sat down at his desk, grateful for the privacy wall between them. He filed an application for a search warrant on Tyler's and Amy's phone records. "Aren't you jumping the gun a bit?" Ian said behind the wall.

"It can't hurt," Ben said.

* * *

At noon, Amy returned to the police station. It had been quiet when she arrived early in the morning, but now the whole place was bustling with people and activity.

Detective Collins led her past the busy command centre where Amy knew Ben would be, down a corridor to a private room. Steve, the forensic artist, a slim man with a full head of brown hair and a moustache, got up from his chair, smiled and shook her hand. "Nice to meet you, Amelia."

Steve wanted to know countless things about Tyler, some of which Amy had to dig deep in her blocked memories to find her answers. She picked out the shape of head and facial features from a facial ID catalogue. They talked about colouring, special markings, hair and the kind of hats he wore.

Amy's head was spinning by the time Steve asked her to go and have a coffee while he put it all together. "Give me forty minutes."

She went to Collins's office and knocked on the doorframe. Collins looked up over her glasses. "Hi."

"Steve's putting it together," Amy said. "Told me to be back in forty minutes. I'm going out for a coffee."

"Sure. See you later."

Amy went to a department store across the street and used the pay phone in the entrance to call Willa. At least this time she wouldn't be lying to her outright, just withholding part of the story. But that reasoning didn't make her feel any better.

"Did you tell the police about Tyler?" Willa asked.

"Yes, I talked to a policewoman this morning – told her pretty much what I told you."

"Did you describe him?"

"Yes. To a forensic artist."

"Wow. You know, my parents and I've never seen him."

"Lucky you."

"So … tell me all about your dinner date with Ben."

"It wasn't a date, Willa. We had tapas while I told him about the other police interview."

"Are you going out with him again?"

"No, I'm not planning to, if that's what you mean. If I decide to, I promise to let you know. Will that make you stop this matchmaking nonsense?"

"Fine, I'll stop."

"So the weekend is coming up. Do you have a hot date?"

"No such luck. I'm working long shifts, which rules out any kind of social life. What about you?"

"I'm going to my parents for dinner tomorrow night, which I'm dreading. And I'm thinking of calling one of my old friends from high school to see if we can go hiking or go to a movie on Saturday. Oh, that reminds me, I have to get a new cell."

"What are you getting?"

"I'm thinking an iPhone, but it's a bit pricey. Something similar. I'll see. Well, don't work too hard. Talk to you next week."

After checking new books in the store, Amy bought a coffee and went back to Steve. "Wow," she said when she saw the drawing. "It almost looks like him."

"Almost isn't good enough," he said. "Now we do the fine-tuning."

Over the next hour, Amy watched Tyler's face emerging. "There!" she said at last. "That's it. Wow. It looks just like him."

"Good." Steve shook her hand. "Thanks for your help. Let's hope someone else recognizes him as well."

"When is it going out?"

"It'll be distributed to media and other law enforcement agencies as soon as possible." He looked at the time. "Probably some time in the morning."

Steve went to talk to Collins. Amy waited by the door, not sure if she was done yet. A moment later, Steve came out, waved goodbye to Amy and left.

Collins came out of her office. "Thanks, Amy. Good work. Are you driving?"

"No I'm walking. It's not far from here."

"Can you wait a few minutes while I scan the composite? I'd like to drive you home."

"Sure, thanks."

While she waited, Amy peeked into the buzzing command centre, lit up in fluorescent light, where police officers, some in uniform and some in shirtsleeves and loosened ties, were moving about, working on computers, talking on the phone, arguing. The countless desks in the room were cluttered with papers and files. A row of video screens stretching across the room, showed maps of city areas, analysis mapping, surveillance and security. She looked around, but didn't see Ben.

"There you are." Seeing Collins, reminded Amy of the drawing. She felt a chill. *It'll be all over the news in the morning.* Thankfully, Officer Collins was her safe driver home.

Chapter 30

Amy tossed and turned all night. When the alarm went off at six, she felt she hadn't slept at all. She hurried to turn on the TV news and got ready for work with one eye on the screen. The sketch didn't show on the six or the seven o'clock news. Amy waited impatiently for the eight o'clock news. The sight of Tyler's face gave her a jolt. His cold stare made her skin crawl. She turned the TV off, wondering who would recognize him. Her parents? Well, she'd find out when she went there for dinner after work.

Meg looked up when Amy walked into the salon. "Are you all right?" she asked, her grey eyes judging Amy.

"A bit tired. Didn't sleep much."

"How did it go at the police station yesterday?"

"It went well. I'll tell you about it in a minute. How did it go here?"

"I was filled up, so when one of your customers had to postpone her appointment, it worked out perfectly."

* * *

Tyler woke up at nine in the morning with a headache. His diminishing supply of beer told him why. In a rush to get going, he started to pull out on the highway just as a cop car drove past in the other direction. Alarmed, Tyler backed up as far as he could without getting stuck in the thicket, then waited. They were looking for him. If the cop saw him, he might be coming back and check him out, or check the license plate for stolen cars.

Tyler took his backpack, left the car and trekked through the brush to a place near the highway where he could check on the police car. When it hadn't returned two hours later, he got back in his car and pulled out.

Driving through a small town in the afternoon, he saw a beer & wine store and pulled in. He was about to go inside when he looked through the window and saw his face on a TV mounted on the wall. He whipped around and had to force himself to walk normally back to his car and drive out of there without attracting attention. Not that he looked much like the guy on the drawing anymore, but he wouldn't take the chance to find out.

"Arrogant, hypocritical *bitch!*" he raged, shaking the steering wheel as he sped away from the store.

She'd described him after all. He should've cut her tongue out. And now he couldn't go near her. The pigs would be all over, watching her, knowing he'd be aching for revenge. This made it harder for him. The cutthroats chasing him would increase their efforts to get him now that the cops were after him, too. This put more pressure on him. He had no time to lose. He took a shortcut along a dirt road leading to the rural highway he knew would lead him to his uncle's cabin. His uncle, who died a few years ago, used to take him there hunting when he was in his mid teens, teaching him how to shoot and set traps.

Tyler reached the highway, turned east, and kept driving, slowing down and examining every opening in the trees for the road leading to the cabin. Suddenly he jolted. He found it! He drove into an opening between pine trees, overgrown with underbrush, but still familiar. The shrubbery scraped the bottom of his car, sometimes getting him stuck, but he always managed to pull free. A few minutes later, he cheered as he saw the double-trunked tree in front of a green door. The pealing paint was dulled, but visible enough for him to know he was safe.

The cabin reminded him a bit of the one he'd used with Amy – almost invisible in the dense underbrush. He removed the debris cluttering the entrance and opened the door. A damp and musty odour permeated the room. Critters scampered off as he stepped inside. The floors creaked as he walked around, remembering. It didn't look like anyone had been there for years. Except for the mouldy beds, the deteriorating wood and layers of dust everywhere, the room looked as if time had stood still. A small wooden stool, an armchair with only three legs and a small wood table were the only furnishings apart from the two beds. The bucket on the rusty iron stove, used for cleaning and washing, was still there, looking grimy.

He unpacked the few groceries and beers he had brought and put it out on top of the stove. He pulled out his stash of coke, amphetamines and money from his backpack, put some drugs aside for his own use and cash to last him for a few months. The rest of his stash he hid in a box of rock salt under the cabin at the back. His life insurance.

* * *

The police located Tyler's parents in Grand Forks, halfway

across the province. They were estranged from their son, had barely talked for years. Hadn't seen him for nearly two years and had no idea of where he could be. They'd seen the composite drawing on the news, but found it hard to believe that it could be their son.

"I'll send you a photo, the latest one we have, and you'll see what I mean," Mr. Corman said.

Shortly after, Harrison received an email with Tyler's high school graduation photo attached. It showed a smiling, good-looking young man, holding his graduation cap. He didn't look much like the man in the police sketch. Harrison shook his head in sadness at how wrong things could go.

* * *

Amy and Meg were fully booked, and time flew by. Amy had a sandwich on the fly at noon, and as she seated her next customer, she happened to see Ben getting out of his car across the street. He pointed to his eyes to let her know he was watching her and walked into the café next-door. She smiled, feeling comforted.

* * *

The investigating team went ahead, started a background check on Tyler Corman. One of his friends seemed to have disappeared. Two friends were found and questioned. Neither recognized the man in the drawing, and neither admitted to knowing the man who'd disappeared. The officers returned to the station and reported their findings.

"You believe them?" Ian asked.

"No, but whatever we asked them, all we got was 'fuck off.'"

Ian grinned. "Now, *there's* a reaction I can work with."

"Go fetch," said Ben.

Ian checked the time. "Nah. It's Friday night. Time to go for a beer." He looked around. "Anyone with me?"

"You got it," the two officers echoed.

Ian turned to Wilson, sitting beside him, staring into space, chewing on his knuckles. "Looks like you could use a beer, Curly? Want to come along?"

Wilson let his hand drop and shook his head. "Nah. I've got too much to do."

Collins came up to Ben. "He'd better be in tomorrow," she said, watching Ian head out the door with the two young officers in tow. "Did you send for Tyler's records?"

"They should be here on Monday morning."

"Do you want to go for a bite to eat?"

"I need to do a little research. Raincheck?"

"Sure."

Chapter 31

"You look beat," Meg said when Amy finished with her last customer.

"I feel it."

"I hope you're not getting a bug. Why don't you go home and get some rest? I'll clean up."

"Thanks, Doc. But you've done enough."

They were done at seven and left through the back door. "See you at nine tomorrow."

On her way from Tresses, Amy debated cancelling the dinner with her parents, but knowing she'd never hear the end of it, she decided to go ahead. She noticed a police car parked on the other side of the street pull out and drive off as she passed. Two blocks later, she saw another patrol car approaching. They were keeping an eye on her. She buttoned up her coat and hurried down Larch Street, cutting through the park to arrive at her parents' house fifteen minutes later. On her way there, she'd decided to tell them about Tyler if they asked about the drawing. Now, as she rang the doorbell, she could feel the tension in her shoulders and jaw.

Her father opened the door, looking relaxed and pleased to

see her. He took her coat, saying he and her mother just arrived home from a whole day of sailing. "Your mother is changing."

Amy barely dared to hope they hadn't seen the drawing. *I should be so lucky.*

"There you are." Her mother hurried up to her, looking elegant in a cobalt blue dress and heels.

"You look very nice," Amy said.

"Thank you, dear. Let's go and see how Elsa is doing."

Elsa, her parents' part-time maid and cook, was making a salad in the kitchen. "Nice to see you, Amy," she said. "Dinner's almost ready."

Amy's father poured his pre-dinner Glen Fiddich and a whisky sour for her mother. "What would you like to drink?" he asked Amy.

"Nothing now, thanks," Amy said. "I'll have a glass of wine with dinner. So tell me about your day on the water."

Her parents were eager to tell her about the new sailboat their friends just bought, about their gourmet breakfast on board before leaving, their lunch at a seafood restaurant on Gabriola Island.

"Mrs. Robinson," Elsa said. "All done."

"Thank you, Elsa." Amy's mother gestured to the dining room. "Let's sit down."

Dinner proved pleasant enough, the conversation revolving around her parents' social functions and her father's thriving machine-tool business, as well as his mediocre golf scores. Amy, relieved that they hadn't seen the drawing of Tyler, mostly listened, thankful for the peace – and distraction.

After dinner, they all sat down with their coffee in the living room. "How's business?" her father asked.

"I'm making a few changes," Amy said. "Meg will become my

partner instead of my employee. She'll be her own boss at the salon. We'll share the costs of the business, like rent, utility and equipment." She explained how the arrangement would benefit them both. "We just booked a meeting with an accountant to set it all up."

Her father stiffened in his chair. "Excuse me?" he said. "How can you make those kinds of decisions without consulting me? After all, I've invested in your business. Is this another one of your brilliant snap decisions?"

"What do you mean by that?"

"Well, how many surprises have we had in the past few months? We had the rush engagement, the rush breakup, and now we have a rush decision about a business change."

Amy crossed her arms. "So my private life was screwed up. I've learned from that, and I've made changes. As for my business, I've run it for nearly two years now, mostly without your help, and I've done quite well. I thought my businessman father would be proud of me for that. Instead, you harass me for making decisions on my own."

"You shouldn't have let Tyler get away," her mother said, puckering up as if sucking on a lemon.

"What?" Amy stared at her incredulously.

Her mother refused to meet her eyes. "You heard me."

Amy put her coffee down and went to stand in front of her mother. "Let me tell you about Tyler," she said, her voice quavering. "Before we broke up, he wanted me to terminate my pregnancy, begged me to abort the baby, said we couldn't really afford it. I told him I couldn't believe he'd say that when we were supposedly planning a future together. I should have left him, but then he showered me with affection. I wanted to believe him when he swore he regretted what he'd said."

She turned to her father. "But it didn't last. One morning, I walked into the den and saw him with a large bag of drugs. He screamed at me to get out, then pushed me around until I lost my balance. I hit my stomach on the corner of the dining table. I lost my baby a few hours later." She looked back at her mother. "That's the kind of man you wished I'd kept."

"I never knew," her mother whispered, shock written all over her face. "I'm sorry … oh God … I didn't mean what I said when you told me about the miscarriage. You must have hated me." Her voice began to crack with emotion. "Please forgive me."

But Amy had closed her ears to her mother. She stared at her father for a moment. He stared back, white-faced and speechless. Amy said goodnight and left.

"I'll call you in the morning," her mother said after her.

"Don't bother."

Despondent, Amy made her way home. She was upset about the argument, mad at herself for losing control, and felt guilty for not saying yes when her mother asked for forgiveness.

The wind picked up, sending a chill through her bones. She pulled the hood up over her head and quickened her pace through the park.

Suddenly, an arm clutched her neck. Next she felt a small, piercing pain, like a pin prick.

Chapter 32

At the command centre, Ben leaned back in his chair and stretched. It had been a long day. No one had called in on the sketch. When he'd pushed for a decision on police protection for Amy, Harrison said he'd do it the next day. Ben, impatient with Harrison's dawdling, had kept an eye on Amy whenever he had a chance over the day. Even his partner Ian had taken a turn to check on her as she walked home from work.

He should call Willa, then go home to get some rest. Using his private cell phone, he dialled, but got voicemail. He didn't leave a message as he thought she might be working a longer shift. He'd try again later. Switching off the computer, he swept up his coat and left.

* * *

Willa dropped into an armchair when she came home from work on Friday night. It had been an unusually busy day at the hospital, and she didn't care if she fell asleep right there with her clothes on. Her cell rang. She scrambled for it in her purse and answered.

"Hi, it's Ben. Can you give Amy a message from me?"

"Yeah sure, if it's not urgent. She went to her parents for dinner."

"Oh, I see. Would she still be there, do you think?"

Willa looked at the time. "She could be, or she's on the way home. I can call her. Anything special you want her to know?"

"No. I just wanted to touch base with her, make sure everything's okay. Do you know if she got a new cell phone?"

"She talked about getting one, but I don't know if she did or not. If she isn't home, I'll call my aunt and get back to you."

"Thanks Willa, I appreciate it."

Willa called Amy and got voicemail. She left a message to call her, then called her aunt. "Hi, Aunt Lou. Is Amy there?"

"No, she left early, about half an hour ago – we had a bit of a tiff. She was walking, but should be home by now … unless she met a friend on the way and stopped for a drink somewhere."

"Do you know her friends?"

"Dear Willa, Amy doesn't want us to know anything about her private life. Why are you asking?"

"Oh, I just had a question, that's all."

Willa called Ben back and relayed the information. "Why don't you call her in the morning? She told me she might go to a movie with a friend in the evening, but she should be at Tresses all day."

"I see. Do you know any of her friends?"

"Sorry, no. Amy and I got back in touch only a couple of months before the kayaking trip. I don't know much about her life before that – except for when we were kids."

"Okay. Thanks Willa. Let me know if you hear from her."

* * *

Ben put his cell down and rubbed his face. It was Friday night. Amy had probably gone to a friend's place after leaving her parents' house.

Still, something didn't feel right. He ran his fingers through his hair, rolling tense shoulders. Paul had gone to a party and wouldn't be home until after midnight. He might as well try to get some rest.

Chapter 33

Amy's head was spinning. She opened her eyes, stared into blackness, then closed them, waiting for the spinning to subside. *What's wrong with me? Why am I so dizzy?*

Moments later she looked up again, feeling less dizzy, but still unable to see anything. She waited for her eyes to adjust, but they didn't. Had she been in an accident? Her heartbeat sped up. *Am I blind?*

Her right cheek pressed into something hard and scratchy. She tried to move her arms and legs, but they wouldn't budge. She could move her head, but only a little bit. She felt something hard under her right hand and managed to move her fingertips over … her door keys in her coat pocket? She wasn't in a hospital. *Where am I? What's going on?*

She tried to remember where she'd been last. She'd gone to her parents' … stormed out … through the park … She gasped for air. Someone had tried to strangle her. She'd been kidnapped! She hyperventilated through her nose until she blacked out.

She woke up to a wheezing sound. A moment later, she realized it came from her own nose. She'd been gagged! Panic returned, building more mucus in her nose. She tried to clear it in order to breathe, then found she could suck some air through the gag. *Not tape.*

Her pulse slowed a few beats. She rocked her body back and forth, trying to roll onto her back, but she seemed to be tied to something that kept her on her side.

She flinched as a door slammed nearby. Her pulse speeded up again as heavy footsteps tramped across a bare floor. A refrigerator opened and closed. *Who's there?* She heard glass clinking, chairs being dragged, a television. *It can't be the cabin.*

She strained her ears as she heard a man say something, his voice a low drone, making the words hard to decipher.

"The bartender at their Squamish hangout said Mike Polanco expected Tyler to show last Friday night," another man said in a loud, squeaky voice. "Said Mike took off all of a sudden. Hadn't seen him since. Said Tyler never showed; swore he didn't know where to find him. We called him a liar, threatened to shoot him, still nothing. I took out my gun, yelled if he was that fucking useless … might as well kill him. That's when he told us … the hairdresser bitch Tyler hung with."

Amy held her breath.

The other man mumbled something.

"Busted our asses to find her." The squeaky voice sounded high-pitched and defensive. "Only had her first name. This fucking city is lousy with hairdressers."

Amy's pounding heart drowned the rest of the conversation. She stared into the dark, struggling to comprehend. *Who are these people? Who's Mike?*

Then she realized these must be the people Tyler had warned her about. They'd already known about her days ago. Her stomach turned. *No, don't.* She concentrated on breathing through her nose until her stomach calmed down. *Ben, where are you? Find me! Help me!*

"Have to find out who's skimming ... Borelli ... we'll be in deep shit," the squeaky voice said.

Brelly?

The quiet voice came closer. "Time to get the bitch to talk."

Shaking and sweating, Amy listened to a clattering of dishes, then the sound of water pouring into a glass. Somewhere behind her, a door opened. A wall in front of her face became visible in a weak light.

I can see! She was on the floor, wrapped in ... it smelled like an old carpet.

Footsteps approached from behind. Someone kicked her back. "Hey!" growled a menacing voice. "Snap out of it!"

Amy moaned behind the gag. She let out a muffled scream as the man kicked her shoulder.

"That's better."

She braced herself for another kick.

"You and I have a mutual interest," the kicker said. "Your boyfriend. I want to talk to him. You know where he is."

Amy held her breath.

"You're gonna tell me where to find him, or you'll die. Understand?"

Kicker's nails scratched her face as he pulled the gag down.

"*Do. You. Understand?*" he yelled in her ear, so close she felt the heat from his breath.

Amy tried to say yes, but her tongue had stuck to her gums.

He grabbed her hair, lifted her head, and threw water in her face. Amy sputtered and choked, but managed to swallow enough to unstick her tongue.

"*Talk!*" he yelled, flinging her head down. When it hit the floor, a bright light flashed behind her eyes, and a dull ache spread across the back of her head and into one ear.

Block the pain.

"We ... we broke ... up ... months ago," she said, each word echoing like sonar pinging in her ear. "Haven't ... seen him ... since."

"You lying bitch!" Kicker yelled. "You're digging your own grave. We went to your boyfriend's hangout in Squamish. A bit of pressure ... the bartender told us about you. So here we are."

Amy felt her legs trembling against her hands inside the tight truss. She swallowed and took a deep breath. "I don't know any bartenders," she said in a shaky voice. "I haven't seen Tyler in four months."

"Who the fuck do you think you're dealing with? Defiant little bitch!" He whacked her head so hard she blacked out.

He was still there when she came to, yelling something, throwing water in her face again. "I'm losing my patience with you, bitch!"

"Please," Amy whispered. "I can't tell you where he is ... I wish I knew ... I left him because he hurt me ... I *hate* him ... why would I help him?"

Out of breath, her body shaking violently, she couldn't talk any longer. She braced herself for another attack, but heard Kicker leaving, slamming the door. She whimpered, relieved.

Chapter 34

Ben dialled Amy's number as soon as he woke up on Saturday morning. No answer. He swung his feet out of bed, thinking she would have called him if she'd slept over somewhere.

He jumped into his sweat suit and went outside, passing Paul's closed door on the way. Today, he needed to run alone. He picked up the *Vancouver Sun* outside the front door, tossed it onto the hall floor and left. He set off through the West End and down to English Bay Beach, heading for the cool sea air of Stanley Park. As he entered the park, a shimmer of peach lined the horizon. A moment later, he entered the shaded part of the seawall, a road between the ocean and a wall of hemlock, fir and cedar.

He checked his pocket to make sure he'd brought his cell phone, and thought back to what Amy had told him about Tyler. Even then, he'd considered the possibility that the thugs chasing Tyler might know about her already. That's why he'd been pushing to get a surveillance car. It surprised him that even Collins thought that move was premature.

He sped up and ran until exhaustion dulled his anxiety, then slowed his pace and made a wide turn. He barely noticed the dawn approaching as he jogged on, lost in thoughts of Amy and planning for the day ahead.

He turned left and ran along Lost Lagoon. The grass around its shore was streaked with early-morning sunlight, filtering through the trees along Georgia Street. Soft willow branches stretched toward their reflection in the water. Terns rested on the grass, and ducks waddled about. A beautiful day. Hopefully a good omen.

He ran the last stretch of the lagoon, passing into the West End and heading back to his apartment. The newspaper was still on the hall floor. He flung it on the dining table, turned on the coffeemaker and went for a shower. When he emerged from his bedroom, dressed for the day, he found Paul in the kitchen, looking bleary-eyed and confused. "Did you have a rough night, Doc?"

Paul scratched his shoulder. "I'm not sure."

Ben made two toast slices with jam and held one out to Paul. Paul waved it away.

"Whenever." Ben put it on the counter. He poured coffee and brought his breakfast to the dining table, eating while he scanned the local news. Paul joined him at the table, yawned and reached for the business section.

"I'm off," Ben said a moment later. "Are you planning to be home today?"

"Yes." Paul cocked his head toward a pile of medical books on the coffee table.

"Good. If anyone calls for me, and I mean *anyone*, call me right away. If I don't answer, call the station. It's very important."

"I hear you. Where are you …"

"I'll tell you later. Don't work too hard." Ben grabbed an apple from a basket on the coffee table and left.

He called Willa on his way to the station and left a message asking her to call him the moment she had a chance.

* * *

Amy started when she heard the door reopen. "You got one chance to save your sorry ass!" Kicker said. "I want names – who your boyfriend knows, talks to, talks about – friends, associates, enemies, whoever. Every. Fucking. One. You have five minutes." The door closed.

Names? She had the ones she gave to Ben. *Enemies?* She had no idea. *Associates?* She supposed the ones who'd been arrested were his associates, but Kicker would know about them, wouldn't he? Who did he talk to? She had to come up with someone. In less than five minutes.

Events, times and places bounced around like trapped flies in Amy's head as she tried to remember who Tyler had been hanging out with. She wished she hadn't tried so hard to forget all those people.

Suddenly a scene in a nightclub came back to her: she was coming out of the Ladies room and saw Tyler talking covertly with a man near the end of the bar. She studied the man's face as she approached, to see if she recognized him. He had a thick scar across his eyebrow and looked like a thug. She wondered why Tyler would be talking to a thug. Suddenly another man forced himself between them. His hands shot out and grabbed the upper arms of the man with the scar, got into his face and growled something Amy couldn't hear. Tyler backed off, looking uncomfortable. He hurried over to Amy, said they should leave and escorted her out. She asked who the men were, but Tyler refused to say anything about them. She'd been upset about that.

Yes, she could describe those men.

The door opened again. "Your five minutes are up," Kicker said as he approached.

Amy gave him the names of Tyler's friends. When she paused to recall details about the two men, he kicked her in the back, knocking the wind out of her. "Spill it, bitch!" he yelled.

"Two men … don't know names … can describe," Amy managed to say between gasps.

"Go on."

Struggling to speak loud enough for him to hear, she described both men. When she detailed the scar above one man's left eye, Kicker yelled, "Sonofa*bitch*," stormed out and banged the door shut.

* * *

Ben called Tresses at nine on Saturday morning. Meg told him that Amy should arrive any minute and promised to ask her to give him a call right away.

Wilson banged the phone down hard. "Stupid broad!"

"What's the problem, Curly?" Collins asked behind her privacy wall. It never ceased to amaze her how someone looking like a cute chipmunk could have such a foul mouth.

"Some dumb cow responding to the composite drawing said she just saw the guy, then described him as being black. What would you call that?"

The detectives were getting frustrated. So far, all public response to the composite drawing had led to dead ends, and no tangible evidence had been found by undercover officers.

When Ben hadn't heard from Amy by ten, he called Tresses again. "She hasn't shown up yet," Meg said, sounding stressed.

"I haven't heard anything, so I don't know what's holding her up."

"Do you have her cell number?" Ben asked.

"Yes, but she lost her cell and hasn't got around to buying a new one yet. I promise to call you as soon as I hear from her."

"Thanks."

Harrison came and handed Ben a piece of paper. "That's Robinson's number. I've been trying to reach her to double-check on some information she gave us, but she isn't answering her phone. Do you have a number for that cousin of hers? She might know where I can reach her."

"I can get it and check with her."

"Thank you."

Ben stared at the number he'd been calling a million times, obsessively tapping his pen on his desk.

"Hey."

Ben looked up at Stephanie Collins balancing two mugs of coffee and a small paper bag, her glasses hanging from a string around her neck. He waved her into his cubicle. She handed him one of the coffees and perched on his desk, letting her legs dangle. She opened the bag and held it out. "Cinnamon bun?"

Ben declined, but picked up the coffee mug.

Collins munched on a bun, studying Ben's face. "Looks like you didn't get much sleep last night. What's up?"

Ben waved it off. "It's nothing. I've been trying to reach Amy, but I can't get hold of her."

"Uh-huh." Collins's look told him she wasn't buying it. "That's today." She dropped the half-finished bun in the bag and licked her fingers. "What kept you from sleeping last night?"

He gave her a look that said: Back off. "I don't know. Couldn't stop the brain from scheming, I guess."

Ben and Collins turned at the sound of an argument behind them. Wilson was poking Krucik's chest with his stubby finger. "You *talked* to her and came up with *shit!*"

"Stop jerking around, Curly," Collins said. "This isn't about you."

* * *

A door slammed, waking Amy from a nightmare. The pain in her ear had become a metallic pinging, and it hurt to breathe. *But I'm still alive.*

She took shallow breaths to ease the pain while she listened to the commotion in the other room. It sounded like three of them in there now.

"Ken fucking Ross vanished," a man with a French accent said. "Who knows where that scumbag is."

"Gavin's checking the bar in Squamish," Kicker said. "The owner's seen one of his regulars talking to Ken. I'm guessing Tyler."

"Those bastards are holding out together with our loot," a gruff voice said.

Two new voices, Amy thought. Frenchie and Gruff. *Who's Gavin?*

"Not for long." Kicker said. "Let's put some incentive on our favourite rats. Find the double-crossing sonsofbitches."

"Oui. What about la bitch, Tony?" Frenchie asked.

Amy stopped breathing.

"She isn't going anywhere," Kicker said. "Let's go."

Conversation ceased, chairs scraped, then the sound of footsteps faded into the distance.

So Kicker's name is Tony. Amy's heart was racing as if about to self-destruct. What were they planning to do with her? "Help me," she tried to yell, but the pain cut her yell to a squeal.

Urgent steps approached. The door swung open, hitting the wall. "Shut la bouche," Frenchie commanded. He pulled the gag up over her mouth and left the room. A moment later, Amy heard a car start up and drive away.

There were no voices to distract her now. Only fear and pain clamouring for her attention. *But I'm alive, and I'm going to stay alive, even if it kills me.* She let out a weak snicker at that. The brief amusement felt good.

Doing her best to block out the pain, Amy listened to the house. She struggled to stay awake, but soon drifted off to a symphony of hums from the refrigerator, clicks from the plumbing and the rustle of leaves in the wind outside.

Chapter 35

On Saturday afternoon, Willa walked out of the OR, pale-faced and shaky, soaked in sweat. They'd lost a man. Wounded in a traffic accident, his life had slipped through their fingers.

When they told her to stop giving CPR, she'd dropped her arms to her sides and asked the patient to forgive her. She could still smell the burning hairs on his chest from the shock paddles.

They sent her to a trauma counsellor.

"It's a normal, healthy reaction to grieve when you lose someone you've worked so hard to save," the counsellor told her. "Eventually, you get used to it." They talked for a long time. Willa had heard it all before in class, but found that it helped to hear it again after having actually gone through it.

She was surprised to see Ben waiting for her when she left the counsellor's office, looking handsome in a suit and tie. "Willa, sit down," he said, in a tone that sent a chill down her spine.

She stared at him as she lowered herself onto a chair. "What's wrong?"

"I don't want you to panic, but we have reason to be concerned for Amy's safety. We need to find her."

"Safety? Why? What do you mean, find her? Isn't she at Tresses?"

"No. She never showed up. I just talked to Meg for the third time today."

"What did she say?"

"Only that Amy seemed tired yesterday. Meg thought she had a bug and told her to go home and rest, but Amy wanted to help clean up before going to her parents' for dinner. When they left, Amy said she'd see her in the morning."

"Maybe she had an accident when she walked home from her parents' house. Did you check the hospitals?"

"Yes, we did."

"But … I don't understand. Why are you concerned about her safety?"

"We know that Amy told you that she planned to talk to a detective on our squad about Tyler."

Willa nodded.

Ben raced out his terse update. "At the time, she also described Tyler to a forensic artist – the drawing you might have seen on the news. But what she didn't tell you is that Tyler was on the run from a gang. He'd extorted money from her to pay for someone's help in disappearing from them. He'd threatened her, saying that if she told anyone about the money, they would find out and come after her to get to him. She was scared, Willa. The detective told her that arrangements would be made for her safety when we released the composite drawing to the media. And now we can't find her."

"But Ben, I don't know where she is. What makes you think she isn't hiding out at a friend's place?"

"She knew we were concerned about her. If she planned to be gone for a couple of days, she would've called the detective she talked to earlier and let her know."

"Maybe she's so scared that she doesn't want anyone to know where she is."

"I know there's a remote chance she's hiding somewhere, but we have a bad case scenario here. We can't be sure that the thugs don't know about her yet. We're racing against time to get her into safety."

"But I don't get it. Why did she go to the police station? Why didn't she just call you?"

"Maybe she tried to. But she did the right thing. She got the information to us right away. So if you can think of anyone she could have been in contact with, please let me know. We'll be talking to her parents, her superintendent and Meg this afternoon. But we'll also need help from her friends and acquaintances."

"Oh, my ... yes, absolutely. Okay. I'll go through my contacts and notes. Surely something should come up. I'll call you as soon as I'm done."

"Good. Do you have phone numbers for our friends in the kayaking group?"

"I do. Just a sec." Willa pulled up the information on her cell and gave it to him.

"Thanks, Willa." Ben put his hand on her arm. "Are you going to be okay?"

Willa nodded.

"I'll catch you later." Ben headed off down the corridor.

Willa leaned back in the chair, closing her eyes. "Ohmygod," she whispered. "What a day."

* * *

Back at the station, the detectives continued to look for leads. Ian was trying to track down the last person on Amy's list of Tyler's friends.

Ben put a trace on Amy's cell phone. Now that he had her home phone number, officially given to him by Harrison, he could call it directly. And he did, over and over, obsessively tapping his pen on his desk – always getting voicemail. A clock kept ticking in his mind – he didn't know when Amy's time would run out. It had been eighteen hours since she'd left her parents' house. He sighed, trying to dismiss thoughts that some gang member had caught up with her, or that Tyler had abducted her again.

"Something wrong?" Ian asked from behind the wall.

"What? Are you a mind reader now?"

"You're tapping your pen again." Ian stood up and leaned over the partition, peering at Ben with bloodshot eyes. "Well?"

Ben dropped his pencil on the desk and rolled his chair to get away from the stench of garlic and old booze. "You really need to do something about your breath."

Ian moved back a bit from the wall. "Well?" he asked again.

"Harrison asked me to get hold of Amy Robinson for him. I've been at it for hours. I'm starting to wonder if something's happened to her."

Harrison came out of his office. "Team." His dark, raspy voice demanded attention. He held up a manila envelope. "Mr. and Mrs. Corman have given us a list of Tyler Corman's high school friends and some personal info. Let's get records: telephone, bank, tax, everything we can get our hands on. Check his background. Find and question his connections. Have another chat with his friends." He turned to Ben. "Anything yet?"

"Nothing."

Harrison checked the time, then returned to his office and

called the Public Affairs Section, filling them in. "I want to get this out to the media tonight. No, *tonight!*" Ben heard him banging on his desk. "It's not too late in the day for you to prepare a media briefing," he thundered. "This is an active investigation of a serious crime in progress, and we need information about what's happening, *now!*"

Ben raced out to question Amy's superintendent and to pick up a copy of Amy's client list at Tresses on his way.

* * *

When Willa came home from work she called Tresses. "Oh, Willa, thank God." Meg sounded near tears. "I've been so worried. Amy didn't show up this morning, and then the police called to ask questions about her. It freaked me out so much I almost cut a customer's ear off! And just a moment ago, the police came here to ask for her client list. What's going on?"

Willa repeated what Ben had told her. "If we haven't heard from Amy by Monday morning, how will you manage?"

"I'll find a temp. I'll take care of the business. Not to worry."

"You rock. Give me your home number, and I promise to call as soon as I have any news."

After the call, Willa pulled out her calendars, journals and notes and checked them for any references to Amy. She wrote them down, including the names of her high school, her hair-design college and fitness club. Finally, she wrote down what Amy had told her about Tyler.

She looked it over and called Ben. "I've written down everything I have," she said when Ben arrived twenty minutes later. "If I'd used half my brain, I would've known Tyler could be dangerous. I should never have let her drive home alone."

"Don't blame yourself, Willa. You've never seen the man, and you've only recently heard what he did to her. How could you predict what he'd do next?"

Ben read through Willa's notes, told her he found it to be useful and thanked her for putting it together. "Did Tyler ever call you?"

"I think he called my cell the morning we left Vancouver. We'd just stopped at a gas station. Amy told me not to answer, suspecting it was Tyler – he'd called her a few minutes earlier – said he might try to reach me to get to her. So … I didn't answer. Another time he left a message on my cell. I'm not sure when. It could have been when Amy and I went out to dinner in Williams Lake the first night, or the next morning when we had breakfast in the motel. As soon as I heard his name, I hung up and turned my cell off. I never even listened to the message."

"We'll check your phone records to make sure," Ben said. "Let us know if someone strange calls, so we can get on top of it right away. The same thing goes for your parents. Don't give out any information unless you know who you're talking to and trust them. I'll tell Amy's parents and Meg the same thing. Again, if something else comes up, call the station or try me at home."

"I will."

Willa and her parents had just finished eating when the doorbell rang. Willa answered to find two plainclothes police officers on the porch, holding up badges. Her parents came to the door as the officers introduced themselves, wondering if they could ask a few questions.

Willa's father nodded, letting them in.

The detectives asked if they knew a man named Tyler Corman.

"Yes," Willa's father said. "Or rather, we know of him."

"Your daughter gave one of our officers some information about Amy Robinson and Tyler Corman this afternoon," the officer said. He turned to Willa. "Are you Willa Robinson?"

"Yes."

"We just started our investigation into Ms. Robinson's disappearance. We're looking for anything that might help us find her. Has something else come up since you spoke to Officer Malik?"

"Nothing yet. Sorry."

"So none of you have met Tyler Corman then?"

Willa shook her head. "No."

"I haven't, either," her father said, then turned to Willa's mother. "Did you ever meet him, Carol?"

"No. The two of them shied away from family gatherings. At least, the boyfriend never showed up when we were there. The next thing we knew, they'd broken up. That was several months ago. We just found out about him tonight."

"I see." The officer held up the composite drawing. "Have you seen this?"

Willa stared at it. "That's Tyler?"

"James, my husband and I saw it on the news this morning," her mother said. "The name sounded familiar, but we didn't think it could be *that* Tyler. Like I said, we just found out about him this evening."

"What does all this mean?" Willa's father asked tensely. "Is there a connection between that man and my niece's disappearance?"

"We don't know yet, sir."

After the police left, Willa's parents listened in anguish as Willa related what Amy had told her about Tyler. Later, they settled down to watch the late-evening news, dominated by

Amy's disappearance and her connection with the wanted gang member Tyler Corman.

A photo of Amy appeared on the screen. "At nine o'clock on Friday night," a newswoman announced, "Amelia Robinson went missing in Vancouver, somewhere between Sixth and Fourteenth avenues and Yew and Trafalgar streets. Miss Robinson is 5'-8", weighs 130 lbs., has shoulder-length auburn hair and green eyes. She was last seen wearing black leggings and a purple tank top under a black, hooded knee-length coat and black boots. Police report that Amy had been threatened and are treating her disappearance as suspicious. They would not speculate further on this active investigation."

The camera closed in on Sergeant Harrison talking to media outside the police station. "As of now, Amy Robinson has been missing for twenty-four hours," he said. "It's imperative that we find her as soon as possible. If you know anything about Ms. Robinson's whereabouts, please come forward. All information will be treated as confidential."

* * *

Tyler found a couple of news stations on his transistor radio, but the static made it hard to hear what people were saying. When he walked closer to the highway, however, he could hear one of the stations quite well. He was out there on Saturday night listening to the announcement about Amy's disappearance.

"Suspicious disappearance?" he scowled as he walked back to the cabin. "Bunch of pussies." He knew Matzera must have taken her and wondered who'd told him about her. It wouldn't take Matzera long to squeeze info out of her. But then, what could she say that Matzera didn't already know? She had no idea who his friends and associates were. Besides, they wouldn't know where he was now either.

So she'd described him. Fuck the sketch. That wouldn't help anybody, including Ken Ross, to find him – not the way he looked now anyway. So Matzera hadn't found Ken yet. That's why he'd picked Amy up.

He lit another cigarette and relaxed. He just had to lay low, wait it out. He had the cash. He had the junk. He even felt a bit appreciative toward Amy for providing him with this opportunity. Thinking about her reaction when she heard he'd be around, somewhere nearby, made him feel good. Real good.

Chapter 36

Amy woke to angry voices. Her captors had returned. She had no concept of day or time. Her arms tingled and the wrap around her body felt tighter, like a python choking off her air supply.

A phone rang. Tony and Frenchie were arguing. Amy couldn't make out the words. Squeaky kept yelling for everyone to listen. The high pitch of his voice made the words seem strained.

"What the hell is it?" Tony yelled.

"That Borelli on the phone," Squeaky said. "More than three kilos … his coke … missing, we find who's milking … or we're dead."

Amy cowered and let go of her bladder as the air seemed to explode with angry curses. Something shattered against a wall.

"You assholes better find Ken!" Tony yelled. "I want him here, *now!*"

The phone rang again. "Oui," Frenchie said. "Where? On our way."

"What?" Tony said.

"Mario spotted Ken Ross."

"Let's go," said Tony.

Who's Ken?

Chairs scraped, followed by hurried steps and a door closing.

Amy tried to calm herself. *Don't clog up your mind with fear. Keep it clear and get ready to fight for your life.*

* * *

Before leaving the station on Saturday evening, Harrison had announced he expected everyone back at work bright and early on Sunday morning. "But that's my day off," Ian had argued.

"Especially you," Harrison replied.

When Ian finally showed up on Sunday morning, unshaven and hung over, he cursed at a note from Harrison on his desk, informing him that all Robinson-spotting calls would be directed to him. Ben had seen the note. He needed those calls to be handled well, and it didn't sound like Ian was in the mood for polite conversations with strangers this morning.

Ian let out a grunt when his phone rang, restraining his temper as he took the first call. After several more, he slammed down the receiver. "What a waste of time."

"Problem?" Ben asked.

"They've all seen her with a guy, and then they describe him: 'Short and fat.' 'Tall and skinny.' 'Wore a black coat.' 'A denim jacket.' I haven't had two people saying the same thing about the bastard. This last one saw her with a teenager walking west on Twelfth, but swears it was on Thursday night."

"Don't let it get to you, just write it all down. We have to follow up."

The team worked late into the evening, calling friends and acquaintances listed by Willa and Meg. Detectives made another search of Amy's apartment and her car, seized her laptop, and checked her e-mail and phone messages. They talked to her sparring coach and other members of her fitness club, to people at her high school and to students who had been at the hair design college with her. They monitored chat rooms on the Internet. Unmarked cars were stationed outside the homes of Amy and Willa's parents.

They found nothing. The different RCMP detachments had nothing new to report.

Every chance he had, Ben dialled Amy's number, hoping someone – anyone – would answer. But no one did.

"You look like hell," Ian said, slipping into his coat. "Get some rest." Ben looked up at him with heavy eyelids and slack jaw. "I rest my case," said Ian, and left. Ben checked for emails and phone messages one more time before leaving.

After tossing and turning for three hours, Ben gave up and went for a run in the dark. The only sounds he heard were the slaps of his running shoes on the pavement, his own breathing and the odd police siren in the distance. Avoiding Stanley Park, he circled the West End and jogged back to his apartment – nearly crashing into Paul as he went inside.

Paul leaped back, startled. "Goddammit, Ben! Watch where you're going!"

Ben ducked into the bathroom.

"Hey!" Paul jiggled the door handle. "I was on my way in there."

Ben slept for two hours, got up, showered and drove to the station slurping his second cup of coffee. Signing in on his computer, he saw that Tyler's and Amy's phone records had arrived. He checked Tyler's records first and saw why he had taken Amy's cell – his own had been cut off and his account cancelled the previous month.

Amy's home phone records showed a few calls placed from a payphone the day before she left on her trip, and one had been placed from her home phone to Tresses after she left.

He recognized the numbers of other calls: Willa's, VPD's, Tresses', his own. Three recent calls came from payphones. He checked another number and found it to be to Amy's parents'.

Next he moved to Amy's cell records and concentrated on the calls coming in or made after the girls left on their trip. Several had been placed to her number, but every single one came from a payphone. Amy had placed a call to her parents in the morning of the day she left Bowron Park. Another one went to the Bowron Lodge Registration Centre the evening she checked into the motel in Clinton.

Ben's heart started to race at the sight of the two last calls recorded the following evening – only minutes apart – to a bar in Squamish. He called and filled the Squamish RCMP in, then went to tell Harrison about it. "They're going to look for the employee who took the calls and get back to us."

Ben put a trace on Amy's cell, but it wasn't transmitting. The phone company told him the phone was pre GPS. He just had to keep calling, hoping that someone would pick up.

* * *

Amy squirmed in her tight packaging, feeling very uncomfortable. She touched her urine-soaked clothing with her fingertips, felt a stinging sensation around her bottom and suspected a rash was forming.

A sudden commotion made her jump. It sounded like several people entering the other room at the same time. "Are you gonna talk, or am I gonna bust your balls?" Tony yelled.

A man said something Amy couldn't hear.

"Don't you ever try to fuck me, Ken," Tony growled.

She heard the slamming and smashing of fists or boots or weapon, the agonized screams of a man.

"Where's our coke?" Tony yelled, as the beating continued. "Where did you put it?"

Amy's stomach started to heave. She tried to block out the sounds of cracking, gurgling and moaning. Suddenly the man's screams became muffled.

"Do you hear me, Ken?" Tony roared. "You sonofabitch!" Something crashed into the wall. "You think you can fuck me and get away with it?"

Amy heard a defiant mumble of a reply.

"Fucking cockroach!"

She heard a muffled pop followed by a drawn-out moan, and then two more muffled pops.

Amy tried to calm her racing heart as she listened to something being dragged across the floor.

"Alain, mop up," Gruff ordered.

"Tabarnac," Frenchie muttered.

"*Now!*" Gruff yelled.

So Frenchie's name is Alain.

"Get bags," Squeaky said.

Amy trembled. *Am I next?*

Chapter 37

Ben kept dialing Amy's cell and home numbers, without success. He felt strained. Sleep deprivation came with the territory, but the stress about Amy was getting to him.

He stepped away from his desk just long enough to get coffee, then tried Amy's cell again. He reached to stab down on the END button when a woman's voice said. "Allo. Housekeeping."

Ben jumped up, slopping coffee over his desk. He scribbled TRACE on a paper and held it in the air. A hush went through the room.

"Yes, hello. Who am I speaking to?"

"Housekeeper."

"Hi, I'm looking for —"

"You calling for phone?"

"Yes!"

"I just a come in to clean a your room, heard it a buzzing. I found it on floor. Must've dropped it, eh? Well, don' worry. You can get it at front desk when you come back."

"Listen, my name is Benjamin Malik," Ben said, struggling to contain his excitement. "I'm a sergeant with the Vancouver Police Department. We need to take a look at that room you're in, so please don't touch anything. Do you understand?"

"Oh … but I hav'a tell my boss."

"We'll call him and explain. What's the number to the motel?"

"Don' remember. Jus' a look up Highway Motel."

Ben held his hand over the mouthpiece. "Do we have a location yet?"

The tracing officer hurried over with an address. "It's in Pouce Coupe, BC."

Ben gestured to him to get Squamish on the phone. "Highway Motel in Pouce Coupe, right?" he said to the housekeeper.

"That's a right."

Ben thanked her, hung up and got on the line with the Squamish RCMP. He explained the situation, said he thought Tyler Corman was renting the room, and gave them the address.

"Got it," the receiving detective said. "We'll pass on the information to the Dawson Creek detachment."

At twelve after four, the Squamish RCMP called back. "We just heard back from Dawson Creek. They rolled an undercover car to the address, talked to the motel staff and showed them the composite sketch. The desk clerk had only seen him briefly when he checked in and didn't recognize him. He'd signed in with another name, paid cash for three nights, kept to his room and didn't want to be disturbed. They're checking the room right now. They'll courier the cell phone and fax his signature. Every officer in the area has been put on high alert."

* * *

Amy smelled food. Hearing the men in the other room – slurping and smacking and arguing with their mouths full, like a pack of savages after torturing someone to death – made her stomach heave. She jerked as a phone rang.

"What's keeping you?" she heard Gruff saying. "Get your ass over here. Pull up to the back door."

"Okay," Tony said. "Pack up. Make sure everything's cleaned out."

"What about the stiff?" Squeaky asked.

"One thing at a time," Tony said.

With her heart racing, Amy listened as the men moved about without speaking.

"Prep the bitch and untie her," Tony said.

"Why bother?" Squeaky said. "Why don't we just take her out and leave her?"

Amy's heart skipped a few beats.

"The cops are looking for her," Tony said. "We don't need more noise. I don't want her traced to this fucking place."

Amy heard water pouring.

Someone came into the room, blindfolded her and flipped her onto her stomach. She heard a few rips, felt a tug, and in the next instant, she was rolled out of the wrap. "Oof ... *shit!*" Gruff cried. "You're stinking piss!"

He grabbed her under the arms, dragged her into a corner and pulled the gag down. Amy gulped air. The throbbing pain in her back from Tony's kicks felt worse without the wrap. She tried to keep herself upright with her hands, numb and tingling from being under pressure.

"Drink some water," Gruff said, tilting her head back.

Water! She felt glass touch her lips. Suddenly her mind became crystal clear. She hadn't asked for water. They must have drugged it! She took a deep breath, held it, and opened her mouth. Water poured in. As she pretended to drink, some escaped down her throat, but most of it ran out the sides of her mouth and down her chin.

"Hey! Stop drooling," Gruff said.

But there in the darkness, Amy knew he'd missed much of the water running down her neck and inside her coat.

She let her head droop, pretending to be dizzy. "Have to pee," she slurred, realizing it wasn't entirely an act.

"Wait! I don't want no fucking piss stink in my car." Gruff picked her up, carried her a few paces and put her down on a toilet, pulling up her coat. "Piss through your pants," he said and left her there, holding onto the bowl to keep from falling off.

When he came back, Amy sat deep in the bowl, head lolling, pretending to be almost unconscious.

"Fucking job," Gruff said, flung her limp body over his shoulder, carried her back to the corner and dropped her in a heap.

* * *

At two in the afternoon, the Squamish RCMP was back on the speaker phone. "We talked to the bar employee who took the call at seven-thirty the night of the murder. He said some guy had asked for Mike Polanco, one of the regulars. He couldn't tell for sure, but thought the caller could have been Corman, whom he'd seen with Polanco before. Polanco left the bar right after the call. We're questioning the bar owner, a bit of a shady type. We find something, we'll let you know."

"Thank you," said Ben. "We appreciate it."

Chapter 38

Amy propped herself up in the corner of the room. They were planning to take her somewhere – that might give her a chance to escape. She tugged the blindfold down enough to see out, but saw only darkness. She heard a car pull up outside and yanked the blindfold back up.

"Alain's here," she heard Squeaky say.

She listened to dragging sounds and the odd groan from the other room, movements outside. *This is it. They're moving out.*

"Get the bitch," Tony said. "Ditch her on the highway a few miles from here. Make it look like an accident. Meet up at the club in an hour."

Knowing she would have to get out of the car somehow, Amy tried to get herself into a focused state of mind, like before entering a race. She heard a sound outside the door and slumped, pretending to be unconscious. Someone entered the room, grabbed her arms and heaved her onto a shoulder. *Don't look. Don't move a muscle.* She felt rain and chill air on the back of her head. A moment later, she was flipped off the shoulder. Her head hit something hard, knocking her out.

* * *

Squamish RCMP called back on the speakerphone at 6:00 p.m. They had interrogated Joe Casey, a smalltime hood associated with Mike Polanco. He'd told them that Tyler Corman was on the run from a Vancouver drug dealer named Tony Matzera.

Matzera, well known to the Vancouver police, had an extensive criminal record. A frantic buzz filled the centre as the team scrambled for information on Matzera's current whereabouts.

Ben learned from an informant that a man associated with Matzera rented a house in Richmond, a suburb just south of Vancouver. He picked up the phone to contact the Richmond RCMP when Ian handed him another phone. "You should hear this."

A nosy suburban neighbour told Ben that he'd just seen what looked suspiciously like a body being thrown into the trunk of a brown '90 Chevy Caprice across the street from his house. He gave Ben a Richmond address – the same one mentioned by his informant. Ben passed the information to Sergeant Harrison and alerted Richmond RCMP, before heading out to meet them at the house.

* * *

Amy came to in the dark, her head throbbing. Something was pushing into her face. She sniffed. *What's the smell? Is it me?* She couldn't see anything. She reached over, felt a boot inside a plastic bag and tried to push it away. It wouldn't budge. She tried to lift her shoulders above it and bumped her head into something hard. She lay back down, looked up and saw the dim glow of an emergency latch. *I'm in the trunk with their luggage. Get out!*

She reached up to release the latch – and froze at the sound of approaching steps. *Too late.* Anguished, she let her arm fall back. The car bounced as people got in. A moment later, they began moving. The luggage shifted, lodging even closer against her. She grabbed it, intending to shove it to the far back of the trunk – then yanked her hands away, stifling a scream. *A body!* She shook violently, hyperventilating as her mind replayed the screams of the man in the other room.

She heard Gruff, Frenchie and Squeaky talking in the car.

They killed him. They'll do the same to me. Something snapped inside of her. *No! I'm not going to die in some random stinky trunk.*

The car made a sharp turn, the body alongside her sliding sideways. Amy pulled her knees up and moved around to brace her back against the body and her feet against the front of the trunk. She reached up to the glow-in-the-dark release lever and waited. When the conversation in the car heated up, she curled her finger around the lever and pulled. The latch released with a click. She held her breath and listened. No one seemed to have noticed. She cracked the lid open and peeked out into the darkness. Cold air and exhaust seeped into the trunk.

"Take the highway," Gruff said.

The car crossed a bridge and slowed. Seeing a highway to one side, Amy guessed they were slowing for an on-ramp. She would have to get out before they sped up.

The men were arguing about something.

Now. Get ready.

In her head, she pictured the jump, the landing, the roll, the recovery. The men were still arguing. She pushed the trunk lid higher. She saw no cars behind them. Slipping her legs over the trunk lip, she raised the lid all the way up, heaved her body over and pushed off toward the side of the road.

She fought to stay conscious through the pain as she bounced and spiralled across the shoulder and onto wet grass. The car's brakes screeched. She dragged herself farther into the grass, rolled into a ditch and passed out.

Chapter 39

Ben drove south on Oak Street, crossed the Oak Street Bridge into Richmond and headed south. Soon after, two RCMP cruisers fell in behind him, lights flashing. Passing through a wooded area, Ben saw what looked like a Caprice parked on the other side of the highway, a man behind the wheel. He radioed the cruisers behind him. "Look like a Caprice to you?"

All three cars jammed on their brakes and pulled to the side. Ben jumped out and started across the highway. A second man ran from the woods, jumped the ditch and dove into the car as the driver burned rubber. One of the patrol cars peeled off behind him, crossed the median strip and took off in pursuit. The other started to follow, but Ben yelled out, "No! Go to the house."

Ben turned to his car when something caught his eye: movement in the brush.

* * *

Amy woke to the sound of screeching tires. An almost unbearable pain shot through her like an internal cacophony of screams.

She felt nauseous, found it hard to breathe.

A voice in the distance shouted something. More screeching tires. There was the odd swishing movement of sound above her. She became aware of the cold rain pelting her face and neck, tasted blood. It felt like gravel in her mouth – or bits of teeth? She pushed some out with her tongue, letting the rain wash it away. *I'm still alive.*

She opened her eyes, but saw only darkness. She tried to move her fingers, then toes, arms, legs. Everything seemed to work. She moved a hand over coarse grasses slanting upward. She'd landed in a grassy ditch.

She pulled herself up on her feet and tried to drag herself out of the ditch. But the pain in her chest made her weak, her bleeding stiff hands slipped on the wet grass. Moaning in frustration, she slowly slipped to the bottom, where she stood, leaning against the wet slope to gather strength, her arms out to the sides to hold herself in place.

She jumped at a sudden crackle. Gathering all her strength, she dug her fingers deep into the soil and inched herself up, out of the ditch, then lay still and listened to a rustling sound nearby. Someone approaching. Rising to her knees, she crawled through the tall grass into the bushes. Once there, she held her breath and peered through the brush as a figure passed in the ditch below. Numb with cold, she waited. She knew she had to move soon or she'd freeze to death.

After a moment, she crawled off in the opposite direction. She heard movement behind her. Turning, she saw a man with a gun climbing from the ditch. She fell onto her back, as if exhausted, and watched as he approached, gun pointed her way. The man stepped closer. Pushing off with her hands for added strength, Amy swept her foot up to kick him in the crotch, then realized it was Ben – too late. He tilted like a felled tree, crashing to earth beside her. His hand hit a rock, flinging the gun from his grasp.

"Ben! Oh, no, I'm sorry," she lisped.

"Nice job," he croaked back. Overwhelmed by relief, they held each other close.

A shot rent the darkness, the bullet slamming into the ground beside them. Ben scrambled for his gun, swung around and shot a man running toward them. He fell with a groan. Ben helped Amy up, then they stumbled together to his car.

He called Richmond RCMP, updating them. "He's injured or dead, and probably armed," he said, giving his location. "Last known position is marked with a flare on the road. I do not, repeat, do not know where he is now. I can't stay. I have Amy Robinson here. Now I'm taking her to Vancouver General."

Eighteen agonizing minutes later, Ben screeched up to the emergency entrance of the hospital and handed Amy over to the triage nurse, who hurriedly wheeled her away.

After giving a quick story to her doctor, Ben made a call to Amy's parents, then dialed Willa on his way out of the ER. "We have her!" he said. "Alive and conscious." He winced and yanked the phone away from his ear at Willa's happy shriek. "She's at Vancouver General," he continued. "Her parents are on the way. I have to go."

* * *

When Willa and her parents arrived at the hospital, they were escorted to a private waiting room. Amy's parents were already there, arguing with a nurse, demanding to see Amy. Willa listened as the poor woman tried to explain something, but was constantly interrupted by Amy's mother who insisted she had the right to speak with a doctor.

"Mrs. Robinson," the nurse scolded at last. "For the love of God, will you please sit down and listen to what I have to say."

Amy's mother stared at the nurse, tightened her lips and sat down.

"Your daughter is being stabilized in the emergency room," the nurse said in a kinder tone of voice. "She'll have a CT scan, neurology and trauma consults, blood work and an X-ray. A doctor will examine her and treat her injuries. After that, a doctor will come and talk to you, but not until then. Expect to wait at least two to three hours. In the meantime, a social worker will come to go over some things with you." She turned around and left.

A moment later, a police officer came into the room. Amy's mother hurried over to him demanding to know what happened. He told her that all questions would be answered as soon as they'd wrapped up the loose ends of the investigation. "She's safe now," he said. "I came to let you know that two police officers will be placed outside Amy's hospital room until all suspects have been arrested. The officers will have a list of people allowed to visit and will ask for identification from everyone."

"That's absurd," Amy's mother grumbled as the policeman left. "They're expecting her mother to identify …"

She was interrupted by an overhead announcement, loudly stating: "Attention. Security level one has been enacted. ER is on lockdown until further notice."

At two-thirty in the morning, Willa woke up in her chair as a doctor came into the room. He introduced himself to Amy's parents and told them that Amy was resting peacefully. "She's been through quite an ordeal," he said. "She's recovering from mild hypothermia and has a concussion – which is a mild traumatic brain injury – and also has a fractured rib and multiple contusions and abrasions. We expect her to make a full physical recovery, but we will need to keep her under observation for a few days to gauge the true extent of her head injury."

He paused for a moment. "As for her psychological recovery, your daughter has been drugged, terrorized and physically harmed over a period of time. Those are extreme, aggravating circumstances causing trauma that may require special attention …"

"Can we see her now?" Amy's mother interrupted.

The doctor nodded. "Certainly. You should know that she's sedated and likely won't respond to you," he said as they left.

When Willa and her parents came home, they turned on the morning news, watching crime lab investigators moving around a neglected house with dark shades in all windows. A reporter announced that the police had arrested a man trying to flee the house with a loaded gun.

After hearing about the highway chase, the arrest of two armed men and the discovery of a body in the trunk, they went to bed, not wanting any more horror stories in their heads.

Willa lay in the dark picturing Amy in her hospital bed, surrounded by gadgetry, with security guards outside the door. She couldn't begin to imagine what she'd been through. The news hadn't shed much light on what had happened to her in captivity, or how she'd been found.

Chapter 40

Tyler was out by the highway with his transistor radio, listening to the news about the arrests. He could hardly believe his luck. Matzera and two of his goons in the slammer! He knew from Ken Ross there were five core members in the gang, so two must have got away. He guessed the body in the trunk could be Ken's. He didn't worry too much about the one on the loose.

He was still on the hook for Mike's murder, but this new development meant things were looking up. His only regret: it would be too risky to go after Amy. He wouldn't blow his chances to get back into the racket for the sake of revenge.

* * *

When Ben arrived at the station on Tuesday morning, Ian told him the guy he shot was gone when they got there. "We found blood, but not enough to tell which way he went. We took samples for DNA testing and searched the area till midnight."

"We need to find the bullet he fired at Amy Robinson and me," Ben insisted.

"Harrison just sent forensics back with dogs and metal

detectors."

"Good. I heard they hit the jackpot with the highway arrests."

Ian grinned. "Fleeing police with a loaded gun and a dead body in the trunk, yeah. Bail denied."

"Things are turning around."

* * *

"Wake up," urged a faraway voice. "Hello. Amelia!"

What? Amy felt her eyelids flutter.

"Open your eyes."

"Uh." Her face was on fire. She couldn't move her hands.

"Amelia. Just open your eyes for a second, and then you can go back to sleep."

Amy struggled to lift her lids. A kind face looked down at her. "Where am I?" she slurred.

"You're in the hospital, dear. You've been in an accident, but you're going to be fine. You can go back to sleep now."

The next time Amy opened her eyes, she saw her father leaning over her. "She's awake."

Her mother's face appeared beside his. "Amy, you're going to be fine. You rest and get well. Then when you get out of here, you'll come home with us. Your father and I will take good care of you until you're strong enough to be on your own again."

No! That I'll never survive. Amy closed her eyes.

A moment later she heard whispers, followed by a door closing. She opened her eyes. A doctor stood at the foot of her bed, looking at her chart. He must have sensed that Amy was awake. "Hi there," he said, and moved around to the side of the bed. "I'm Dr. Sinclair. How are you doing?"

"Peachy," Amy wheezed.

An amused look flashed across his face. "You must feel better than I thought." He replaced the chart. "Let's have a look." He examined her eyes with a small flashlight, peeked under bandages and lightly pushed on her abdomen and ribs, asking if she felt pain.

"You're doing fine," he said when he'd finished. "There's more family waiting to see you. Also, a Detective Malik. He has a few questions for you, if you feel up to it."

"Sure."

As Dr. Sinclair left, Willa, her Aunt Carol and Uncle James stepped in, clutching a card. They stood around her bed, looking at her, blinking away tears, telling her how happy they were to see her again.

Amy gave them a little smile, protecting her lips. "Me too. So what does the card say?" She motioned to her bandaged hands.

"Oh, let me." Willa opened the card and read it in a cheery, sing-song tone.

"Beautiful," Amy said. "Thank you."

A few minutes later, they all waved goodbye and left, holding the door for Ben.

He came over to her, his face showing the pain he felt at seeing her so beaten up. "Hi Amy," he whispered.

"Is this an official visit?" she lisped.

Ben sat down on a chair by the bed, telling her they'd taken three suspects into custody. "One of them, his name's Tony Matzera, was arrested as he fled the house in Richmond with a loaded gun in his pocket."

"You got Tony!" Amy grinned, then cried out as a sharp pain cut through her cracked, bruised lips. After recovering, she said,

"Did you find a dead body in the trunk? I think they killed a man in that house."

Ben nodded. "We have the body. The suspects were caught before they had a chance to get rid of it. We're looking to match it with blood found in the house. We're also hoping to match Tony Matzera's gun to three bullets found in the body – and of course, any other unsolved cases with good ballistics."

"I think his name was Ken," Amy said through half-closed lips. "Ken Ross." Painful thoughts contorted her face. "So they held me in Richmond … so close … Are they all locked up now?"

"We're still looking for the guy who shot at us when I found you. I'm here so you know I won't be on the sidelines while the search is on."

"Don't you trust them to do it?"

"Everyone's a bit overworked right now. I just don't want anything overlooked. I wouldn't worry too much. The good news is they found blood at the scene, and there are no reports of gunshot wounds at local hospitals."

"Meaning what?"

"For all we know, he could be dead. Best to be safe, though. Just in case."

"So when you find him, do you have them all?"

"As far as we know, yes."

"What about Tyler? Now, that he doesn't have to worry about them, he'll come after me."

"We're hoping to find him soon, but for now, we have two policemen stationed outside your door at all times. You're safe here."

"Knowing him, he won't make it easy for you to find him."

"RCMP detachments across BC are working with us to track him down as he moves around the province. Detachments in

Alberta have been alerted as well. We'll get him. So far, we've collected samples for DNA testing and lifted his prints from a motel in northern BC and from the cabin. Your prints were found at the cabin as well."

They heard a knock at the door.

"My two minutes are up." Ben stood up.

"Ben, thanks." She reached for his hand and held it to her cheek. "Thanks for saving my life."

He smiled and threw her a kiss. "My pleasure. I'll be back."

* * *

After leaving Amy's room, Ben called Forensic Staff Sergeant Chang to get an update on the field team's progress. "We dug a bullet out of the ditch lip and picked up a trail of blood farther away," Chang said. "We followed it with the dogs, but the trail stopped at the edge of a street in the nearby industrial park. Your guy must have been picked up, or maybe carjacked someone." Ben made a mental note to check for cell calls from that location, in case their quarry had called a friend for help. "We searched the whole area with metal detectors, but didn't find a gun," Chang finished.

Before heading back to the station, Ben decided to check up on Amy's security. Sergeant Harrison called. "Where are you?" he asked.

"At VGH," Ben said.

"Good. We may have found your guy. A surgeon just called. A man was brought in an hour ago with a bullet in his chest. They're prepping him for surgery as we speak. The guy who drove him in said the patient flagged him down near the scene of your little shootout."

"Which hospital?"

"You're standing in it. No ID, so he probably ditched it."

"Did anyone talk to the surgeon, tell him not to damage the bullet?"

"He knows the drill. We also need to question the driver who picked the guy up. He'd said something about being late for a meeting and took off."

"I'll see if the ER took down his name."

"Can't get a warrant without ID or ballistics," Harrison continued. "And ballistics may be crap if the bullet's a mess. So right now he's just some schmuck who got shot. But I've got him under guard."

"I'll pick up the bullet as soon as it's available."

"Going to need your gun to match with the bullet. Sign it in and pick up a replacement from the armoury."

Ben went to the ER and found the nurse who'd admitted the suspect. "Did you get the name of the driver?" he asked.

"Yes I did." She looked it up in a ledger. "His name is Henry Murdock. He said he planned to report it to the police; he definitely wanted someone to pay for cleaning the blood off his car seat."

Ben let that pass without comment. "Do you know what kind of car he drove?"

"Not really, we had our hands full. But it was small, red sedan, if that helps."

Ben passed the nurse's information on to Harrison, who started a search for the driver.

Chapter 41

Ben picked up the bullet taken from the suspect and delivered it to the lab for DNA testing. When he returned to the command centre, Harrison waved him into his office. "We still don't know who the man is, but we do know he was in the Caprice that fled the scene of your shooting. So it's a good bet he's the guy you shot. We've doubled the security around him. He'll be transferred to the prison infirmary after surgery."

"Good," Ben said. "That reminds me, I still have to take my gun down to ballistics."

On his way back from ballistics, Ben passed behind the reception desk and overheard a man introducing himself as Henry Murdock.

Ben took him to see Harrison, who thanked Murdock for his unselfish act. "The man you picked up is under suspicion for kidnapping," Harrison told him. "We'll need to check your car for his fingerprints. You'll get it back tomorrow."

Murdock, looking disappointed, gave them a statement and drew a map showing the spot where he'd been flagged down, and his route to the hospital. "He asked me to stop along the way, though," he said. "Needed to throw up. When I stopped, I said to just open the door and lean out, but he got out of the car and stumbled off into the bushes."

"Where about?" Ben asked.

Murdock pointed on the drawing. "Somewhere around here, along a wooded area. I didn't pay much attention. Anyway, he was back in a minute."

Harrison thanked him for the information and offered him a lift home. Murdock declined the lift, but asked if someone could clean up the blood before returning the car. Harrison said he'd see what he could do.

"It's already getting dark," Harrison said after Murdock left. "Get a good night's sleep. First thing in the morning, we'll comb the area where the suspect stepped away from Murdock's car."

* * *

On Wednesday morning, a nurse came into Amy's room toting a large poster board covered with photographs and notes. She sat it down beside the bed, saying that Amy's friend Kaley had dropped it off a minute ago. Amy looked at the pictures and read the comments scribbled around them, touched by her friends' concern. Her parents arrived. "Can I have a look?" her mother came around to look at the poster. "Who are all these people?"

"Friends from the kayaking trip."

Her mother pointed to a photo of Ben gazing at Amy. "And who is this?"

"A friend," Amy said, seeing her mother stiffen and aim a grim look at her father. When he bent over to examine the photo, his lips formed a tight line. At that moment, Willa, wearing her blue scrubs, walked in.

Amy's father took her mother's arm. "Lou, I think it's time to go." He nodded to Willa on the way out.

"Did I come at a bad time?" Willa asked when they left.

Amy shrugged. "Not really. Their noses went out of joint when they saw that." Amy pointed to the picture.

Willa moved forward for a closer look. "Why?"

Amy sighed. "Never mind. I forget you don't know my parents all that well. Count your blessings."

They sat together and read what their friends had written on the poster board. Some made Amy laugh, causing her to pinch her lips shut to prevent them from splitting.

"I bought you something," Willa said when they were done. She pulled a new hairbrush from her pocket. "Do you want me to brush your hair?"

"Mmm, that would be nice."

"Have you talked to Meg?" Amy asked, as Willa ran the brush gently through her hair.

"Yes, I stopped in at the shop yesterday to see how things were going. She said great, and that you're making lots of money. She asked about you. I told her you were feeling better. She said not to worry about anything, just get well, show up when you're ready, even joked she might let you have your customers back. I think you have a good friend in her. You know that?"

"More and more. You're a good friend, too." Amy stretched her arms out to Willa. "Come here. Let me give you a hug."

* * *

Harrison called his team together, showed the map Henry Murdock had made and ordered an immediate search for the gun used to shoot at Ben. "Check out metal detectors and start at the wooded area."

Ben pulled out of the station, first in a line of cruisers heading for the Riverside Industrial Park in Richmond. The team arrived at the park, cordoned off the area indicated on Murdock's map and began the search. Within two hours, they found the gun, partially buried under a rock.

"Three cheers for Murdock," Ben said, high fiving Ian and Stephanie Collins.

"And if the bullet you picked up from the hospital came out of this gun," Ian said to Ben, "we'll have him on DNA, gun and bullet."

"Yeah." Collins grinned. "Let's see him get out of that."

* * *

Mario Borelli, a stocky man in his early fifties with thinning dark hair and a pockmarked face, sat in his office, smoking a cigar. Pounding music, shouts and whistles bled through the walls from the strip club downstairs. Borelli squinted under puffy eyelids at a newscast about the arrest of three suspects and Amy Robinson's recovery at Vancouver General Hospital. Police were searching for a fourth man who had escaped after being shot. He cursed and reached for his phone.

Chapter 42

On Thursday morning, Sergeant Harrison told the team about a call he'd received from an attorney whose client had been subpoenaed to testify against Tony Matzera. His client had been threatened over the phone by a stranger, telling him his throat would be cut if he testified against Matzera.

"This threat confirms our suspicion that another suspect remains at large," Harrison concluded. "We've known for some time that several area gangs – including Tony Matzera's – are run by the same person. We need to find this 'boss'."

Ben thought about Mario Borelli. Though they had arrested Borelli for drug trafficking before, there had never been enough evidence to convict. "What about Borelli," Ben asked. "We haven't been able to connect him to this or anything else major because there's been no one to ask. But now we have people in custody."

"You're right," Harrison said. "You and Krucik have a talk with them. Borelli's a suspect in the witness threats. Track him down and keep him in sight until we have enough to bring him in and hold him. Whoever did this, we need to find them. Check the witness's phone records."

A few hours later, Ben and Krucik reported back to Harrison. The men in custody refused to cooperate, insisted they knew nothing about Borelli and then stopped talking altogether.

"One of them showed a flick of alarm when I mentioned Borelli's name," Ben said. "I'll check with Amy if she heard his name mentioned in the house."

"Just don't give her the name yourself," Harrison said. "See if she comes up with it. We don't want our balls in a wringer when we get to court."

* * *

Mario Borelli was sitting in conversation with his strip-club manager when he had a call from one of his prison contacts. He shooed his manager off like a fly, told him to close the door behind him, then got back on the phone. The contact had heard that the Robinson bitch, just rescued and in Vancouver General Hospital, had seen Borelli interfering in a conversation between her fiancé Tyler Corman and Ken Ross in a downtown Vancouver bar about a year ago. She'd given a very detailed description of Borelli to Matzera.

Borelli grunted a thank you and hung up. He thought for a moment, then picked up again and dialled. "I need you to take care of someone for me."

* * *

Ben went to the hospital to see Amy. "Good news," he said, smiling as he sat down beside her, happy to see colour in her cheeks again. "All four suspects are now under arrest."

Amy let out a big sigh of relief. "Thank you."

"So, how're you feeling?"

"They told me I have to stay here two more days."

"And?"

"I feel fine. I should be able to go home."

"You're getting bored. Good sign. But your doctor probably needs another couple of days to observe your head injury. He wants to make sure it's safe for you to leave."

"What makes you think it's safe for me to stay?"

"Everyone on this floor is looking out for you."

Amy's gaze shifted to the coat rack by the door. "Where's my coat? My house keys are in the pocket."

"At the crime lab. The forensic team is checking your clothes for anything that could place you in that house – fibres from the carpet, grime, hair. They have your keys, too."

"The keys I need. Tell them to burn the coat."

"All right, I'll make it happen," Ben promised. "Is it too early for you to talk about what took place in the house? I'd like to know what you heard and how you escaped."

"No, it's not too early. Just let me gather my thoughts."

While Amy silently called up the memories she'd pushed away, Ben took out his notepad and a pen. After a moment, Amy looked into his blue eyes, feeling safe as she began telling him – for the record this time – everything she remembered about her time at the house, including the details of her escape from the car.

When she finished, Ben leaned back in his chair and looked at her healing face. "I can't believe you did that," he said. "You're incredibly brave, Amy. I'm speechless. But I'm very happy that it worked."

"Thanks, Ben, but without you showing up in your shining armour, I'd be in a box instead of a bed right now. So in my book, you're pretty brave yourself."

"Do you remember any other names?"

Amy thought about it. "I know I heard a different name mentioned once or twice. An unusual name …" She shook her head. "I can't remember it right now. I'll think about it."

Ben wanted to ask if it was "Borelli," but knew that if he supplied the name, the defence could argue that it came from him and not from Amy – that he planted the name in her mind. "All right," he said simply. "I'm going to check on something. I'll be back in a minute."

Ben arranged a few changes to strengthen the security around Amy, then called Harrison and told him what Amy had said. "All right," Harrison said. "I'll send forensics back to the house and have them go over the Caprice again."

Ben told him about the security changes.

"What the hell," Harrison snapped. "You're supposed to check with me before you make decisions like that."

"I couldn't justify wasting time after what she told me."

Harrison grunted. "I'll authorize it. As of now, the search for Borelli is our number-one priority."

"Thank you." About time, Ben thought, and went to check on Amy.

Chapter 43

The receptionist at the hospital information desk picked up a ringing phone. "Vancouver General, how can I help you?" she said, for the thousandth time that day.

"I'd like to send some flowers to Amy Robinson," said the man on the line, "but I don't remember the room number. I was hoping you could tell me."

The receptionist pulled up the information on a computer. "And who are you?" she asked the caller.

"I'm a friend of the family."

"All right. What's your name and code?"

"Oh yeah, the code ... now where did I put it? Listen, I'll find it and call you back."

The receptionist hung up and moved to the next call.

Sitting in a car in the parking lot, the man on the other end of the line flipped his cell phone shut. Taking a last look at a photo of Amy and her parents, he grabbed a bouquet of flowers from the seat and strolled into the hospital.

When Amy's parents arrived about an hour later, they took little notice of the man with the flowers, seated in the waiting area just inside the main entrance. But he noticed them and followed as they stepped into the elevator. He watched to see which floor they got off, then rode the elevator up to the top and down again, exiting on the same floor they had.

Glancing at the names on the whiteboard behind the nurses' station, he saw that one of the entries contained the letters "NIC" in place of a name. He smiled inwardly, knowing it meant No Information Client – which explained why he'd not been able to get Amy's room number over the phone. When a nurse approached, he stepped back into the elevator and pushed the button for the ground floor.

A few minutes later, he was in the hospital changing room, clipping an ID badge to the lapel of his orderly's uniform. He struggled to close the locker concealing the unconscious orderly whose clothes he now wore. Moving to the washroom, he pulled Amy's photo from his breast pocket. He studied her features for a moment, then burned the picture and flushed the remains. Afterward, he stopped at the nearby supply room, scooped up a pile of clean linens and made his way to the nearest corridor where he disappeared into the bustling hospital foot traffic.

* * *

Inside Amy's room, Ben looked around to make sure she had everything she needed. "Looking good," he said. "I'm off to the station now, but I'll be back in a few hours."

"You'll be just in time for dinner. We're having porridge and mashed bananas today. I can't wait."

Ben laughed. "You'll be able to eat other foods soon."

Amy listened to him talk briefly to a guard outside the door, wishing he didn't have to go.

Ben moved down the hallway and stepped into the elevator,

getting off at the ground floor. A hospital orderly stepped in as he left, holding a stack of fresh sheets. Ben made his way toward the exit.

* * *

Inside the elevator, the man with the sheets watched the lights as others entered and departed, impatient to be done with this. It took several minutes to reach the right floor. He exited the elevator into a T-shaped hallway. His eyes flicked to the empty nurse's station to his left and then to his right, where a uniformed officer chatted up a nurse by a hand-washing station. The cop seemed too busy with her to notice anything else.

Checking the sign on the wall in front of him for directions, the orderly strode quickly past the nurse's station.

* * *

Downstairs, Ben had stopped to help an elderly man with directions. He had resumed his trek toward the door when his phone rang.

* * *

The man with the sheets checked the room numbers as he went, noting the fire stairs at the end of the hall. He'd use them when he left, to avoid walking past the cop again. He spotted the room on the left. An empty chair sat just outside the door, no doubt meant to hold the ass of the cop in the other hall. Checking the way behind him, he reached out and pushed the door open. He slipped into the room, dropped the sheets and fired the suppressed 9mm in his hand. Three shots: one to the head, two to the body. But no blood. He stepped forward, jerked the sheets back and saw a medical doll of some sort with an auburn wig. He turned to run as the door burst open in front of him, spilling cops into the room, disarming and pinning him to the floor in seconds. A man in plain clothes entered then, snapping a cell phone closed. He'd seen this man before somewhere – downstairs, stepping off the elevator.

Ben smiled down at Amy's would-be killer. "Surprise, asshole."

Ben watched the would-be assassin being handcuffed, and accompanied the officers who escorted him from the room. The man carried no wallet or ID. Fingerprints might tell them who he was, but Ben already knew who he wasn't: Mario Borelli.

Moments later, as they escorted the suspect from the elevator on the ground floor, Ben asked, "Where's Borelli?"

"Fuck you."

A phone rang as they stepped outside. Reaching into the man's pocket, Ben found a cell phone. Instructing an officer to place the suspect in a waiting patrol car, Ben answered the phone, doing his best to sound like the man they'd just arrested. "Yeah?"

"Is it done?" a gravelly voice said.

"Yeah, I got her."

"You made sure?"

"Sure did."

"Good." The man hung up.

Ben found the number of the phone in his hand, called headquarters and asked for a trace on the call. Spotting the hospital ID tag on the would-be hit man's coveralls, Ben opened the cruiser's door and took it from the suspect. He eyed the real orderly's name and photo. "What happened to him?"

The hit man just smiled back at him. Ben left him in the car and returned to the hospital, checking the phone for anything that might prove useful. He asked the hospital to conduct a staff search for the missing orderly.

Chapter 44

Ben was on his way back to Amy's room when his phone rang. The cell call had been traced to an East Vancouver strip club named East Dix Candy. Ben sent a plainclothes unit there with Borelli's picture to have a look around. A moment later, he stepped into Amy's room.

"Back already?" Her smile waned. "Why the grim look?"

Ben raked his fingers through his hair. "I hate to tell you this, Amy, but there's another gang member at large."

Amy swallowed. "Another one? Did one of them escape, or is someone else out there, coming after me?"

"There's someone else out there, yes. But I'm not going to let him get to you. We thought we had them all until a lawyer called to say that his client, a witness for the prosecution, had been threatened over the phone. We think we know who made the threats, but we're not sure yet."

"Who is it?"

"He's big in the drug-running business. We've been trying to nail him for months, but we haven't been able to prove anything, didn't know he was connected to this particular gang. He knows we have something on him now, so he's laying low somewhere.

We're doing everything we can to find him. But like I said, I'm not taking any chances."

"There's something you're not telling me."

"Well, it looks like he hired someone to come after you, here at the hospital."

Amy's face turned pale with shock. "That's why you changed my room today? Without telling me?"

Ben nodded. "I couldn't be sure. I didn't want to worry you."

"Where is he now?"

"The cops are taking him to the station. I'll know more about him when I get back there."

"What did he do? No. I don't want to know." Amy took Ben's hand and held it to her cheek with both of hers. "You saved my life, again." She lowered their hands to her lap. "Is there any way I can help?"

"I have something to show you," Ben said, with a regretful look at his hand in Amy's.

Amy smiled, moving her hands away. "Let's see it."

"Be right back." Ben went outside and got a copy of a photo lineup of Borelli and similar-looking men from the cop in the hallway. "Do you recognize any of these men?"

Amy scanned each photo, then stopped and pointed to a man with a square head and puffy eyelids. "Him," she said. "Number five. I've seen him before somewhere. I just don't remember where."

"Let me know if it comes to you." Ben leaned over and kissed Amy's forehead. "I'm off. See you soon."

Ben had just left the hospital when Sergeant Harrison called. "The owner of the strip club is Mario Borelli," Harrison reported. "And your missing orderly has been found."

"Alive?"

"Surprise. He's got a nice goose egg on his head, but he'll survive."

Twenty minutes later, Ben walked into Harrison's office. "Did they get Borelli?"

"No. They were processing the photo through the club when someone said he'd just seen him. When they got to his office, the only trace of him was a hot meal on his desk. The morning papers will run his mug shot, asking readers to come forward with information."

"Shouldn't we prepare a contingency plan for protective custody on Robinson?"

Harrison thought about it for a moment. "I'm concerned about the cost. I'm not ready to commit to it yet."

"Remember Clisby?" Ben said, referring to a case whose guilty-as-sin suspect was now walking free because he – or someone he'd hired – had shot the only witness who could testify against him.

Harrison's lips tightened. "Yeah, I remember. I'll think about it."

"Someone just tried to kill her." Ben struggled to keep his voice down. "What's there to think about?"

"I'll submit the request. It has to be approved."

"Why wait? Just do it. If they say no, I'll foot the bill."

Harrison leaned back in his chair. "Something you're not telling me?"

"Yes, there is."

Harrison nodded to a chair. "Take a seat."

"I'd rather stand." Ben told Harrison that he'd fallen in love with Amy. "I'm more interested in her safety than anyone else, because it's more than just a job to me." He said he expected to be pulled off the case and would do everything he could to make up for his earlier decision to keep quiet.

Harrison sat up in his chair and looked at Ben for a moment, then nodded. "Okay. I'm glad you came forward. I feel you're the best man for the job because you came up with the idea to switch rooms for Robinson, which saved her. If she'd died, I'd be in the shitter, and we'd have nothing on Borelli. So I won't be pulling you off the case. Not just yet, anyway."

"All right," Ben said. "Then I'd like to be one of the officers staying with her in protective custody." He held up a hand. "Before you say anything, I want to tell you that the feeling is not mutual. She doesn't feel the same way about me, but we've become friends and she trusts me."

"Women," Harrison grunted. "Okay, fine, go nuts."

Amy lit up when Ben returned. "Did you find him?"

"Not yet. But we've decided to put you in protective custody. You'll be taken directly from the hospital to a safe house tomorrow morning. Harrison has agreed to let me stay with you."

Amy gaped. "He agreed? You mean you asked him?"

Ben pulled up a chair and sat down. "I told him about my feelings for you, and that it wasn't mutual."

Amy looked away, confused by her feelings, hearing this. They were changing, and she wanted to tell him that, but she didn't know how.

"What will happen to your job?"

"Nothing. He decided not to hold it against me."

"What changed?"

"Switching your room made him look good, so he owes me."

Amy smiled. She felt her face get hot and covered her cheeks with her hands, but couldn't stop smiling. "We'll be living together?"

Ben laughed. "Not really. I'll be there with you during the day, and a policewoman, Penny, will be with you at night. I think you'll like her. She's a good cop and a lot of fun. We'll have two apartments, right next-door to each other. When I'm with you, Penny will rest in the other apartment and vice versa."

"For how long?"

"A few days. Make a list of things you want to bring – clothes, books, medication, whatever you'll need for a week. I'll assign an officer to get them from your place."

"I don't want some stranger going through my stuff, picking out underwear for me."

"I was thinking a female officer."

"I'll ask Willa to do it. She knows my place and what to bring."

"All right, ask Willa. I'll get your door keys from the crime lab and give them to her. If she has any questions, tell her to talk to me. I'll have a plainclothes cop bring her in case your place is being watched. She can drop your things off at the station, with the desk sergeant." Ben reached out and brushed a strand of hair behind her ear. "Gotta go. See you soon."

Amy called Willa.

"A safe house? Why?"

"They're looking for another gang member."

"Oh Amy, I'm so sorry. What happened?"

"Don't ask. Talk to Ben. The police will talk to my parents. But please let Meg know that I'll be away for a few more days. Can you pick out some clothes and bathroom stuff for me? A cop will take you to my apartment. Ben will give you the keys and tell you where to drop my things off."

"Sure, I'll call Meg right away, and I can do your place at

lunch. I'll be at the ICU all afternoon, but I'll come by to see you before you leave in the morning."

"You'd better check about that with Ben. Even I don't know which room I'm in."

Chapter 45

Amy's parents came for a visit after dinner. They had been talking to the police. "Do these cops know what they're doing?" her father asked, tugging at his navy tie. "One minute they have all the suspects, and the next they don't."

"I'd say they know what they're doing," Amy said, trying to keep her voice calm. "I'm alive because of them. They're working day and night trying to nab this guy."

"So who's going to be with you in hiding?" her mother asked.

"A policewoman will be with me during the night and another officer during the day."

"Will you call us? Keep in touch?"

"I don't think I'll be allowed to call, but I'll keep in touch, somehow. Don't worry."

* * *

Detectives at the command centre tried to link the hit man, Art Chapman, according to his fingerprints, to the rest of the gang. But they couldn't find a connection. "I'd like to see you and Krucik take him on," Harrison said to Ben. "Would good cop/bad cop work?"

"Not a chance," Ben said. "This guy's a seasoned pro. He'll be on to us in a second."

When Ben and Krucik entered the interrogation room, Chapman glared at Ben, who in turn nodded and said, "Hi."

While Ben stayed off to the side, Krucik sat down at the table across from Chapman, fingered the birthmark on his forehead for a moment, then, without a word, started a recorder.

"So Chapman," he said, giving him a hawkish stare, "why are you willing to take the rap for a certifiable cutthroat like Borelli?"

"Fuck off."

"If you think he's going to get you out of here, you're dumber than I thought. Guys like him don't give a shit about guys like you. He's more likely to send someone to kill you for bungling the job. We can protect you, if we want to. Give us something useful."

"Cut the bullshit."

"Do you really think a man like Borelli will just sit back, hoping you don't give him away? Think about it. You can bet he's thinking about it."

Chapman refused to cooperate. Eventually, he asked for a lawyer and stopped talking.

When Krucik turned the recorder off, Ben came and leaned on the table. "So this is where we're at," he said. "Your gun is not registered. It has your prints on it. We're going to book you on attempted murder, weapons charges, kidnapping, assault of the orderly at the hospital, and trespassing. There will be no bail." He and Krucik walked out of the room and nodded to the guards to take Chapman back to his cell.

* * *

Amy couldn't sleep. She felt vulnerable in the darkened hospital room, listening to a respirator sighing and monitors beeping at the nursing station. Every time she drifted off, it seemed the officers outside her room said something or moved in their chairs, dragging her back to consciousness.

She had only pretended to take her medication at bedtime, fearing that some cutthroat madman would burst into her room during the night. Time and again, she checked to make sure the alarm button was close at hand. She couldn't wait to get out of there and into the safe house, to be near Ben.

She woke at dawn, soaked in sweat. It seemed she'd listened all night to the policemen outside her door, but she'd fallen asleep after all. Good thing. She needed to become strong for her continuing ordeal, which had started to feel like the endless miles of the one-and-only marathon she ran.

She peeled the sheet free of her damp nightgown and went to the bathroom. Leaning over the sink, she inspected her lips. They were healing, slowly. Her face, overrun by scratches, looked like a drawing rejected by an angry five-year-old.

She pulled her nightgown off, dropped it in the laundry basket, then stopped cold at the sight of her shoulders in the mirror. She turned and inspected her back. Angry bruises, green, yellow and purple everywhere – on her hips, bottom, shoulders and rib cage. She'd felt it happening, but hadn't seen it until now. Queasy and faint, she held on to the sink, fighting back the memories. *I'll be fine. Don't think about it. I'll be fine.*

She filled the sink with warm water. Dipping her hair, she washed it carefully, avoiding the shaved, bandaged areas on her scalp. Then she cleaned her body with a washcloth, taking care to avoid scratches and cuts. The effort left her exhausted, and she sat down to rest.

"Amy," someone called, knocking on the door. "Are you all right in there?"

"Yes … I'm okay."

"Someone left a change of clothes for you. I'll put it on the bed. There's a carry-on bag here for you, too."

"Thank you."

Amy had just finished breakfast when Willa arrived.

"You look a bit hollow-eyed," she said. "Are you all right?"

"I didn't sleep."

"Isn't the medication working?"

"I didn't take it."

"Why?"

"I can't swallow the damned things. My throat hurts. Besides … it gives me nightmares."

"You need the medication to help you rest and get better. Where is it?"

"Under the pillow. On the floor. I don't know."

Willa found two tablets under the pillow. "How many are you supposed to take?"

"Two."

Willa crushed the tablets between two spoons and dribbled honey over the pieces.

"What are you doing?"

"You behave like a child, I'll treat you like one." She held the spoon in front of Amy's mouth. "Open up."

Amy laughed and grimaced at the pain this caused. "I never expected you to push drugs down my throat." She washed it down with water.

"When are you leaving?"

"Around ten, I think. I have to meet with my doctors first." She motioned to the carry-on bag. "Thanks for bringing my stuff."

"You're welcome."

Amy sighed. "All this sucks."

"I know. Just hang in there. You'll be in a safe place until this is all over."

A nurse came to pick Amy up for her appointment with Dr. Thomas. "You're supposed to bring your belongings," she said.

Amy moved into the wheelchair and put the carry-on in her lap with the poster board on top.

Willa hugged her. "Let's hope they catch that guy soon."

Amy nodded.

Willa blinked back tears as she watched the nurse wheel Amy from the room accompanied by the police officer.

Chapter 46

Amy had met with Dr. Thomas, the hospital psychologist, three times before, and had come to trust her. She'd learned from each session how to be in more control of herself and her demons.

But this time the session with the doctor turned out to be different. She was putting more pressure on Amy, making her frustrated. "Why do you keep probing about my life?" she asked. "I've told you everything."

But her questions kept coming. Amy listened to them, but refused to answer. They touched a nerve. She found herself clenching her teeth and struggling to stay calm.

Dr. Thomas stopped asking questions and started to talk in a warm, compassionate tone about the sadness she could hear in Amy's voice. About something she hadn't dealt with yet. She touched on everything Amy had told her.

Amy looked away. She didn't want to cry, fought it. But the tears flowed anyway. Her sobbing intensified into uncontrollable crying. And then it all came out: the resentment, the grief, the loss, the guilt, the real sorrow.

Afterwards, Amy leaned back in the chair, exhausted and bleary-eyed. Calm came gradually as she listened to Dr.

Thomas's soothing empathy. Amy started to understand, on a deeper level, what the doctor was trying to say, and it left her with an unusual feeling of peace.

Dr. Thomas hugged her. "Call me if you need me," she said, and she handed Amy a small container. "This is a short-term minor tranquilizer, similar to what you've been getting here at the hospital. Make sure you take the tablets as prescribed for the next four days."

After going through Discharge Planning, Amy was wheeled to a room where Ben waited with a husky, dark blonde policewoman. The policewoman approached Amy. "Hi, Amy. I'm Penny, your temporary roommate. Nice to meet you."

"Hi." Amy shook Penny's hand, thinking she looked very young.

"Penny and I have met with your doctor," Ben said. "I picked up your prescription. We're all set. Are you ready?"

Amy nodded. Ben and Penny whisked her off to an unmarked car waiting in a secured area of the parking garage. Ben waved to an officer waiting nearby in another car.

"Who's that?" Amy asked.

"My partner, Ian," Ben said. "He's escorting us as security."

Moments later, they were on their way to the safe house.

Amy sat quietly in the back seat as they drove through the bustling city, looking out at people through dark-tinted windows. Suddenly she recoiled in fear as a man walking on the sidewalk seemed to stare straight at her. She looked away and sank down in the seat.

After driving around for an hour, making random turns to be sure they weren't being followed, Ben turned into another underground garage and parked beside an elevator. Ian held the door while Ben, Penny and Amy got in with groceries and luggage. They got off at the second floor. Near the end of the hall, Ben turned to Penny and pointed to apartment 203.

"You go ahead."

Penny used a nickel-plated key to unlock the door and went inside with her luggage.

Ben unlocked apartment 204 with a brass-coloured key. While he and Ian brought in the luggage and groceries, Amy, feeling a bit overwhelmed, went to the bathroom.

Ian had left when she came out. "Are you all right?" Ben asked, hanging his suit jacket over the back of a dining chair.

"I suppose," she said.

"Penny's coming over. We thought we'd make lunch. Would you like some?"

Amy shook her head. "You guys go ahead. I don't feel much like eating right now. Maybe later."

"All right."

Amy looked around the apartment. She'd thought that being there would make her feel safer, but she felt more trapped than protected. The drapes in the living room and bedroom should not be opened. Lamps in the living room and kitchen should not be turned off. There was a real fireplace with tools in the living room, but no logs. The furnishings consisted of a rustic coffee table with a large candleholder, a brown sofa and two matching chairs on a blue rug. A lamp and a telephone sat on a side table, a TV on a stand and four pin chairs placed around a small dining table. There were no pictures on the walls, only a shelf with a few paperbacks held upright between stone bookends crudely shaped to look like duck necks.

So quiet. She longed for the daily happy chatter and clutter at her Tresses. She peeked out behind the drapes at other apartment buildings. *Stacks of concrete filled with strangers.* She moved away and shuddered, now afraid of the city and its strangers.

Apart from clothes and bathroom stuff, Willa had packed books and a few magazines. Amy smiled when she saw two chocolate bars and a bag of her favourite cookies at the bottom of the case. *Awesome Willa.* She put her clothes away and brought her toiletries bag to the bathroom. The sink faucet was dripping and two of the five light bulbs on a metal rod over the mirror didn't work. She looked at herself in the mirror. Tried a toothy smile. *Ugh.*

Finding Penny and Ben in the kitchen making ham and cheese sandwiches with lettuce and red peppers, she suddenly felt hungry. "That's a big leap from hospital food."

Penny talked about her cat while they ate. "He's a tabby with very special preferences," she said. "He'll pick out the one person in a crowd who doesn't like cats. Never fails. Then he'll spend the rest of the evening finding ways to end up in that person's lap, or on top of his feet, or around his neck. You can hear him purring while his victim recoils."

Penny's steady stream of cat stories kept Ben and Amy entertained for the rest of the meal. After lunch, Penny left to get some shuteye before her nightshift, starting at eleven. Amy wrapped herself in a blanket on the sofa and fell asleep within minutes. When she woke two hours later, Ben was sitting at the dining table, talking on the house phone and typing away on his laptop.

"Talking to your girlfriend?" she asked with a lopsided smile when he got off the phone.

"Aha, you're awake. I was just checking up, getting the latest from headquarters."

Amy sat up. "So what's the latest?"

"The forensic team found your prints in the car trunk and on the toilet bowl in the house."

Amy swallowed her smile, trying to dismiss the image. "Good. That should be another nail in their coffin."

"And our suspect has been spotted in Alberta, near Calgary."

"Are they closing in on him?"

"He's a slippery bastard, but they'll get him."

"What about Tyler?"

"He's on our most-wanted list as well. We have people all over the map looking for him. Don't worry; we won't let him come near you."

Amy smiled faintly. "Thanks, detective." She got up and paced around the apartment, feeling the need to move. After a few laps, she sat down on the sofa, picked up one of the books Willa had packed and did her best to get lost in its pages. But she couldn't concentrate on the story, and nodded off, to wake up every time Ben went to check the area outside, spoke with his colleagues on the phone, or listened to the walls.

Not tired anymore, and restless, Amy riffled through a magazine, checked news channels on TV, then reached for the book to give it another try.

Ben closed his laptop. "Are you ready for dinner?"

"Yeah. Dying for a steak."

"Later. Your doctor thought you should start with something easier to chew." Ben disappeared into the kitchen.

"I'm sick of pureed food and porridge."

"We're having spaghetti and meat sauce."

"That sounds good." Amy joined Ben in the kitchen. "Cute," she grinned, looking at him with white sleeves rolled up, an apron tied around his waist. "I'll make a salad. Is Penny coming?"

"She prefers to eat later, so we'll save some for her."

They ate their dinner at the coffee table, watching a movie.

When Penny knocked on the door at ten, Amy was asleep on the sofa. She started to wake up when Ben carried her to bed.

"Penny's here," he whispered, kissed her cheek and left.

Trying to go back to sleep, Amy listened to sounds in the building: someone walking in the hallway, muffled voices seeping through the walls, the clatter of dishes, rain pounding the window.

Penny peeked in the door to check on her. "Oh hi, you're awake."

"I'm not used to the sounds around here."

"Yeah, well, there's a party going on below us."

"Do they know I'm here?"

"Nobody knows. You're safe here, Amy. Don't worry. Try to get some sleep."

Soon the sounds gave way to silence as the last guests left the party with loud goodbyes and car doors slamming.

Amy drifted in and out of troubled dreams. She found herself at a party, biting into a hard cracker. A tooth came loose. Panicked, she spit it out into a napkin and checked her teeth with her tongue. More teeth were coming loose as she struggled to make her way through the crowd to leave without anyone noticing.

Amy jerked upright in a panic and checked her teeth with trembling fingers. They were all there. Relieved, she fell back on her pillow, back to sleep.

Chapter 47

On Saturday morning, Amy woke up sobbing. A nightmare about her breaking down and becoming hysterical in court still lingered in her mind. It took her a moment to remember where she was. Looking at sunlight seeping in through a crack between the drapes that she wasn't allowed to open, made her feel like a caged animal. She dabbed her face and neck on her sheet, vaguely remembering Penny wiping her forehead during the night.

Penny's head appeared by the door. "Good morning, Amy. Ben will be here in ten minutes."

"Thanks." Amy got out of bed, picked up a change of clothes and shuffled to the bathroom. Shedding the sweat suit she'd been wearing since she left the hospital, she showered, changed bandages and brushed her teeth. She leaned forward to examine her face in the mirror.

Suddenly, a flashback of plowing through wet gravel in the dark hit her, making her pull back in panic, her heart racing. *Where did that come from?* She waited for her heart to slow down, then leaned closer again. Nothing happened. Her breathing slowed down. She looked at her crusted face and tried a smile.

Not a pretty sight.

She took out her hairbrush and raised it toward her hair – and gasped as another flashback hit, this time of her crawling in the dark, her hair dripping wet and tangled with grasses. She backed up against the door and slid to the bathroom floor, wondering what was going on. Then she remembered Dr. Sinclair cautioning her that something like this might happen. But she hadn't thought it'd be like living in a minefield. She stayed on the floor while struggling into her clothes, then carefully stood up holding onto the doorframe.

She went to the kitchen to find Ben in shirtsleeves, gun holstered on his hip, reading the label on her pill bottle. "Keep your hands off my dope."

Ben looked up and smiled. "Hey, how're you doing?"

"I'm okay." Her stomach grumbled.

"You need something to eat." He shook out two pills and handed her a glass of water. "Start with these."

Amy crushed the tablets, poured them into a soupspoon and filled it with maple syrup. "Willa's recipe," she said, popped it in her mouth and swallowed.

Ben let out a soft chuckle. "Whatever works." He poured coffee into mugs, handed one to Amy and started to prepare an omelette.

"Can I help?"

"You can slice this." Ben put a tomato on a carving board.

"Ben, how did you find me that night?" Amy asked as she sliced. "How did you happen to be in that ditch?"

"It's a long story that involves the RCMP and a private citizen. I can't tell you much more than that right now." Ben divided the omelette in two, put the pieces on plates and added tomato slices.

"Why? If you can't tell me now, when can you?"

"Actually, you and I shouldn't discuss the case at all." He picked up the plates. "Let's sit down and eat."

Amy started in on her food. "Why can't we discuss it?"

"Because there's a good chance that both of us will be called to testify in court, and we don't want to be accused of altering our story to agree with the other."

"Oh." Amy ate in silence. *Testify in court.* She'd been afraid that would come up.

"I'll be happy to tell you all the details, just not before the trial."

After they washed and dried the dishes, Amy curled up on the sofa and watched as Ben checked the grounds below, then got back on the phone. She played with her nails, fretting about testifying. She had a million questions, but they would have to wait. She got up and paced the floor, lap after lap. When she couldn't take another step, she lay down on the sofa, and soon fell into a dreamless sleep.

She woke with a start to the sound of a ringing phone and waited for Ben to pick it up. It rang again. She sat up, wondering where he could be. At the third ring, she was about to answer when Ben hurried out from the bathroom. "Thanks for not picking up," he said, and took the call.

A few minutes later, he hung up, looking out at nothing, tapping his pen on the table.

"What are you thinking?" Amy asked, snapping him out of his thoughts.

"Oh … that was the station calling. Mr. Corman, Tyler's father, had just called. He'd thought of something. His brother, who'd passed away, used to have a cabin in the woods somewhere east of Mt. Currie. He didn't know where, he'd never been there, but his brother used to take Tyler there to go hunting when Tyler was in his teens. He recalled Tyler describing it, but all he remembered was that it had a bright green door. He said if it's still standing, we might find Tyler hiding out there."

"Do you think they can find it?"

"The station contacted Squamish RCMP. They're going to send someone out and ask around."

"So what else is happening?"

"It seems our suspect got away. They think he might have slipped back into BC. The RCMP is patrolling the roads near the border. There's an APB out on him, and Harrison has every man on the squad looking for him. We're just waiting for him to make a mistake. Sooner or later, he will."

"What about the guys in custody? How long can you hold them?"

"Don't worry. They've all been denied bail and will remain in custody until the trial, months from now."

"Tell me, why do you always use the house phone?"

"There's always a risk the guy we're looking for finds out what cell number I have. If he does, he can trace my calls. With the house phone, on the other hand, he'd have to know which apartment we're in to begin with." Ben gazed at her. "Are you bored, Amy?"

"You guessed it. I wish I could go outside for a run, breathe some fresh air, catch some crooks. By the way, did you have a look at the poster board our friends made for me?"

"I saw some of the pictures, but I haven't read the notes. Do you want to show me?"

"Sure." Amy dashed off to the bedroom and picked it up. "You're going to love this," she said, coming back. She watched Ben as he read the notes filled with affectionate get-well wishes, sometimes throwing his head back and laughing, other times quietly reading with a smile dancing around the corners of his mouth.

"You're a popular lady," he said, catching Amy off guard with an affectionate look on her face. He gave her a questioning glance.

She flicked him a self-conscious smile and took the poster away before he could see her blushing.

Chapter 48

Amy picked up her book and pretended to read as she studied Ben; how well he filled that shirt, about his slight need for a hair cut, how it would feel holding his gorgeous male body against hers. She'd never known anyone like him – the way he cared for her and only asked for friendship in return. She didn't know what to think of how it affected her. It more than moved her. It touched her, unsettled her, stirred her, even.

Ben looked up and smiled at her. "What are you thinking about?"

"Why?"

"You're always playing with your nails when you're thinking about something."

Amy looked at her fingers picking at her nails. "I do?" She looked at the book in her lap. She hadn't turned a page. "I can't get into this book," she said, turned the TV on and found a movie.

But, instead of concentrating on the movie, she sat through most of it trying to sort out her feelings for Ben. Had she started to fall in love with him? Or did she think so because he was protecting her? Yet she realized it was too late. But how could she trust another man? By the end of the movie, she had a headache. She turned the TV off and massaged her temples.

"You have a headache?" Ben asked.

"I'll be fine."

"You need some food." Ben put his laptop away and disappeared into the kitchen.

Amy got up and followed. "Can I help?"

"Sure, thanks, but there isn't much to do." Ben pointed to a vegetarian pizza on the counter. "I'm taking the easy way out. I thought I'd just add some stuff on top." He took olives and mushrooms from the fridge. "If you'd slice the mushrooms, that would be great."

"Be happy to." Amy rinsed the mushrooms and started to slice them. "I'd like to talk to my parents," she said. "Can I call them?"

Ben gave her a regretful look. "Amy, I'm going to be totally paranoid and presume that our fugitive has my cell number by now, and your parents' information as well. I don't want to use any phone that can be traced to you. If you call your parents from this phone, that can be traced. Your parents can come to the police station, so you can call them there, or you can write them, then I'll have someone email it from the station. Whatever works for you."

"All right." Amy finished slicing the mushrooms. "I'm done. Do you have a piece of paper?"

"Pull a sheet from the note pad by the laptop. There's a pen by the phone."

Amy sat down on the sofa and wrote a letter telling her parents that she was in good hands. "I love you and never meant to cause you this much grief," she wrote. "I look forward to seeing you as soon as I'm out of hiding. Don't worry about me. Love,

Amy."

She read it over, blushing at the thought of how easy that had been to say on paper, not sure that she did love them. She went back to the kitchen where Ben was slicing olives and showed him the note. "How's this?"

He read it and handed it back to her. "Short n' sweet."

"Thanks. I don't have the greatest relationship with my parents, but I'm trying to normalize it enough to introduce them to an important person in my life." She pointed to Ben.

He gave her a curious look.

"More than just a friend," she added.

Amy gasped when she saw the kitchen knife slip, cutting his little finger. Her mind flashed back to the scene in the nightclub with Tyler talking to a thug and another thug forced himself between them. "I know where I saw him!" she burst out, her eyes on Ben's finger as he rinsed off the blood and wrapped a tissue around it.

Ben gave her a confused glance.

"The man in the photo lineup. The one you showed me at the hospital. I did see him before. With Tyler. In a nightclub."

Ben turned the oven down. "I want to hear this." He wrapped another tissue around his finger. "Let's go and sit down."

"Shouldn't you put a bandage on that first?"

"Later." They sat down in the living room.

"Remember when I told you what happened at the house?" Amy said. "How Tony reacted when I described the man with the scar?"

"I do."

"But when I described the second man, he didn't react at all, so I figured the second man didn't interest him, that he was just another troublemaker."

She told Ben about the incident in the nightclub. "His face seemed familiar when you showed me the picture, but I couldn't place it until you cut your finger."

Ben lit up and grinned.

"What?"

"I think I know what's coming, but I want to hear it from you, so I'm not influencing what you say. Go on."

"Okay. So when he grabbed the other man's arm, I saw that he had only four fingers on his left hand. He didn't have a little finger. And he had a tattoo on top of his hand and wrist."

Ben straightened up. "Oh? Can you describe the tattoo?"

"Yes, I can still see that open eagle-foot clutching the top of his hand as if it had caught prey – it was so lifelike. Anyway, Tyler saw me staring, so he came and told me we were leaving. I glanced back and saw the man looking back at us." Amy shuddered. "Now he turns out to be the worst of them all."

Ben caressed her cheek. "Thanks Amy. We were hoping you'd seen him, and we didn't know about the tattoo. He must have gotten it after the mugshot." He reached for the phone. "I'll let Harrison know."

Amy pointed to his finger. "I'll get something for that."

She returned with antiseptic and bandages. While she waited for Ben to finish the call, she cut the rest of the olives and put the pizza in the hot oven. She jumped when she saw Ben standing in the door opening watching her intensely. "You startled me."

"Sorry, I didn't mean to."

"Come here. Let me look at your finger."

"His name is Mario Borelli," Ben said softly as she bandaged it.

"Borelli?" Amy looked up at him. "That sounds familiar." Suddenly she lit up. "Brelly! I knew I'd heard something like that."

"Thank you, nurse." Ben put his hands on her cheeks and looked at her searchingly. "More than just a friend?"

Amy's excited smile turned tender. "I'm afraid so."

Ben pulled her into his arms and buried his face in her hair. "I'm a lucky man." He moved his head back and smiled. "So you want to introduce me to your parents, eh?"

Amy leaned her forehead on his chest and moaned. "I'm not sure you'd like to meet them."

"What do you mean?"

"They're both … intolerant … discriminating."

"Oh, I see. Just wondering where this might be leading. If your parents won't accept me, how will that affect the two of us?"

"It doesn't have to change anything as far as I'm concerned. I was scared to tell you because I thought you might think less of me after hearing about my screwed-up parents."

"See, that's where you got it wrong, Amy, I think more of you for being the person you are, in spite of what you grew up with."

Chapter 49

"I worry about the trial," Amy said as she and Ben prepared their Sunday morning breakfast. "On top of the flashbacks, I've started to have really scary nightmares about the trial."

Ben put his arms around her waist from behind, watching her slice a banana for her cereal. "Anything specific you're afraid of?"

"That I'll be a basket case in court, screw up my testimony, get shot … Take a pick."

Ben kissed the back of her neck. Amy closed her eyes. *That feels so good, so very good.*

"What can I tell you about it that'll make it seem less scary?" he asked.

"Mmm. Everything. How it works, when it starts."

"Okay. Let's get our breakfast on the table first."

Amy poured milk on her cereal and ate, waiting for Ben to tell her everything. "I know you've testified in court many times …"

"Well, it being part of my job," Ben said, chewing on a piece of toast.

"So tell me about it. When does the trial start?"

Ben swallowed and wiped his mouth. "I don't know. It's a long process. First, the case goes to the Crown Counsel for charge approval. At that point, the police will disclose everything discovered during the investigation. Photos, witnesses, statements, notes taken, everything. Then the Crown Counsel will give a copy of all that evidence to the judge and the defence, so they can review it.

"What photos?"

"Mugshots, pictures of your injuries taken at the hospital, that sort of thing."

"Are they showing photos of me in court?"

"If the judge rules them admissible, your doctor might want to show certain ones to explain a point. But they'll be of your injuries, like a bruise, not of other parts of your body." Ben winked.

"Okay. And then?"

"The accused will appear in court to hear the charges. They'll be asked how they want to be tried. If they plead not guilty, which they probably will, a date is set for a preliminary hearing. That's like a mini trial where the prosecution presents evidence to a Provincial Court Judge. Then the judge has to decide whether there's enough evidence against them to justify a trial."

Amy groaned. "You mean there might not be enough evidence to go to trial?"

"I really don't think we have to worry about that in this case. They're all being charged with serious offences. I'm just trying to explain a small part of the judicial process, or what I know of it."

"Why do you think they'll plead not guilty?"

"They'll want a jury. Their only hope of a lesser verdict is if a jury disagrees with some of the evidence."

"Should I be at the mini trial?"

"If you get a subpoena to testify."

"How can I testify against people I haven't seen?"

"Your fingerprints connect you to their car and the house. Just tell the court what you heard. When you told me about your captivity and escape earlier, you proved you have an unusual ability to remember details. Trust yourself, Amy. When the time comes, the prosecutor will tell you what to do."

"But, if they're in custody for months, they'll have plenty of time to discuss what to say, won't they?"

"No, they won't be allowed to communicate with each other."

"Do you think they'll go to jail for a long time?"

"We're working on it. They don't know we have proof that you were in that house. But we do. Not only your fingerprints. We have your DNA on your urine and on a few strands of hair caught in the cracks of the hardwood floor, in one of the rooms. Also we have another witness who saw three of them going in and out of that house several times over the past few weeks. Still – we may need something more concrete."

"Like having me identifying their voices?"

"Exactly."

"All right. I'm not going to let those bastards victimize me anymore. I want them behind bars for the rest of their lives."

Ben reached for her hand and kissed it. "You never let them victimize you."

"I have to admit I thought about not testifying … but just for a moment."

"That's only human."

* * *

Just before dawn on Monday morning, Mario Borelli drove into an industrial park in south Vancouver. He scanned the surroundings through drizzling rain, then pulled up behind a black sedan parked under the overpass. A man stepped from the black car. Borelli got out to greet him. They spoke briefly, and Borelli handed over an envelope. The man opened it, nodding at what he saw inside. Borelli's hand slid into his coat pocket.

* * *

Ben arose early and took a quick shower. He'd decided to surprise Amy with a steak for dinner and wanted to slip out to a nearby supermarket before his shift began. Hurrying downstairs, he jumped into his unmarked car and sped off toward the market.

Suddenly an "officer down" call came over the radio, the location an industrial park a few blocks away. Ben made a hard left, flipped on the siren and sped toward the park.

* * *

Penny had just put a pot of water on the stove when the apartment's intercom buzzed. She stiffened. None of her colleagues would contact her that way. She checked her watch. Ben's shift would start in ten minutes. She pushed the intercom. A panicky male voice introduced himself as Henry Gonzales and said that Ben's partner Ian Burke had sent him. They had a security problem, and the phones weren't secure.

Penny didn't know any Henry Gonzales, but Ian was a friend, so she asked Gonzales to wait a moment. She hurried to the other apartment and called inside. When Ben didn't answer, she went in and checked. Not there. Thinking he might have gone to the grocery store for something, and certain he'd arrive at any minute, Penny asked Gonzales to go around to the emergency exit and show himself in the window.

She went out in the hallway and looked down the stairs. She saw a man pressing a badge to the glass, the shaded doorway obscuring his features. Penny locked both apartments, pulled her gun and went down the stairs. Glancing at the badge, she shouted through the door, "What's the problem?"

Gonzales's face, contorted in distress, tried to explain with a thick Mexican accent something about leaving, changing safe house, alerting Ben. Penny couldn't make sense of what he said. She opened the door a few inches with her gun aimed at Gonzales, only to have the door slam into her head, knocking her unconscious.

Chapter 50

Ben raced through the industrial park and skidded to a stop beside a black sedan. He spotted a body slumped behind the wheel, jammed the shifter into park, took a quick look around and rushed to the sedan. He recognized the driver immediately.

"Ian. *No!*" Ben went down on his knees, trying to stop the blood seeping from the gash in Ian's neck, looking at his partner's closed eyes. "Look at me, Ian! Stay with me." Ben slapped his cheek. "Look at me!"

Ian's eyelids twitched.

"There you go, buddy!" Ben rocked him gently. "Hang on, hang on. Help's coming." To make sure of that, he got on the radio himself and called dispatch, giving location and situation and requesting an ambulance.

"Sorry," Ian said in a slurred whisper. "Tell my wife ... Sorry ..."

"Ian, just stay with me, and you can tell her yourself. Sorry for what? Who did this to you?"

"Borelli ... paid ... Amy ... safe house ... Forgive me." Ben turned cold with shock.

Ian's eyes rolled back in his head as his pulse disappeared. Ben heard sirens in the distance. "I forgive you," he said and ran back to his car. He hit the siren again and raced from the lot while trying to reach Penny on her cell. No answer. He dialled the apartment phone, crazy with rage and anguish. "Come *on!* Answer!" Was Borelli already there? Why did Ian betray him?

* * *

Mario Borelli slipped in through the door and pulled it shut behind him. He took Penny's keys, slipped her gun into his belt and started up the stairs. The sound of Penny's cell phone made him rush back down to turn it off.

* * *

Amy stepped from the shower, dried herself off and slipped into a robe before moving to the bedroom. A sputtering sound from the kitchen made her stop halfway. "Penny? Are you there?" No answer. Puzzled, Amy went to check it out. The phone rang.

* * *

Mario Borelli heard sirens, but ignored them. He knew the police were going to the dead cop and not to him. Climbing to the second floor, he quickly found apartment 204. Pulling his gun, he tried one of Penny's keys to unlock the door. It didn't fit. The other key worked, and he eased his way inside. The phone rang as he entered a short hall. He saw a living room in front of him, another hall to the left, and what looked like a walk-through kitchen to the right. Moving swiftly, he lifted the phone off the hook and set it down on the side table.

* * *

"Pick up the phone, dammit!" Ben yelled as he sped through the city. A block from the apartment, someone picked up. "Amy! Hello!"

But no one answered.

* * *

Amy decided to let the answering machine take over when she saw a pot of boiling water splattering on the stove. She hurried over, thinking Penny must have gone next door for something. She moved the pot aside, then suddenly froze. The answering machine hadn't picked up.

* * *

Borelli heard a sound from the kitchen. She must be there. Another few seconds, then he'd have her. He edged toward the kitchen, quiet as a whisper, then swung around the doorframe, bringing up the gun.

Before he'd even focused on the woman, his face erupted in a ball of fire, or so it felt. Through the pain, he saw the bitch drop an empty pot and run from the far side of the kitchen, and realized she'd thrown boiling water in his face. He stumbled after her, blinking furiously, trying to clear his sight enough to get a decent shot off.

There – he saw a shape moving through the living room.

* * *

Amy saw the man coming after her and grabbed the iron candleholder from the coffee table, hurled it at him. She heard a clanging of metal, the man cried out in pain and clutched the top of his forehead as blood seeped through his fingers and into his eyes.

Amy knew she'd blinded him for the moment. That, at least, gave her a chance. Looking to escape, she knew she couldn't get past him as he stood blocking the way to the front door. Not wanting to get trapped in the bedroom, she quickly scanned for something she could use as a weapon, grabbed one of the duck bookends and slipped back into the kitchen while the man was still dabbing at blood running down his forehead.

"Fucking *bitch!*" he roared.

Amy heard him coming closer. She quietly moved to the other end of the kitchen and peeked out. She couldn't see him and made a mad dash for the front door, but before she reached the hallway, he was there, blocking it, throwing himself on top of her, flattening her to the floor.

With the speed of lightning, she'd smashed the bookend into his face, sending the beak of the duck through his nostril. His body slackened for a moment, reacting to the pain. Amy kneed him hard in the groin, tore loose and scrambled to get away as he folded with a groan.

The man flung his arm out, got hold of one of Amy's feet and pulled her back. Dragging her with him, avoiding her swinging arms, he moved to brace himself against a wall.

Exhausted, Amy stared up at the bloody mess that used to be his face, not knowing how much longer she'd be able to fend the man off. He was too strong for her, she had nothing left to fight him with … Unless …

She scrunched up her face as if about to cry in defeat while tightening her grip around the neck of the bookend. The man leered at her and reached to grab her hair. Amy's right arm shot through the air like a comet. The man ducked, and the bookend hit the back of his head.

As he swayed, looking dazed, Amy kicked herself loose and scrambled out of reach. Knowing he'd catch her if she tried to get to the front hall, she locked herself in the bathroom. She found a bottle of liquid plumbing cleaner under the sink, unscrewed the cap, then moved into a corner behind the door. Breathing hard, she braced herself for another battle. *I'm trapped.*

Ben! Where are you? Suddenly she froze. Ben wouldn't leave her for that long. Something must have happened to him. *I'm going to die.*

She jumped as a bullet shattered the lock. When the door swung open, she threw a pile of towels into the opening. The man fired, the bullet ripping through the towels, ricocheting off the tiles over the bathtub and lodging into the vanity. Amy quickly swung the plumbing cleaner around the door, splashing the liquid as far and wide as she could before the man had time to send off another shot. As he screamed and thrashed about, trying to wipe the burning liquid off his face and eyes, Amy slid past him and ran toward the kitchen. He came after her, aiming his gun at her head. "You're dead!" he roared. At the instant he fired, something crashed into his side.

Ben's flying tackle bounced both men off the kitchen counter. Amy was thrown to the side and quickly escaped into the living room. Borelli's gun fired once, shattering a window. Ben pressed his gun-hand to the hot burner. He heard the flesh sizzle before the gun released. The two men spun into the living room, tripped over the coffee table and fell by the fireplace.

Ben tried to draw his gun as Borelli climbed on top of him. Borelli's unburnt hand clamped down on Ben's as the gun came out, smashing Ben's wrist against the stone fireplace. Ben felt the gun fly from his grasp.

Borelli's left hand went to his waist – and Penny's service pistol. Ben twisted the gun in Borelli's four-fingered grip until he heard the bone in the trigger finger snap like dry wood. Both men went for the gun, but it spun out of their reach.

Still straddling Ben, Borelli managed to pull the fireplace poker from its holder with his three working fingers and raised it high over Ben's chest, like a spear poised for the killing blow.

The world exploded with sound. Borelli swayed for a moment, dropping the poker – then falling sideways. Looking up, Ben saw Amy holding Borelli's gun. Her hands trembled as she stood frozen for a moment, smoke rising from the barrel.

"Ben!" she cried, dropping the gun to the floor and rushing to his side. Ben pushed Borelli's legs off him and sat up, taking Amy in his arms.

"I'm fine," he said, holding her close. "Thank you, darling. Thank you."

Penny raced through the door a moment later, holding a can of Mace, looking beat up with caked blood around her nose and a large bruise on her forehead. "I woke up downstairs. Sounded like gunshots?"

Ben indicated the body on the floor, felt for a pulse and found none. "I'll call it in," he said. "Wait in the hallway with your badge showing, to keep the neighbours away from the scene."

He saw Amy staring at the mangled fingers grasped in an eagle-foot tattoo. "I didn't know it was him," she said, as if in a trance. "I never had time to notice."

"Everything's all right now," Ben said, stroking her hair. "It's over."

He called Sergeant Harrison. "I found Borelli."

"No shit. Where?"

"Dead on the safe house floor."

Harrison arrived at the safe house. While he and Ben went to the other apartment to talk about what happened, Amy was examined by paramedics, then whisked off to the hospital for further examination.

"I'm sorry about Ian," Harrison said.

Ben nodded. "Yeah."

"I don't see the connection."

Ben's eyes clouded over. He looked down at the floor and shook his head. "There were rumours about him having gambling debts. I asked him about it. He said he was dealing with it, getting it under control."

"I see ... Gambling ... hmm." Harrison loosened his tie and sighed. "Brings out the worst in people." He put his hand on Ben's shoulder. "Anyway, it appears the danger's over. There's no need for protective custody anymore. Also the approval just came through, so you're off the hook on the tab."

"Corman's still out there. How can we keep her safe from that lunatic?"

"There's a manhunt for him, and he knows it. Hell, he'll be too busy saving his own ass to come after Robinson. I'm sure you'll think of something." Harrison pointed to Ben's hand. "Get that looked after. And take the rest of the day off."

"What about Ian's wife?"

"We'll talk to her. She'll have his insurance. And his pension will go to her, too. Hopefully that'll cover it."

Penny stuck her head in the door. "Medics want to drag me to the hospital," she said.

"Then you'll go," said Harrison.

"It's just a bump on the head," she replied, but she let the medics have their way.

"You should get checked out at the hospital as well," Harrison said to Ben. "I'll have patrol take you over there."

Chapter 51

After a brief physical evaluation, Amy went to see Dr. Thomas. When she came out, Ben was waiting for her, his hand in a brace. "How are you doing?" he asked, putting his arm around her.

"I feel all right, considering." She motioned to his hand. "What's the verdict?"

"Banged up and torn. Just need to baby it for a while. Can I give you a lift home?"

"Home." Amy smiled. "What a beautiful sound. Yes, please."

Inside Amy's apartment, Ben pulled the brace off his hand, tossed it on the sofa and wrapped his arms around Amy. "Oh, Amy," he whispered, rocking her gently. "What a warrior you are! I love you so much."

"I love you, too."

Ben pulled back at the sound of tears in her voice. "What's wrong?"

"I told Dr. Thomas what I'd done. I was shaking when I came to her office. Like it had just dawned on me that I'd killed someone. I had to talk about it. I mean I *had* to kill him or he would've killed you. But now I don't know how to live with it. I took a life."

Ben held her gently. "You were in a terrible situation. You saved yourself, me, and anyone else he might have harmed if he'd gotten away. You did the right thing. No one can doubt that – least of all you."

"What am I going to tell my parents, my friends?"

"That the police found Borelli, and that he's dead. Nothing else. We'll give a statement to the media. We're in the middle of an investigation, so you can't disclose any details."

"Will I be arrested?"

"Are you kidding? You saved a cop's life. You'll be lucky if they don't give you a medal."

"What about Tyler? Now that there's nothing to stop him from harassing me … or something worse."

"Finding him is our top priority now." Ben fell silent, looking thoughtful.

"What are you thinking?" Amy said.

"I have an idea. Paul and I have an apartment in the West End. Our mother downsized to a townhouse about nine years ago, and helped us finance the condo purchase. It's a temporary arrangement. Eventually Paul will earn enough to buy me out, or vice versa. I'd feel a lot better if you'd stay with me in our apartment for a while. I'm sure Paul won't mind staying with our mother for a couple of weeks. You can have his room. What do you think?"

Amy thought about it. "I'd feel safer with you around, but I don't want you to kick Paul out," she said. "Why don't you stay here with me for a while instead? I have a small den, and a mattress in my storage space in the garage."

"When you put it that way, I'd love to."

Amy grinned. "Now that we've saved each other from certain death, you have to get ready to meet my parents."

"I'm ready."

"You'd go there after what I told you?"

"Absolutely. I'll follow you anywhere."

Amy shook her head. "Well, I'm not. Not yet, anyway." She went to unpack.

Ben brought her poster to the bedroom. "Where do you want this?"

Amy looked around the room. "On the wall over the dresser would be good. Can you help me hang it?"

"Sure."

"I'll get the toolbox."

Ben called Harrison, arranged to have Amy's apartment under observation while he was away and gave Harrison his new temporary address. "Starting today … You gave me the afternoon off, remember?"

"Take your time," Harrison said. "Take the rest of the day. See you in the morning."

Ben shook his head after the call. "He's giving me my afternoon off, all off."

Amy handed him a small toolbox. He looked inside. "Is this all you have?"

"Well, yeah."

"I'll call Paul later and ask him to bring a few things over. Some clothes, tools, groceries …"

"Hey, you owe me a steak."

"That, too."

Chapter 52

On Tuesday morning, Tyler left the cabin to stock up on food. When he headed back, new tire tracks in the mud tipped him off that someone else had been this way. He hid his car, sneaked up to the cabin on foot and saw it swarming with cops. He watched as they found his drugs and cash, and had to keep from flipping out and screaming, right there. He finally sneaked off.

Now he had no money or drugs to buy his way out of the country. He felt an insane rage at Amy for 'siccing' the cops on him, something he'd make her pay for sooner or later.

* * *

Amy woke to the sound of rain pelting the window. After breakfast, she caught up on her voice mail and returned phone calls. The first one went to Willa to let her know that Ben was going to stay with her in her apartment until Tyler had been arrested. Amy had to yank the phone away from her ear as Willa squealed in excitement. "Slow down, Willa, I didn't say he proposed."

"It's just that … I know. Sorry. I'm so happy you're safe. When can I see you?"

"We need a few days to get settled. I plan to tell my parents about Ben staying here. If I'm still alive after that, I'd love to get together."

"Good luck. Call and let me know how it went."

Next, she called Meg to apologize for missing their appointment with the accountant. "Do I have any customers left?"

"Oh, Amy, your customers have been incredibly supportive and understanding."

"That's a relief. Meg, I'd like to come and talk to you after you close tonight. Will that work for you?"

"Absolutely. I should be done by six-thirty. I can't wait to see you."

After the call, Amy sat and looked at the phone. She had to let her parents know about her new living arrangement before they heard it from someone else. She agonized over what to say, then dialled. The answering machine came on and Amy left a message.

Her father called back at two in the afternoon. He'd just got her message. "Good to finally hear from you," he said. "The police called and told us what happened and that you were okay. They wouldn't give us any details because of the investigation. But that was yesterday. Why didn't you answer the phone?"

"I came home late from the hospital," Amy said.

"Are you hurt?"

"Just a few extra bruises. They thought I should have a checkup before they took me home. Is Mother there?"

"No, she's at a luncheon. She's a bit upset she didn't hear from you."

"Yeah, I'm sorry. I wrote a letter, but it never got sent because I had to leave the safe house in a rush."

"So they finally got that last gang member. What's happening now?"

"I just wanted you to know that a policeman is staying with me at my apartment until they've arrested Tyler."

"A police*man*?"

"Yes. A close friend."

"I see. Do I know him?"

"No, but you saw a picture of him on the poster board from the kayaking trip."

Her father was silent for a moment. "The black guy?"

"Black? His skin isn't much darker than yours, as if that has anything to do with it."

"He looked pretty dark to me."

"Call him what you like, but his name is Ben Malik. I want you to know that he's the best thing that ever happened to me. He saved my life. Twice."

"He's a cop. It was his job to save your life. You don't owe him anything."

"Owe him? I said he's the best thing that ever happened to me."

"Sounds like he's there permanently."

"Possibly."

"I see. And what do his parents have to say about that?"

"Ben's father is dead. I haven't met his mother yet, but by the sound of it, the two of us will get along very well."

"You presume. What do you know about her?"

"She used to be a social worker before retiring, born and raised in Sweden."

"Sweden, eh? I heard about those women."

Amy gasped. "What? First black people and now Swedes? Of all the racist, bigoted people …" She took a deep breath to be able to finish her sentence. "I thought the trauma you've been through over the past couple of weeks made you realize there are more important things in life than skin colour, but you haven't changed. It's sad. I have nothing more to say to you."

She hung up, buried her face in her hands and cried in frustration. When she calmed down a bit, she called Willa. "Sorry for disturbing you at work, but I just told my father about Ben living in my apartment," she said.

"Umm … you sound a bit riled up. What happened?"

Willa listened in silence as Amy told her what had been said.

"How *dare* he?" Willa exploded. "I'm proud of you for standing up to him like that."

"What else could I do? I'm so upset right now, I can't think straight. I'm disgusted with him …"

Willa sighed. "Amy, do you mind if I tell my parents what you just told me?"

"No. Go ahead."

"So … you'll be okay?"

"Yeah. Thanks for letting me vent. I feel a bit better now."

She had just hung up when Ben called. "I have some good news and some bad news," he said. "The good news is the Squamish RCMP located the cabin today. Tyler had cleared out, but they found and confiscated his stash."

"*Yes!* So they got him where it hurts most … And the bad news?"

"The forensic firearms examiner has confirmed that Ian Burke was shot with Mario Borelli's gun. "They found an envelope containing $10,000 cash in Borelli's car. It had Ian's fingerprints on it."

"Ian's?" Amy whispered. "You mean that Ian … but why?"

"He had a problem," Ben said, his voice husky with emotion.

"Borelli took advantage of it, and here we are."

"Ben, I'm so sorry."

"So am I."

Amy was shocked. What insurmountable problem did Ian have, to do this to his partner and to her? Feeling overwhelmed by bad news, she thought about cancelling the meeting with Meg. But she knew Meg was looking forward to it, and she'd been taking care of the business for a long time – it would be selfish to ask her to wait again. She called Ben and told him about the meeting, and that she'd be home at seven-thirty.

"Take a cab, okay?"

"No, I've decided to walk. I need it, Ben. I haven't been outdoors for weeks. If Tyler is around, he won't recognize me. I'll be all covered up in a raincoat with a hood. I'll leave early, so I can pick up a cell phone on the way. Don't worry. Meg will drive me home."

"All right. See you tonight."

* * *

Home from work, Willa hurried to find her parents. "Amy called today. You need to hear what she told me," she demanded, crossing her arms.

"You have our complete attention," her father said.

"Ben, one of the guys who drove me home from the kayaking trip, is a policeman. He and Amy have become close, and he moved in with her after they came home from the safe house. So … she called her parents to tell them about it. Didn't want them to hear it from someone else." Willa's tears welled up. She pulled her glasses off and wiped her eyes. "I've never heard her sound so sad. And after all she's been through lately. Right now, I hate

Aunt Lou and Uncle John."

She repeated what Amy had told her. As she spoke, she saw her father's face turn red. Suddenly the flats of his hands bore down hard on the armrests, making his chair tip over as he pushed himself up.

"*Bastard!*" he growled and stormed out of the house, leaving the chair on the floor.

Willa and her mother stared wide-eyed at each other.

"Is he going to hurt Uncle John?" Willa asked.

"He probably needs to walk it off."

"Mom, his face was red. Don't you worry about his heart?"

"He has a good heart."

* * *

Amy zipped her raincoat and pulled up the hood. She hadn't seen or heard from Tyler for a long time. If he was looking for her, he'd be looking for her Kia, especially in this weather. She walked east along Fourth Avenue, pelted by the rain, and loving it. The change of scenery and to be out walking in her city again changed her mood. People hurried past in the downpour, too preoccupied to pay attention to someone looking like she'd been in a fight with a grater. It felt wonderful, freeing. In the electronics store, she tried to ignore that the salesman stared at her scratched up face instead of into her eyes when he spoke to her. She bought a phone, then continued on to Tresses.

When she entered the shop, Meg ran up to her and practically squeezed the life out of her. "It's so good to see you."

Amy winced in pain. "I've been thinking about you," she said when Meg let go.

"I know. Willa kept me in the loop. I hope you haven't been

too worried about the business."

"No, I trusted you. Are we still on for a partnership or are you burnt out by now?"

"Lightly toasted, but not burned. Actually, Mary Thompson, the accountant, called me after the news about your escape from those horrible gangsters. Holy shit, Amy … Sorry. Where was I? Yes, Mary Thompson's standing by, waiting for your go-ahead."

"Great. Ask if she's free tomorrow night."

While Meg made the call to the accountant, Amy checked the ledger. It was decided that they meet at Mary Thompson's house at seven the next evening.

"The paperwork is up-to-date," Amy said when Meg hung up. "Everything around here looks neat and shiny. I'm impressed."

"Thanks." Meg looked proud.

"Meg, I want to make myself useful in our business, but only in the background and after hours, until my face and hands have healed. So I propose that I'll do the bookkeeping, meet with the accountant, make purchases and see that bills are paid. And I'll help you clean up every day after closing. That will only make up for part of what you've done for me, but it's a start. What do you say?"

"Oh, Amy, I can't tell you how happy I'll be just to have you here. You don't have to clean up after me, for heaven's sake."

"I know I don't have to, but I want to. Just let me give you a bit of a break."

"Okay." Meg moved to hug Amy.

Amy held her hands up. "No more hugs, okay? Don't forget, broken ribs here."

Meg pulled her arms tight to her body as if they'd shoot out and grab Amy of their own accord. "I'll be good."

"I have some good news," Amy said to Ben when she came home from the meeting. "Weirdly, Tyler stealing my money had the fortunate side-effect of me making a new business partner and a friend." Amy told him about her business proposition to Meg and that they were meeting with the accountant the next evening. "She'll pick me up and drive me home."

"Fantastic!" Ben kissed her.

Amy gazed at him affectionately. It had been a pretty rough morning, but at the end of the day, she had this. "I'll be right back," she said. She went into the den and picked up his pillow. Clutching it to her chest, she went back to Ben. "I'm madly in love with you, Ben, so if you don't mind …" She went to the bedroom and put his pillow beside hers.

Chapter 53

Tyler franticly searched rural areas near small lakes in the interior BC, looking for a new 'safe' place to settle in for a few months over the winter. So far, nothing had been said on the news about money and drugs being found. The sight of the cops picking up his stash had made him physically sick. He had to stop thinking about it – it turned him into a reckless driver.

In the early afternoon, he found a furnished cabin at the end of a gravel road, looking like it had been closed for the winter. He broke in and checked it out. It had a living room adjacent to a kitchen area. The sink, attached to a pump, had been disconnected. He found folded towels and blankets on top of a double bed in the bedroom. A small washroom off the bedroom had a non-electric composting toilet that ran on food waste for fuel. Two large flashlights and a big box of batteries would do for light. The fridge had been cleaned out. A portable gas stove sat on top of an old-fashioned stove. He found a half full propane tank, a shovel and fishing gear locked into a shed at the back. This was a major step up from the cabin in the woods!

On his way to a grocery store, an hour away, he checked the other cabins around the lake and found they had all been closed for the winter. There were no signs of human life in the area. He should be safe from the cops there. He had enough drugs and cash to make it for three to four months ... But what would happen after that?

He bought a transistor radio, a small propane heater, stocked up on canned food, snacks and beer and settled in. He found a news station and was ecstatic to hear that Borelli had been killed. That left only the cops looking for him. Sooner or later they'd find more urgent cases to concentrate on. He'll just hang back and wait for his chance to start all over, and when things calm down, pick up the slack with some like-minded people operating in rural BC.

* * *

On Thursday morning, Amy lingered in bed, thinking about the meeting with Mary Thompson the night before. It had been very productive, giving clear preparatory steps for her and Meg's business partnership. Even a lawyer had been contacted to prepare legal documents. She loved how things had been set in motion so amicably. She jumped at the sound of the door buzzer. *Who'd that be?* She didn't expect anyone. She went and pushed the talk button.

"Amy, it's me," her father said into the speaker. "I'd like to talk to you."

Amy stiffened. "I think enough was said yesterday."

"Amy, please. I've come to apologize."

She hesitated. "Fine," she snapped, and buzzed him in. *Apologize?*

She opened the door and stared at her father, standing there looking hollow-eyed and embarrassed. She moved to the side and crossed her arms. "Come in."

He stepped inside and stopped there. Clearing his throat, he said, "Your Uncle James came to see me last night. Amy … I … your mother and I are sorry for being insensitive and tactless. We wonder if you can forgive us. We also wonder if you would introduce your police friend to us. Come over for a drink, the two of you. Whenever you're ready for it."

Amy stared at him, stunned. "I don't get it." She looked away for a moment to collect her thoughts, control her feelings. She turned back. "How can you expect me to believe that, after all you said last night? You want to meet him, have a drink with him? Why? What changed all of a sudden, and what makes you think I would subject someone I care about to your attitudes?"

"I was wrong. I understand that now. Please let me make it up to you?"

Amy hesitated. Then she sighed. "We'll see. I'll talk to Ben about it, but not for a while."

Her father looked relieved. "Thank you." He put his hand on her shoulder for a moment, then turned and walked out.

Amy looked at the closed door, thinking she must be dreaming. A moment later, she hurried to the window and watched him drive off.

She called Willa at work. "What did you say to your parents?"

"I just repeated what you told me, and my dad shot out of the house like a cannonball on speed. Mom and I waited for hours. Finally, I went to bed. I didn't hear him come back. So … what happened?"

"My father came here. He just left. He and my mother were sorry they'd been tactless. Did you hear that, Willa? Tactless. He wanted to make it up to me. Asked me to introduce Ben to them, come for a drink some time. I've never seen him like that before. I don't know what to think."

"My goodness. That sounds promising to me."

"I don't know. I'm still mad at him. At this point I'm not ready to forgive him for being blatantly offensive in order to go there for a drink, let alone to pretend closeness and rapport. And I'm not ready to tell Ben about him, either. This isn't the first time he's tried to push his screwed-up values on me, you know."

"But it's the first time he's apologized like that. Maybe give him another chance?"

"Maybe when things calm down … when I calm down."

"Good plan. Listen, I've got to go back to work. I'll check with Dad tonight and call you."

* * *

Home from work, Willa found her father reading the newspaper in the kitchen. She sat down on a chair beside him, elbows on the table, chin in her hands, gazing at him. He ignored her, but she could tell from the slight twitching around his mouth that he felt her staring.

"Dad. Whatever you said to Uncle John worked. Amy and Ben have been invited over for a drink. Amy isn't ready to take them up on it yet, but still, you're a hero. What on earth did you say to him?"

He threw her a quick grin and went back to his paper.

"Dad?"

"All right." He put the paper down. "You'll be surprised to know that I've recently learned from my genealogy research that we have at least one black ancestor." He stopped for a moment, waiting for a reaction. When none came forward, he continued,

"My brother and I were never told about that. Now he knows. Does that answer your question?"

Willa threw her arms around him. "Oh, Dad, I love you so much. Thank you." She hurried off to tell Amy.

Chapter 54

November arrived, chilling the air. Dying leaves swirled around Amy as she hurried home from work, vivid colours dancing in the wind. It seemed Tyler had disappeared from the face of the earth. She still hadn't seen or heard from him and started to relax, thinking he might have heard that she lived with a policeman.

Ben still worried when she was out on her own. But Amy needed the freedom and assured him about her added awareness of what's going on around her. She always kept to busy sidewalks and never went out at night alone.

She found Ben already home, going through the mail. He kissed her before handing her a letter. "Wish I had a bunch of roses for you instead of a subpoena."

She cringed, opening the envelope. "Did you get one as well?"

He nodded. "Ya."

After reading the subpoena from Mr. Mackenzie, the Crown Counsel prosecuting the case, she looked at Ben. "What a slew of charges those guys are facing."

"And we can't talk about it."

"What about my killing Borelli?"

"The police report to the district attorney's going to say it was in self defense. You did everything you could to stay away from him, but he came to you. It doesn't hurt to have a police witness, either."

"Thanks." Amy hugged him. "That's a big load off my mind." She went back to the report. "The prosecutor wants me to call tomorrow to set up a time to meet. I have to ask you something."

"Go ahead."

"He wants to make preparations for the trial. Do I have to tell him everything that happened in that house? Like some of it is quite personal."

"He wants to meet with you, so he can tell you exactly what he needs from you, which will include everything that happened to you in that house."

"I don't really want to talk about it."

"Honey, the forensics took samples from the carpet and your clothing. They have your DNA. Right now, the prosecutor needs to hear how you say things, how you think. That'll make it easier for him to prepare his case. So don't hold back. Tell him everything. At the trial, he'll only ask you about things that are relevant to the case."

Amy tossed and turned between nightmares all night and woke up in the morning completely exhausted. Ben kissed her, said he'd made an extra strong batch of coffee, and left for work.

Amy shuffled to the kitchen, filled a large mug with coffee and looked through the morning paper. She topped up her coffee, then went to have a shower. By the time she left for the prosecutor's office, she was high wired on caffeine and ready to tell him her life story.

After the meeting, she walked to Tresses with the prosecutor's instructions and questions ringing in her ears. "What happened first, what happened next, give me details, dates, times, descriptions, actions, exact words …" He'd given her copies of the statements she'd made earlier and asked her to memorize them all well enough to repeat in her sleep. "The defence lawyer is allowed to look at your statements while you're testifying," he told her. "But you are not."

"The whole thing was mind-boggling," Amy said to Meg when she arrived at Tresses. "There's a lot more to being a witness than I thought. When he's put everything together, he'll look it over and come up with trial questions. Then the two of us will have a mock trial."

Meg looked confused. "What's a mock trial?"

"It means that first he'll ask me the same questions he's planning to ask me in court. After that, he'll pretend to be the defence lawyer and ask me questions that can only be answered with a yes or a no. He warned me that I should 'count on a less friendly approach'. I can just see the defence lawyer point to the statement and say, 'It says here that you said holy shit at 2:43 p.m. on Thursday the eleventh. Yes or no?'"

Meg giggled. "Amy, let's close the salon the day you're testifying. I want to be there with you."

Amy sighed. "Thanks, buddy. I'll need every friendly face I can get."

"I'm sure most of your friends will be there. And your family, of course."

"Family? Damn. I forgot about that. I've gotten used to the idea of telling everybody what I heard in that house, except my parents." Amy let her head fall back and laughed.

"What's so funny?"

"I'm just picturing using their colourful language in front of my parents. I'm not going to make up my own version to keep them from fainting."

"We'll be there rooting for you."

"Thanks. You'll probably have to scrape me off the floor when I'm done."

* * *

Amy studied her statements so fervently that by the time she met with Mackenzie for the mock trial, she felt like her words were tattooed on her brain.

"I'll be standing close to the jury when I question you at the trial," Mackenzie said. "So right now, I want you to imagine the jury behind me. Face me and answer confidently. We want to make sure they hear every word you say to believe you as a reliable witness."

"All right."

Mackenzie started his questioning.

Amy answered with focus and self-confidence. Mackenzie made a few notes and asked her to clarify some of her answers. "You did very well," he said when they were done. "Now, it's the defence's turn."

After the meeting, Amy walked out of Mackenzie's office a bit bewildered. He'd shown her what questions and insinuations to expect from the defence, and she'd been unsure of how to deal with that.

"You should've seen the transformation in the man," she said to Ben at the dinner table. "His disposition, his voice, his facial expression. Everything changed."

Ben shot her a fake ominous look under his dark eyebrows and growled, "He wanted you to have a taste of the enemy."

Amy laughed. "You're not kidding. At first, his questions rattled me. He noticed and told me to stay confident no matter how harshly he tried to put me down or insisted I was lying. 'Don't buy it,' he said. 'And don't let it bother you. He'll try to confuse you. That's inevitable. Know that. Then shrug it off and go back to your truth.'"

"Good advice."

"You know, now that I'm familiar with the process, I won't let myself be intimidated by someone trying to shake me about what I know is true."

Ben pulled her close. "Would you like to be familiar and not intimidated with me?"

Chapter 55

A few days before Christmas, Amy woke up thinking everything seemed strangely quiet. She pulled the drapes and was almost blinded as rays from the sun, rising over the house-tops across the street, shot through the room like laser beams. Gusts of wind sent light snow swirling and sparkling in the air like Tinker Bell on a rampage. It was a beautiful and unusual sight in Vancouver. But it wouldn't last long. She could see the layer of snow shrinking as the sun rose, and the new flakes melting as they landed on sun-drenched cars before draining away into storm sewers. Somehow, that sight moved her to decide it was time to make peace with her parents and introduce them to Ben.

He was delighted at the opportunity to finally get to meet them, so they went. In the car, going home from an evening with canapés and cocktails at her parents' place, Amy kept glancing at Ben. "What? What are you grinning at?"

Ben burst out laughing and pretended to wipe sweat from his forehead. He looked at Amy staring straight ahead, tightlipped, her arms crossed. "Just kidding," he said, running his hand over her hair. "It's just that that was the closest to a third degree as I've ever been."

"I *told* you." Amy cringed in embarrassment. "Now I'll have to kill myself."

"Come on, honey." Ben tried to look serious. "Don't worry. Your parents were fine. I'm sure we'll all learn to be relaxed around each other one of these days. They're not as bad as you think."

"Easy for you to say."

* * *

Ben's mother invited Amy, Ben and Paul to a Swedish Christmas dinner at her place on December 24th. Driving home, Amy couldn't stop talking about the evening. "The best Christmas Eve I've ever had. I can't get over what a spread of food your mother prepared! I must admit, seeing all those fish dishes gave me a bit of a jolt. But some of them were good, like the smoked eel and the caviar and shrimp toast and that anchovy dish. I didn't care much for the herring and the lutefisk, though."

"But you tasted everything, I'm impressed."

"How can you eat so much without getting fat?"

"Only at Christmas."

"And what's with all the singing? Do you always sing some crazy song before you have a bite of something?"

"Only with the herring."

"And you sang along, too. I thought you'd lost most of the language."

"We've been singing those songs all my life, every Christmas, every midsummer celebration, over and over. It's like a favourite lullaby – you never forget."

"What do the words mean?"

"That's not lullaby material … and not something you use in

everyday conversation."

"Come on, *tell* me."

"I'm really looking forward to the turkey dinner at your parents' tomorrow."

"Let's get back on topic."

Ben kissed her. "Some other time."

Late at night, in bed with Ben's arms around her, Amy felt nostalgic, thinking she'd missed out on her own cultural heritage. Ben, who'd never been to Sweden, seemed to know more about its cultural history than she did about hers. Not that she'd been to Ireland or England, but she felt there should've been some feedback from her parents that would've stuck, made an impression. Instead, she felt like she was in some kind of cultural abyss. She didn't want to blame her parents, really, but every time they'd gone into their "when we grew up" stories, their dreary recollections in a polite society had made her tune out.

* * *

Tyler looked out at the white landscape surrounding him, thinking he hated snow. Early February was dumping another layer, holding him prisoner in this hellhole. The road to the cabin hadn't been plowed. His car was covered in snow. The drugs he'd kept for personal use were almost gone. He'd been using way too much lately, cooped up in the cabin and bored to death.

Convinced that Amy had something to do with the cops finding his stash, he obsessed about a way of getting back at her. He had to get out somehow. Maybe use the shovel in the shed to dig himself out to a plowed road.

He bundled up, snorted a line of coke and pushed through the snow to the shed. Using his hands and arms, he pushed enough snow away so he could force the door open, grabbed the shovel and went to work. An hour later, he was ready to drop – his arms wouldn't lift a snowflake. He rested for a while, had something to eat, swallowed his last two amphetamines and went back to shovelling.

The next day, it was still snowing. Tyler stormed outside and shovelled at a furious pace. The shovel broke. He went berserk and started to walk over the snow to tramp it down. Back and forth he went. But as the snow kept falling, he finally gave up, deciding he could wait until it thawed. He just had to cut down on the drugs to make them last, that's all….

He heard a sound. The moment he looked back, he slapped a hand over his neck as a stalking cougar sprang through the air onto his back. He tried to shake himself loose, then screamed in agony as the cougar's teeth ripped through his hand.

Chapter 56

Spring arrived early and suddenly, as it often does in BC. The abundance of cherry trees, lining avenues in Vancouver and its surrounding housing areas, blossomed with a ferocity that almost made you swoon.

In contrast to all that loveliness – with the snow gone – a hunter made a gruesome discovery near a cabin area in the interior BC, 400 kilometres north of Vancouver: a human hand, obviously crushed and partly eaten by a cougar. The police hadn't found any remnants of a body in the vicinity and thought the cougar might have buried or dragged it off to feed on throughout the winter. They hoped DNA would show a match to any missing person.

The first day of the trial arrived. Amy kissed Ben good luck on his way to court as one of the first to testify. He had been told to check in at the courthouse at nine in the morning, even though he wasn't slotted to testify until the afternoon. Amy would be the Crown's first witness the following day, and had been told to be at the courthouse at eight in the morning.

Amy got ready for work, glad she'd booked a full day at Tresses to keep her thoughts occupied. The salon would be closed on Thursday, so Meg could be at the courthouse for Amy's turn on the witness stand.

* * *

While Ben waited his turn at the courthouse, Mackenzie called the gang's neighbour in Richmond to the stand. He asked the man to tell the court what he'd seen at 6:55 p.m. on Sunday, September seventeenth.

"The people livin' across the street from me at the time were always comin' and goin'," the man said. "Their place looked like a dump – knee-high weeds, boarded-up windows. Always slammin' car doors, takin' off with screechin' tires, keepin' people up at all hours. I wasn't the only one wonderin' who they were, or what's goin' on over there. But at least the other neighbours didn't have to look at the eyesore behind the high hedges lining the sides and the back of it.

"Anyway, that day, sometime in the middle of the afternoon, I heard a bigger racket than usual. A lot of yellin' and screamin'. I thought I heard shots and almost called the cops. Then it calmed down for about an hour or so. The wife and I'd just finished dinner when we heard some kind of commotion. I went and looked out the window and saw them luggin' stuff outside and throwin' it in the trunk of their car, a chocolate-brown '90 Chevy Caprice parked at the back. It was pretty dark out, but I still recognized the car. I've seen it before. Then I saw another guy carryin' what looked like a body over his shoulder and dumpin' it into the trunk. That time, I did call the cops. About ten minutes later, three of them got in the car, and they took off."

"Let the record show," Mackenzie said, "that a car of the same make, model, year and colour was apprehended that same evening at 7:42 p.m. – exactly forty-seven minutes after the witness called the police – only three kilometres away from the witness's house, with two of the accused inside. Amy Robinson's fingerprints were found in the trunk."

The defence had no questions, and Judge Dawson excused the neighbour. Dr. Sinclair, Amy's doctor, was sworn in and seated.

"Explain to the court," said Mackenzie, "what the differences are in appearance between an injury stemming from a jump out of a moving vehicle and an injury from a kicking."

The court had given Dr. Sinclair permission to show the photos he'd taken of Amy's injuries on her arrival at the hospital. He now asked to use the overhead screen.

The jury watched as one picture after the other appeared on the screen. Sinclair pointed to different injuries and explained why one looked like it had been caused by a hard kick and another from landing on a hard surface.

"Will you explain to the court," said Mackenzie, "how it can be determined that one injury is recent and another two days old?"

Sinclair pointed out the differences. Mackenzie had no further questions.

Judge Dawson turned to the defence lawyer. "Your witness, Mr. Giacomo."

Giacomo contested Sinclair's theory of bruises. "What makes it so obvious that one bruise is caused by a kick and another by landing on a hard surface? Couldn't it be that a rock on the ground left a similar impression?"

"Yes," Dr. Sinclair said, "but one of those particular bruises clearly shows that it happened two days earlier than the other."

"Surely one or two days can't make such a difference in appearance that you can state the hour a bruise was caused." Giacomo kept contesting Sinclair's explanation of bruise dating until the judge ruled that, as Giacomo had called no medical expert to testify, and not being an expert himself, he should sit down.

Mackenzie next called Detective Stephanie Collins, asking her to tell the court about her meeting with Amy on the morning of Thursday, September fourteenth.

"Amy Robinson called me at the station at seven in the morning," Collins testified. "She wanted to talk about the man on our composite drawing shown on the news the day before. She didn't want to talk about it over the phone, so I asked her to come to the station. She arrived twenty minutes later, very remorseful for having lied to a police officer on September ninth, and wanted to revise her earlier statement and explain why she had lied."

Collins told the court what Amy had said, and Judge Dawson turned the witness over to the defence.

Giacomo eyed Collins as he moved to stand closer to the jury. "Amy must have done an excellent job when she lied to the police," he said, "or they wouldn't have swallowed her whole fairytale. What else is she lying about? And how would we know? How reliable is she, really?"

"There are times when a person feels that she's hearing the truth," Collins said.

"Do you have a degree in psychology?" Giacomo asked.

"No."

Collins was excused at 2:00 p.m., clearing the way for Ben to take the stand. Two hours later, he was excused and left the courthouse.

"How did it go?" Amy asked Ben when she came home from work.

"Giacomo gave me a hard time," Ben said as he slipped a tray with two wraps into the oven. "But I managed to hold my composure and frustrate him a bit."

"Can I ask you about it?"

"Sorry, honey. I'm done, and I'll be in the courtroom when you testify tomorrow, but you're not done yet."

Amy looked troubled, restlessly gathering her hair for an elastic tie, then letting it loose, gathering and letting it loose. "I can't help worrying about him questioning me about Borelli," she said. "About killing him, I mean."

"Sweetheart, you already know what's been decided on that," Ben said, wrapping his arms around her. "Giacomo has had an earful from me about that, so don't worry, all right? The last thing he wants to do is associate his clients with a would-be cop killer." He studied Amy's face for a moment, then added, "I have some other information for you if you're up to it."

Amy looked up at him from under her bangs. "Shoot," she said. "At this point, I think I can take anything."

"All right. Do you remember a hand was found in the interior BC about ten days ago?"

"Yeah. A suspected cougar attack, right?"

"Yes. DNA shows that it's Tyler's. They haven't found his body, and doubt they will, as cougars are known to hide their prey to feed on during the winter."

Amy shuddered. She sat for a moment playing with her nails, then looked up at Ben. "You know, that wasn't so hard to take … all I can feel is relief."

Chapter 57

The next morning, Amy stepped into the shower, every nerve in her body tingling. She'd left the hand shower hanging, so when she turned the water on, the hose and showerhead swung in a wide arc, drenching the bathmat and the towel before she managed to catch it.

When she stepped out of the shower, she slipped on the wet floor and slammed her wrist into the doorframe trying to stop herself from falling. She hopped around, holding her wrist and trying to dry herself with the wet towel. Her ponytail looked like a bird's nest by the time she managed to get an elastic band around it.

"How am I supposed to make a positive impression when every damn thing goes wrong?" she grumbled, as she stormed past Ben into the bedroom.

"Whoa!" Ben swooped her up in his arms and sat down on the bed with Amy on his lap. "Honey, calm down. You'll be fine." He held her tight until her body relaxed.

"Thank you," she whispered and kissed his neck.

She got dressed, grabbed her shoulder bag, notes and statements, and went to get her coat. Ben was waiting by the door with a brown paper bag and two coffees. "Breakfast," he said when he saw Amy eyeing the bag. "Bagels with cream cheese and red-pepper jelly. Never testify on an empty tummy." Amy hugged his arm.

They stepped into the unmarked car waiting to take them to the Supreme Court Building. A second unmarked police car followed close behind.

Holding tight to Ben's hand, Amy looked out at the barren trees and frost-speckled lawns as they drove down a quiet side street, feeling like she was on her way to the death chamber. A moment later, they eased into the stream of vehicles on Broadway and headed downtown.

Ben held a bagel out for her. "You need to eat something."

"I'm too nervous to eat." She took the coffee and sipped at it. "Maybe I'd better." She reached for the bagel.

Ten minutes later, she straightened up in her seat as they turned onto Smithe Street, pulled into a parking space under the overpass between the courthouses and stopped. The sight of the solemn police officers, standing ready to escort them through the wide glass doors just a few steps away, gave her an anxiety rush. This was the moment she'd feared. *Will Borelli still have thugs paid to kill me as I move through the courthouse?*

Dead leaves scuttled past on an icy wind as they hurried through the entrance. They were taken past throngs of security to the sixth floor. Then Ben entered the courtroom through the main doors and joined his mother and Paul, sitting on a bench with Amy's parents. Willa and her parents, Meg and other friends sat on the bench behind them.

Amy smiled hesitantly at family and friends as she was escorted into the courtroom through a side door. She was sworn in and seated. She watched Mr. Mackenzie flipping through his papers and reminded herself of his list of court behaviour: think before you say something, don't blurt things out, answer confidently, no silly quips, sighs or eye rolls, answer questions directly and don't volunteer information.

She glanced at the accused, sitting in a row on a bench in a glassed-in room, all leaning forward, elbows on knees, staring at the floor. Her eyes moved to Mr. Giacomo, the defence lawyer, riffling through papers on his desk, then back to the accused. Her heart bolted as one of the men turned his head, his eyes trained on hers. His threatening gaze iced her spine. She looked away and shuddered. *I'm going up against a bunch of killers. I must be out of my mind.*

Judge Dawson told the prosecution to begin. Mackenzie stood up and moved to stand close to the jury. Remembering what he'd told her, Amy looked directly at him and managed to calm down. He asked the questions from their dress rehearsal, and she answered confidently.

When she told the court about Tyler's demands to withdraw her money from the bank, her voice trembled with emotion. "I didn't have a choice. My parents' lives were in danger." She told the court about the psychopath waiting to hurt them.

She heard a gasp, and glanced at her mother, leaning on her father. Amy looked away. *Stay cool. Don't get distracted.*

After telling the court about the abduction, Mackenzie asked Amy to give an account of the conversations she'd overheard as a captive.

To avoid distraction, Amy fixed her eyes on the wood grain of the jury box, and focused on seeing herself alone in that dark room in Richmond. She recalled the first time someone entered – the sounds of the fridge door opening and closing – and began to disclose what she'd heard.

With the courtroom in complete silence, she repeated the words of her captors. "'You lying bitch!' Kicker yelled. 'You're digging your own fucking grave.'"

She felt her cheeks get hot, but ignored it. She went on and on, disclosing conversations between the different voices: Kicker, Squeaky, Gruff and Frenchie. She described the movements and the different sounds she'd heard – among them the sounds of someone being beaten up. "They called him Ken," she said and described the moaning and the screaming between slamming and smashing sounds. The pops of a gun.

Her eyes followed Mackenzie as he went to his table, picked up a paper, then came and showed it to her. It was a photograph of the man she'd seen talking to Tyler in a nightclub. "Do you recognize this man?" Mackenzie asked.

"Yes."

"What can you say about the scar?"

"I know it well. That's the scar I described to Kicker and to the police."

"Tell the court where you saw this man."

"In the evening of August 16th, 2008, Tyler Corman, my fiancé at the time, and I went to a nightclub called Au Bar on Seymour Street, in Vancouver, to celebrate Tyler's birthday."

"And what happened there?" Mackenzie asked.

"We finished our dinner about nine-thirty. I went to the Ladies room. When I returned ten minutes later, I saw my fiancé speaking in a confidential way with a man at the far end of the bar. As I walked toward them, I studied the other man's face to see if I recognized him. I didn't. But what I did see very clearly was the scar over his left eye – lumpy, pale skin cutting across his black eyebrow in a U-shape, as if he'd been branded by a small horseshoe."

"Thank you." Mr. Mackenzie handed the picture to Judge Dawson. "Now, Amy, can you tell us about the physical abuse you endured as a captive in the house."

Amy looked down. "I recognized the man who beat me as Kicker," she said with a quaver. She swallowed and looked up at Mackenzie. "I later heard the others call him Tony."

She told the court about the death threats, the kicks to her head, shoulders and back as Tony interrogated her about Tyler. How she'd felt relief every time she passed out. She described the pain in her eardrum after her head had been lifted up by the hair, and then flung back against the floor. She spoke of the constant fear for her life. "I drifted in and out of consciousness as they came and went, so after awhile, I never knew the time or how long I'd been there."

She looked at Mackenzie, waiting for him to say something. But all she heard was people clearing their throats, blowing their noses, shifting their feet.

"Thank you," Mr. Mackenzie finally said. "Now, Amy will you please tell the court about your escape from your captors."

Amy glanced at the accused. They were all staring at her. She quickly averted her eyes and turned to Mr. Mackenzie. He nodded encouragement.

Amy told the court that she'd started to prepare herself to fight for her life when she heard Tony say, "Get the bitch. Ditch her on the highway a few miles from here. Make it look like an accident."

"At that point, I was so parched I almost accepted a glass of water before I realized it might have drugs in it." She explained how she managed to avoid drinking most of it being poured into her mouth, and how she'd faked being drugged when they dropped her into a car trunk.

She told the court how she discovered that a large piece of luggage in the trunk beside her was actually a dead body inside a plastic bag. She explained how she found the trunk release, and then later threw herself from the moving vehicle. She spoke of the terrifying chase in the ditch, about being shot at, and a policeman rescuing her. "The next thing I knew, I woke up in the hospital."

Mackenzie listened to the silence in the room for a moment, then said, "Amy, tell the court what happened two days before you left the hospital."

"On Wednesday, September twentieth, I was moved to a different room – normal safety precaution they told me. About an hour later, the police arrested a man who'd fired bullets into the bed in my old room. On Friday morning, September twenty-second, two police officers picked me up at the hospital and drove me to a safe house. The officers stayed with me, to protect me. I stayed there until …" Amy gave Mackenzie a questioning look.

He nodded. "Please tell us what happened on the morning of Monday, September twenty-fifth."

"I'd gone to the kitchen, tending to a pot of boiling water, when a man suddenly appeared, aiming a gun at me. I grabbed the pot, threw the boiling water in his face and ran."

Amy told the court of how she fought for her life until she was finally overpowered. "He aimed his gun at my head. The instant he fired, one of the police officers came crashing into him."

She told the court about the fight, the would-be killer's gun spinning out of his reach, and how she'd picked it up when he was about to stab a fireplace poker into the police officer's chest. "I fired his gun."

"Thank you, Amy. No more questions, Your Honour." Mackenzie returned to his seat.

Judge Dawson turned to the defence. "Your witness, Mr. Giacomo."

Giacomo stood up. "Miss Robinson," he said, walking slowly to the jury box and leafing through his papers. "You claim that you were drugged – which shows on your blood tests – terrorized and beaten unconscious for hours, yet still remember every word spoken in another room in that house."

"They drugged me when they abducted me, and tried to drug me when they took me away. Not in-between …"

"Yes or no?"

"I never said I could repeat every word, only identify the people who said …"

"Yes or no?"

"No."

"It says here in your official statements that you are accusing my clients of physically assaulting you, causing a brain injury, a fractured rib, multiple abrasions and contusions." He looked up at Amy. "Are we to believe that all those injuries were caused in that house? Wouldn't jumping out of a fast-moving car leave those kinds of injuries?"

"A doctor at the hospital said that some of my injuries were, at least, two days old when I arrived there."

"Well, we'll see about that." Giacomo consulted Amy's statements again. "You state here that you were kept blindfolded in the dark and that my clients made you fear for your life." He looked at Amy. "Couldn't that mean that they wanted to prevent you from identifying them – because they planned to let you go after they had questioned you?"

"But he threatened me …"

"Yes or no?"

She couldn't stand it. He had to twist everything. "Yes."

"Miss Robinson," Giacomo said. "Frequenting nightclubs …"

"I don't frequent …"

"… and being engaged to a drug pusher killed in a gang war," he continued loudly, "tells us a bit about your personal preferences."

"Engaged to someone who turned to drugs, yes," Amy said. "But I left him as soon as I found out about his habit."

As Giacomo continued his insinuations to discredit Amy's reputation, Amy noticed a few jury members glaring at him, which strengthened her resolve to keep to her truth no matter what.

Giacomo looked through some papers on his table. Suddenly he turned to Amy. "I challenge you to ID my clients blindfolded, in open court, right here and now."

Amy stared at him, stunned.

Before she could answer, Mackenzie jumped to his feet. "Your Honour, may I approach the bench?"

Judge Dawson waved the two lawyers to the side of the bench, covered the microphone with his hand and leaned over to listen.

Mackenzie was incensed. "This is a complete surprise," he said. "We don't know how it works. I need time to discuss this with my client."

"I have it written here." Giacomo handed Judge Dawson and Mackenzie a paper.

They read through it.

Mackenzie gasped in shock to see that Giacomo expected to have ten impersonators per accused. "Your Honour, this is outrageous!"

Judge Dawson agreed that it was excessive. "Make it two."

"But Your Honour," Giacomo protested. "I need more."

"You get two extra voices, that's all I'm going to allow," Dawson said. "The defense asked for this, and now must live with it."

"That's unacceptable." Giacomo crossed his arms and stared at the judge.

"If you want it to happen today, it's going to have to be this way," Dawson said. "If you prefer to wait, we'll let the prosecution take its time and practice."

"No, no," Giacomo said. "We'll take it. We'll do it now." He circled something on a paper and handed it to Dawson. "This is what I want them to read."

"*She* will choose the lines," Dawson said. "You like surprises. Let her surprise you." Dawson turned to Mackenzie. "We'll take a break for lunch. Have the text ready when you get back." The judge announced lunch, then told the jury to be back by one-thirty.

Chapter 58

Ben followed Mackenzie and Amy into the prosecutor's room. Mackenzie was nervous. He ranted and raved about Giacomo springing a "goddamned stunt" on them. "Now that they've put the idea in the jury's mind, we can't ignore it," he said to Amy. "If you don't do what they ask, you'll appear uncertain. And if you muck it up, you'll seem unreliable. How sure are you? Can you pull this off?"

"Can you have your nervous fit somewhere else?" Ben said to Mackenzie. "I'll talk to her."

"You've got one minute," Mackenzie said and left.

"Listen, Amy," Ben said. "It's not your fault that he's freaking out. Don't feel pressured into doing this. We have other witnesses; we have fingerprints, DNA …"

"I don't want to," Amy interrupted, "but when so much depends on those voices, I have to."

"You don't have to."

"I *do!* I want those guys locked up where they can't hurt innocent people. You said yourself I have an unusual ability to remember details. And I know voices from listening to clients all day from the back of their heads in the salon."

"Yes, but this is different. It'll be intense. Their voices will take you back to that time in a very real way."

"Sometimes I feel like I never left. Maybe this will put an end to that. Whatever happens."

"Come here." Ben pulled her close. "If anyone can do this, you can."

Mackenzie stormed back, looking stressed. "The defence must have thought about this for a long time," he said. "People from casting agencies are lining up in the corridor, practicing lines from Amy's statements." He paced the room staring at Amy. "Have you made a decision?" He stopped in front of her. "It all boils down to this: Can you do it?"

Amy stared back at him. "Yes, I *can*." She told him what she wanted the accused to read. Mackenzie had the lines typed out and copied.

With the court back in session, Mackenzie handed the typewritten lines to the judge and the defence lawyer.

Giacomo was not happy. He slapped the paper with the back of his hand, complaining that the wording implied his clients had said these things and thus were guilty.

"That's what we're here to find out," Judge Dawson said. "And I caution you that your clients were recorded when questioned by the police, so if they try to alter their voices to botch the test, I'll review the recordings, and the jury will be informed of the results."

Ben gave Amy an encouraging wink. Her stomach filled with butterflies when the court clerk came up to her with a blindfold. She looked back at Ben. He made a fist and mouthed, "Go for it, Amy."

She took a deep breath and tried to breathe calmly as the

blindfold covered her eyes. Her heart started to race when the judge asked for complete silence throughout the session. Clasping her hands in her lap to stop them from shaking, she listened to papers being handed out, followed by Judge Dawson's voice. "This is what you will say. Exactly as it's written on the page."

Then, a moment later, "Are you ready, Ms Robinson?"

Amy took a deep breath. "Yes."

The judge told the defence to proceed.

Concentrate. Amy leaned forward.

Giacomo called for voice number one. A man read the phrase Amy had chosen, words she'd heard Tony say: "Do you hear me, Ken? You sonofabitch! You think you can fuck me and get away with it?"

He's trying to impersonate Frenchie, Amy thought. With adrenaline surging, she waited for number two to read. After a few words, she knew. Her face tightened, and she sat back in her seat. In the darkness behind the blindfold, she could hear Ken's screams for mercy, feel his dead body in the plastic bag. She covered her ears.

Mackenzie steepled his hands nervously when he saw Amy's hands over her ears, blocking out the third reader's voice as well.

In the gallery, Willa's father squeezed his brother's shoulder. Amy's friends moved close, holding hands.

Giacomo asked if the voice she'd heard in the house belonged to number one, two or three. He had to repeat the question before Amy snapped out of her unbidden flashback and took her hands from her ears. Her voice broke when she said number two. She cleared her throat and repeated the number in a clear voice, then added, "I call him Frenchie because of his accent, but the others called him Alain."

Mackenzie began to relax.

Amy wiped sweat from the top of her forehead. *Calm down.* The instant the next reader started to speak, she could feel the blows pounding her. She gasped and slumped back in her seat. She wanted to scream. She couldn't stand that voice. "Number *one!*" she blurted out in a loud, angry voice before Tony could finish his line.

Giacomo glanced briefly at Mackenzie, who smiled back at him, waving two fingers.

Amy's pulse pounded in her ears. She really needed to calm down. She turned toward the judge. "Can I have a moment before we go on?" she asked.

The judge told the defence to give her a minute. Amy took a few deep breaths, told herself to relax. *I can do it, only two more. Relax. I can do it.* A moment later she nodded.

The judge told the defence to continue.

Amy listened impatiently to the first two voices, one of which was clearly an actor with a penchant for drama. When the real Gruff read the line, she tightened her lips and crossed her arms. *You should've kept your mouth shut when you handled me.* She called out "Number three" before Giacomo could ask.

"Next." Judge Dawson sounded impatient.

Amy relaxed her arms and concentrated. *The last one. Squeaky. Don't screw up.* But the next three voices sounded too much alike. The actors' impersonations were perfect. Amy's heart sped up. *Don't panic. Focus. Which one is it?* She had to get this right!

Mackenzie was sweating. He could see from Amy's face that she didn't know for sure this time. Amy asked if she could hear the voices again. The judge told the men to read the lines again. Mackenzie stared at Amy as if trying to send the right number through telepathy.

Ben mumbled, "Go, Amy. You can do it."

Amy held her breath as she listened to the first voice. *Not him* ... or at least she didn't think so. She listened to the second voice. *Maybe* ... But when the third voice started to read, she relaxed. The pitch had grown higher. Squeaky was nervous. *Thanks, man.* "Number three," she announced. She heard murmuring in the room. *What's happening?*

She jumped when Dawson banged his gavel and yelled, "Order in the court."

Amy sat stiffly, listening to the silence. It seemed to last forever. Then she heard Giacomo say, "I have no further questions."

Someone came up behind Amy and removed the blindfold. She squinted and blinked in the sudden light, looking at Ben, obviously proud and happy, congratulating her with his fingers in a V.

I did it! Almost dizzy with relief, Amy squeezed her hands in her lap. *Yesss*. She turned to Mackenzie, who smiled at her, dabbing sweat from his forehead.

"Recross, Mr. Mackenzie?" Judge Dawson asked.

"No, Your Honour."

Judge Dawson told Amy she was excused. Court adjourned for the day, and the jury left to deliberate.

Ben hurried over to Amy, grinning hugely. "What a clever warrior you are," he said, hugging her tight. "Giacomo gambled on you messing up, and it backfired!"

Giacomo stuffed papers in his briefcase with a glum look on his face.

Mackenzie shook Amy's hand. "A pleasure working with you, Amy. You have a good ear and an incredible memory. Amazing ... you surely know how to handle pressure. Most impressive."

"Thanks for believing in me," Amy said.

Family and friends surrounded her in the hall outside the courtroom, hugging her and offering congratulations. "You were brilliant," her father said. "I'm proud of you."

She thanked him, then turned to her mother, who stood there looking traumatized. "Oh, my goodness ... Oh, my goodness ... Oh, my ..."

"It's over, Mother," she said, putting an arm around her. "You can relax now."

"You're so brave," her mother said. "I never knew."

Amy gave Ben a fatigued look.

"The car is ready whenever you are," he said.

Amy thanked everyone for being there for her. "It's been an emotional day. I just want to go home and rest." She waved and stepped into the elevator with Ben. A moment later, they were riding in an unmarked car, being taken back to the apartment.

"I wasn't sure I'd survive today," Amy said, snuggling close to Ben in the backseat. "There was a moment ... a look from one of the accused ... I thought someone might put a bullet in me."

"The worst is over now," Ben said softly, stroking her hair.

"When will they announce the verdict?"

"It's hard to say. A few more witnesses are listed to testify, and then we have to wait for the jury to decide."

"I can't wait to go back to a normal life."

Chapter 59

"I feel like celebrating," Ben said before leaving for work on Friday morning. "Let me take you out for dinner tonight. On a real date this time."

"That's sounds wonderful," Amy said. "I'll be done at seven."

Spring was in the air as Amy made her way to Tresses, relieved the trial was over, excited about the upcoming dinner date with Ben. This time, they'd be able to relax, not having to worry about Tyler anymore. Be like normal people, without a death threat hovering over their heads.

Happy to be back at work, Amy hedged questions about the trial from her customers. "I'd rather not talk about it," she said. "I'm trying to put all that behind me – not having to think back on it every time someone asks. It gives me nightmares."

Everyone said they understood. Amy sighed as she noticed them asking Meg about it instead. But she knew Meg could deal with it.

* * *

Ben left the station at six and headed for a jewellery store. This was the night he planned to ask Amy to marry him. He'd even asked her father for her hand. He knew Amy would get a kick out of that. He'd chosen a ring and borrowed one of her rings for sizing. He picked it up and headed for Tresses.

He arrived at the salon fifteen minutes early and decided to go for a coffee across the street. He waited, watching people walking by and listening to Rihanna belting it out on the speaker system. He drifted off in thoughts about the evening coming up, took the box out of his pocket and peeked at the ring. The anticipation was thrilling. He had to cool it or he'd give himself away ahead of time. He watched a woman with shapely legs in ankle boots, skirt, jean jacket and a sunhat with a scarf attached enter the salon. A little girl pulled her hand out of her mother's and sat down on the sidewalk, refusing to get up. Her mother, laden with shopping bags, pleaded with her, then yelled at her to get up and come with her.

He helped himself to a second cup of coffee. Amy Winehouse was singing "Back To Black." He looked at his watch. Almost time to go.

* * *

At the salon, Meg was collecting the waste of the day and putting it outside the back door. Amy, almost finished with her last customer, looked up as a tall blonde woman entered. She was about to say they were closing for the day, when the woman untied the scarf attached to her hat and tossed it into a corner. Amy's eyes turned bright with terror as she saw the white stripy hair, flushed face and streaky beard: a madman with hate in his red eyes.

"Fucking *bitch!*" Tyler hissed, moving closer to Amy. "You *ruined* me! I'm going to *kill* you!"

Amy flung the blow-dryer at him, yelling to her customer and Meg to run as she backed away, bombarding Tyler with aerosol cans, jars, bottles of mousse and hair thickeners, recognizing her advantage: her two hands to his one.

Meg hurried the customer out the backdoor, telling her to get help, then grabbed a large bottle of shampoo, ran past Amy and squirted it far ahead onto the floor in front of Tyler who was busy trying to get his gun out of his shoulder bag. With his gun in hand, Tyler took a couple of steps forward and slipped on the shampoo. Flailing to keep his balance, he latched onto the arm of an overhead hairdryer. His gun went flying as the hairdryer came crashing down, felling him to the floor with it.

Amy grasped the cord of a thick curling iron, swung it around fast like a lasso, crashing the iron into Tyler's head repeatedly until he finally caught the cord and pulled it out of her hands. When he saw Amy clutching scissors, he scrambled to retrieve the gun behind him, but his shoes were slippery, and he had to turn and grasp her arm to stop her from stabbing him.

In the next instant, he ducked as Meg flung a flowerpot at him. It crashed into a mirror behind him and he reached up to protect his head from glass and pieces of earth and pottery shards showering over him. Cursing and swearing, out of his mind with rage and bleeding from several cuts around his head and hand, Tyler used a chair to pull himself up, then threw himself over Amy who was trying to scramble away.

Meg screamed for help as Amy tried to jab the scissors into Tyler's eyes. He yanked them out of her hand and was about to thrust them into her neck as a shot rang out. Without a sound, he fell to the side, a pool of blood forming under his head.

Amy looked up and saw Ben with his gun. She let out a moan of relief, pushed Tyler's legs off her and pulled away from his body. Ben hurried to pick up Tyler's gun and check his pulse, then picked Amy up from the floor. "Oh my god," he whispered, holding her tight. "I didn't see that coming." She could feel his emotion.

They heard Meg sobbing behind them and reached out for her. "Thank you, Meg," Ben said, putting his other arm around her. "You and Amy are two of a kind." Meg smiled through her tears. Amy pulled Meg closer and kissed her cheek. "You're amazing, Meg. I'm so sorry you were dragged into my mess. You've gone way beyond helping."

"But Amy, we're partners!" Meg sniffed. "It was my pleasure … well … you know, to help sending that murderous shithead out of this world."

Amy laughed. "I love you, my friend."

They glanced at people coming into the salon, looking shocked and worried. Police sirens were blaring in the distance. Meg looked around at the mess. "Maybe we should call someone to help clean up this mass of gob."

"This battle station will be turned over to the crime scene investigators for a day or two," Ben said. "I'll let you know when to call in the cleaning crew."

"In the meantime, we'll put in a claim to the insurance company to make up for destroyed stock and equipment," Amy said. "And have another talk with our customers, but right now, I'm dying to know what made you come up with the idea of squirting hair shampoo on the floor."

"Oh, that. Well, when you were kidnapped, the police came to the salon asking questions. That made me so rattled I forgot I was pouring shampoo into my hand to wash my customer's hair.

When my hand filled up, I lost the grip on the bottle, and it fell to the floor. Then I almost killed myself, slipping on the soap as I tried to mop it up, so … you know."

Chapter 60

Ben held back for a more ideal time for a wedding proposal. It came a few days later, when he and Amy went back to court with their families to hear the verdict. Ben had told everyone in advance that he planned to take Amy out on a special date afterwards, so if they wanted to celebrate with her, they'd have to wait till another day. He ignored all the meaningful glances his request caused and made a reservation.

Amy wasn't prepared for what happened when the accused filed in. For a brief moment, the soft sounds in the room were suddenly replaced in her head by loud, threatening voices as if she'd changed channels on the radio. She started to hyperventilate and quickly averted her eyes. *Will this ever stop?* Ben squeezed her hand.

The jury members filed in and took their seats. Judge Dawson asked if they had a verdict.

"Yes, Your Honour," the jury foreman said. A paper was passed to the judge. After reading it, he returned it to the clerk.

Starting with Tony Matzera, the clerk asked the foreman, "How do you find the accused on the count of first degree murder of Ken Ross?"

"We find the accused guilty."

Amy's eyes fixed on the jury foreman as the accused, one after the other, were found guilty of accessory to murder of Ken Ross, kidnapping, unlawful confinement, harassment and assault of Amelia Robinson, possession and trafficking of controlled substances, and possession of firearms and ammunition without a licence.

Alain was also found guilty of attempted murder of Ben Malik.

All accused were sentenced to life in prison. In his verdict, Dawson stressed his abhorrence of the inexcusable violence that was unleashed because of their involvement in smuggling large quantities of drugs.

The accused were escorted out of the courtroom. Dawson thanked the jury for their good work. Amy watched them file out, wanting to run after them and thank them all.

"Now is a good time to celebrate," Ben said as they stood up to leave. "Let me take you out for dinner tonight."

"I'd love to," Amy said. "But please don't make any plans about where to go or when. Every time we plan a date, lately, somebody ends up dea…"

Ben's lips silenced her.

Acknowledgments

I ventured into the world of fiction with the intention of writing an adventure story. When the story seemed to veer off on its own into a dark and dangerous place that I knew nothing about, my curiosity took over, and I took off after it. I would like to thank the following individuals, each one essential to my journey:

My husband, Bo, my sounding board, my love and my strength when I lose it, for putting up with my distractedness; My daughter Ingrid and son Ulf, my pride and joy, with whom I have it all.

Members of my writers' group: Pat Smekal, Madeleine Nattrass, Bert Wolfe, Dan Lundine, Joanna Qureshij, Ann Graham Walker, and former member, Susan Constable (who also came up with the title of the book), for their wisdom and encouragement, which led me to venture out of my box to find my love of writing.
Author John Gould, my Victoria School of Writing workshop teacher, for giving my self-confidence a boost when I most needed it.
Author and friend Gail Crease, (aka Gail Whitiker), for spending hours reading passages of my novel and then giving me her honest and useful critique.

My mentor, author and screenwriter John Robert Marlow, for his diligent advice, his never-ending belief in my book and encouragement to stretch beyond what I thought was possible.

BC poet and author Bernice Lever, my second copy editor, for pointing out my discrepancies and helping me repair them.

My young readers, Ingrid Håkanson and Becky Clarke, for setting this grandmother straight with their thoughtful comments and helpful editing suggestions.

For sharing their professional knowledge, I'm immensely grateful to Civil Engineer Ray Dechene, Police Inspector Gordon Kiloh, Forensic Lab Staff Sergeant Brent Wladichuk, Judge Brian R. Klaver, Criminal Defense Lawyer Paul Ferguson, Counsellor Susan Croskery and Registered Respiratory Therapist Ingrid Håkanson, plus my publisher Mike Roscoe.

And thank you to all my friends who have patiently waited for me to finish the novel and get out of my grotto.

A final note: the Bowron Lake Circuit with its interconnecting lakes and rivers is real, although I had to alter a few campsites to fit the story. Vancouver street names, BC main highways, names of cities and towns along these highways are real. All the rest – characters, businesses, rural places and events – are products of my imagination.

Ulla Håkanson

About the Author

ULLA HAKANSON grew up in Umeå, Sweden. She worked as a draftsperson in Stockholm for six years before moving to Toronto, Canada, where she took a degree in Commercial Art and opened her own graphic design business. Upon retiring, she moved with her husband to Vancouver Island where she turned to writing fiction.

Seduced by the raw power of British Columbia's wilderness, Ulla began using the province's rugged landscape as settings for her novels. Small towns, quaint villages, even thriving cities provide a backdrop, adding to the flavour that is distinctly west coast.

When not writing, Ulla and her husband enjoy exploring these areas with family and friends, as they kayak through the crystal clear waters along the shore, or hike the many trails that wind through the bush.

The Price of Silence is her first novel.

Visit Ulla at **www.ullahakanson.com**

Made in the USA
Charleston, SC
20 July 2013